# THE BOARD

# BOOKS BY KATY FARBER

STANDALONE NOVELS

*The Board*

*The Order of the Trees*

PICTURE BOOKS

*Salamander Sky* (with Meg Sodano)

NONFICTION

*Personalized Learning in the Middle Grades: A Guide for Classroom Teachers and School Leaders*

*Real and Relevant: A Guide for Service and Project-Based Learning*

*Change the World with Service Learning: How to Organize, Lead, and Assess Service-Learning Projects*

*Why Great Teachers Quit and How We Might Stop the Exodus*

# THE BOARD

KATY FARBER

Published in 2025 by Blackstone Publishing
Cover and book design by Larissa Ezell



Printed in the United States of America

First edition: 2025
ISBN 979-8-228-01688-0
Fiction / Thrillers / Psychological

Version 1

Blackstone Publishing
31 Mistletoe Rd.
Ashland, OR 97520

www.BlackstonePublishing.com

"You are not crazy. You are a goddamn cheetah."
—Glennon Doyle, author of *Untamed*

For all the women carrying more than you should have to,
often alone, trying to do better by the next generation,
and working against systems designed to keep you down.
I know you are strong and I know you can do it.

For all of the teachers,
special educators, librarians, nurses, and guidance
counselors helping students and colleagues every single
day despite broken systems and a fractured society.
You are the glue, the inspiration, and the reason
someone feels seen, safe, heard, and valued.

# CHAPTER ONE

"The public comment period is now open. You have two minutes."

The man who had spoken was in his late forties or early fifties. He wore a crisp suit that matched his bolt-upright posture. His small, cold eyes barely moved.

The yellow-blue glare of fluorescent lights in the small school library illuminated the man's shiny, balding head. I pulled my face into a pleasant smile. He didn't return it. The room was silent, except for the rustle of a few of the school board members shifting in their seats.

I twisted my Aunt Esther's ring on my finger and tucked my hair behind my ear. Those wild curls sometimes had a mind of their own.

*It's all right. You got this. Look around the room for some warm eyes and begin.*

Three men and one woman sat at a long table up front. Another woman was off to the side, taking notes, her eyes glued to her computer. There was no eye contact from any of them. Even though I didn't love public speaking (it made my stomach hurt every time), all my life—until now—I could easily size people up, make a connection, share a laugh. But these people kept their eyes downcast on their board packets, their bodies stiff and shifting every so often under the harsh light. Besides the suited man, another of the men wore a tie, the third just a button-up shirt. The suited man was apparently the school principal, and he seemed to be running the show.

*Doesn't the board chair run this meeting? Who* is *the board chair?*

My voice broke the stiff silence.

"Hello. I'm Olivia Wilcox."

Suit-man's small eyes burned like coals as he waited for me to continue, like I was wasting his precious time already. His stare made me feel exposed and jittery, like prey.

I squirmed, pulling at my black wool skirt—I'd had to open about fifteen moving boxes before I finally found it.

Outside, wind pounded at the library windows, and flashes of movement beyond the glass kept catching my eyes. Bursts of leaves swirled around out there, illuminated by a floodlight. *Focus.*

"My daughter Piper and I just moved to Whitebridge from Boston last month," I finally said. "Thanks for all of your hard work on the board. I'm happy to be here."

Here, naturally, I paused, for the recognition, the looking up and the smiles, for the "Welcome to Barnes Elementary!" and the "We're glad you're here!" comments, but there were none. Weird. My dad had taught me: start with a positive comment and gratitude for their time, and it had always worked.

The principal's mouth twitched. The woman next to him, who'd been looking down since I arrived, looked up and gave a tiny nod. Her hair was impeccably straightened and curled under, so it shined and shook slightly in one solid piece like a helmet. Two other women—other moms, it seemed like—sat in folding chairs beyond the long table, near the stacks of books that lined the room. One knitted as she listened. The other looked at her phone.

I blinked and took a breath, barreled on. I'd worked in a courtroom after all. The energy was awkward but not unmovable.

"Well, anyway, Piper is enjoying her time here. It's hard to start at a different school a few weeks into the year, but so far, so good."

My words hung there in the small library. No nods, no "I'm so glad!"-type comments.

Just silence. *Is this just how it is in New Hampshire?*

Their expressions were like the faces of wax dolls.

I gave my head a tiny shake and continued.

"Okay, I'm sure you have a lot going on, so I'll get right to it."

I started to talk faster, trying to fill the silence with words. Without my permission, my voice climbed up an octave, like it always did when I was stressed. I hated it. I sounded like a thirteen-year-old at the mall.

"Piper was happy to meet her classmates and Ms. McCallister and settle into third grade. She was excited to head out to recess to play last week and try to make some new friends. You know how hard it is to meet new people in a small town, where everyone already knows each other and grew up together."

Again, no nods. *What was happening here?* The board woman's mouth pursed, as if she had smelled something disgusting. The principal watched me, eyes narrow and tight.

*Keep going.*

"But Ms. McCallister—and I think it was the testing coordinator, Mr. Bevin—said she would need to stay in all week from recess to take a series of placement tests."

*Why did I say "I think it was"? I know* exactly *who it was.*

Sweat prickled at my armpits. Instantly, I felt small, girl-like.

"Now, I know there are many kids like Piper for whom recess is a release valve, a chance to take a break, to be active and social with friends. Piper is also a little anxious, so the time outside really helps her. And the research says that kids who have recess every day have higher achievement levels than kids who don't."

At the word *research*, the principal cocked his head to the side ever so slightly.

"So, I wanted to ask what the school policy was for missing recess. I couldn't find it on the website, or in the parent handbook. I called last week, left a message. I also sent an email and didn't hear back, so I thought I would just come to this meeting and ask."

I made sure to keep my tone light, uncomplaining, but direct.

After a few moments of silence, I added, my voice softer than I meant it to be, "I used to go to school board meetings in Boston regularly."

The principal's mouth, in a tight line, opened to speak.

"Thank you so much for bringing up this important issue."

The way he said *important*, it was clear he thought the opposite. His tone dripped with sarcasm, as if he'd verbally put air quotes around the word.

He continued, "We have a lot of budgeting and personnel issues to talk about, so coming here to question a decision made by the professionals at the school is a bit . . . refreshing."

Only his lips moved when he said all this. The rest of his face seemed frozen, the tiny lines on his forehead motionless. Whatever he felt about my being here, he didn't appear refreshed.

"And while missing recess might seem like a big deal to a third grader, I assure you that understanding her academic level, abilities, and needs is of far greater concern."

*What? Hell no, he was not going to minimize what I'd said.*

I jumped in, interrupting him, "Yes, of course I understand that but—"

The principal's hand, sudden and violent, shot up to stop me. It worked. As if that hand wielded magical properties, I obeyed and went silent. The room shifted. Now the board members looked up at me, awakened from their comas. The woman's mascaraed eyes were wide, and she shook her head slowly back and forth, like, "How dare you interrupt him?"

The man continued. "Ms. . . . what was it?" His lips curled at the edges now.

"Wilcox."

"Right. Wilcox."

My name hung in his mouth like it wasn't worthy to be there. Sour, rotten.

He continued, "We don't interrupt people here, like maybe they do in Boston." He laughed a bit at his own joke, and the laugh made his face fold at odd angles. "We let the educational leaders finish."

The woman with the iron straight hair, who I guessed was the board chair, smirked at this, two creases appearing in her foundation.

My ears stung. I'm sure they turned bright red. A tell I could never control. Shame filled me top to bottom and took my breath away.

"I'm sorry," I found myself saying, though I was most certainly not sorry. Not one bit.

"Okay then." He nodded once, slowly, as if acknowledging that I'd been put in my place and I knew it. He continued like he was speaking to a small child after a temper tantrum. "I'm sure down in Boston they were very play-focused and wouldn't dream of taking away recess. Here we do things differently. We want to give our students every chance at academic success, even if that means missing a few recesses."

Despite the heat coiling around me, I found myself nodding. Was I making a big deal out of nothing? I thought of Piper coming home, lying deflated on the couch, day after day this last week. I shook my head. No. I'd read the research; they were ignoring the importance of getting outside, of free time for a kid's social and emotional health.

*Get back in there.*

I took a deep breath to jump back in, but it was clear the conversation, if it could be called that, was over. My two minutes were up.

"Now, if we could get back to the business of running a school district, what's on the agenda?" Suit-man looked away from me. Dismissed. Done. The public comment period was over.

One of the listening moms looked up from her phone, smirking. The other, the knitter, glanced up, too, wincing slightly as if she were in pain. Was that empathy?

Hot, feeling trapped, ears burning, I couldn't stay in that library any longer, and it seemed pointless to remain.

I stood, accidentally knocking my chair against the table with my body. It clunked and the note-taking woman, who was reading off the next agenda item, stopped talking. Everyone at the table looked at me like I was an irritating insect that they wished would just go away.

Blood pounded in my ears.

And in my mind's eye, I saw another self-important man: Richard Floss, my former boss and the managing partner of Floss, Deegel & Alter. More hair but the same tone, the same ego. Richard Floss had tried to dismiss me too. And for far too long, he and his law firm had gotten away with it.

I turned and left the library, needing to be outside. I stopped in the lobby to pick up Piper, who'd been waiting there during the meeting.

"Hey, come on, Pipes, let's go."

She looked up from her iPad, shoulder-length jet-black hair in two short pigtails, deep brown eyes half-shut. Wordlessly, she stood up and followed me out of the heavy school doors and into the cool, swirling fall air. Leaves crunched under our feet—a classic New England sound—as we walked to our old red pickup truck, the one my aunt had left in her driveway. A safety light on the building cast long shadows on the ground around us.

I climbed into the truck, sat on the soft gray seat, and tried to breathe. The truck's cab felt like a safe cocoon, away from that florescent, confusing world inside the school. Piper settled in on the small bench seat behind me in the extended cab, headphones wrapped around her head, a story still playing on the iPad. I turned the key in the ignition and looked behind me to pull out.

Suddenly, I realized we weren't alone out here. The woman with the knitting must have followed us. There she was, scuttling across the parking lot toward the truck, her body throwing a giant shadow across the pavement.

I didn't feel like talking after the scene inside. And I certainly didn't want to seem as weak and dismissed as I felt, but it was too late. I couldn't start the car and back up, because the woman, knitting needles in one hand, a striped creation in the other, was making a beeline for us. Probably best not to run someone over right after attending my first board meeting in this town.

I looked at the steering wheel, set my face as I had learned to do in all those meetings, classrooms, and conversations, then rolled down the window and said hello brightly as the knitting woman approached. "Hi," she said, stopping at the truck. She had mousy hair pulled into a low bun and cat-eye eyeglasses. Her eyes were crinkled with concern. She looked into the truck, saw that Piper was wearing headphones, and continued.

"Whew," she said, shaking her head like we were old friends leaving a sporting event after our team had lost the game.

I nodded, trying to think of something to say. "Is that . . . ?" I finally managed after a few beats. "Is that how it always is in there?"

"Yep. No room for discussion or dialogue. Nothing."

"That's just not right."

"It isn't. It's terrifying."

Maybe because I was so new in town, or because the experience had been so awful, I kept talking with this woman even though I wanted to get home.

"But if it's like that, how can parents give feedback and be involved?"

She barked a short laugh, then looked embarrassed at her own volume.

"We don't. The board is run by Bob Stewart, that snake-man, and Brooke, his plastic sidekick. And if we complain about anything, we get put on the list."

"The . . . list? What list?"

"The 'problem' list. Once you and your kid are on there, good luck getting anyone to pay attention to you."

I felt a weight sink into my stomach. I'd already screwed up, and we'd only been in town for a month.

"Then why are you here?" I asked her.

She looked off into the night beyond the truck. "That's a very good question. To keep an eye on it, I guess? I come when I can."

I watched the moths circling the school light. A gust of wind would clear them for a moment, then they'd appear again, flying around and around, their shadows skittering.

"Am I on the list now? And Piper?"

The woman watched the moths too.

"I don't know," she said. "But . . . probably. Sorry." She sighed, shaking her head. "You better keep a low profile for a bit, hope it blows over."

I'd been told that before. Way too many times.

*Keep your head down.*

*Ignore the taunts, the advances. Consider them a compliment.*

*Be easygoing, low maintenance. Don't have strong opinions about anything.* Bullshit.

"Thank you," I said, plastering a smile on my face. "What was your name?

"Laura."

"Nice to meet you, Laura. Thanks for the heads-up."

I backed the truck up and left Laura standing there, holding her knitting, while moths swarmed the light above her.

# CHAPTER TWO

After a late dinner, I stood in the doorway to Piper's room. She was under the soft light, curled around her book, hugging her stuffed hedgehog, Clyde. A few half-opened cardboard boxes sat lined up along the wall of her room, with various toys and clothes spewing out, but the bed was set up, cozy and welcoming. Luckily, there was no school for students tomorrow since it was an in-service day for teachers, so she could sleep in a bit.

Piper's eyes fluttered partway open, shadowed under thick brown lashes, and she muttered, "I'm awake."

"Clearly," I said, laughing slightly, feeling like air had finally returned to my lungs after a long dive underwater. I crawled in and rested my head next to hers, pulling her close, smelling her clean, freshly washed hair. Best smell in the whole wide world.

Maybe it had been a mistake to leave Boston so quickly. To leave Piper's small group of friends that she'd known since preschool.

But didn't we deserve a fresh start?

I shook my head. It would all work out. We just needed to settle in, that's all. And not make waves. The financial settlement from the firm would hold us over for a few months until I could find a job. And then, once I passed the bar, I'd open my own law office, my name on the door. I could see it there in white letters on a black background.

"Everything will be fine, babe," I said and kissed the top of her head as her eyes closed again. "Everything will be fine."

A metallic clunk jarred me awake in the middle of the night.

*Just the heat clicking on.*

Houses have their own language of sounds at night. Creaks, thuds, the wind wheezing and pounding on windows. I didn't know the late-night language of Aunt Esther's house, even though I'd stayed there on occasion growing up.

My mind replayed the school board meeting, like a movie on repeat, with no off switch. The way my own voice climbed up and up, speaking so passively. The way the principal silenced me with a wave of his hand, talked down to me, just like so many other men in my life. And I let it happen. I'd actually apologized! I questioned my own logic, research, and reasoning, just like I'd done before.

I winced and rolled over in bed. The packing boxes threw shadows on the carpet as moonlight streamed in the window. I thought I'd left all those problems behind. The firm. My ex-husband, Tom. All the men who'd held up a hand to me, silenced me, in one way or another, appeared like old photographs in my mind.

I tried the mindfulness strategies I'd seen on all those websites and parenting magazines I'd read to learn how to help

Piper calm her anxiety. Count inhales and exhales. Longer exhales each time.

*The list.*

Piper and I were on "the list." The snake-man, as Laura had called him, surely must have been new to the job or temporary. This couldn't be how a modern school board was run. At Piper's old school, the board was made up of engaged, well-intentioned volunteers working on the budget, deciding when the school would be painted, and how to get more resources for the kids. They even painted the classrooms themselves on weekends and brought coffee and doughnuts for the staff regularly.

I went to those board meetings and felt welcomed to participate, to speak and ask questions, and leave whenever I chose to. They were professional, supportive, respectful.

Community-oriented. Even when we disagreed.

*Just forget it.*

Nope. Not working. I sat up, grabbed my computer, and flipped it open. Typed in "Bob Stewart."

*Let's see who we're dealing with.*

"Mama? Should we have pancakes or French toast? And then can we open up more boxes?"

I rubbed my eyes, pulling myself into consciousness. *When did I fall asleep?*

This little girl, so often silent, chirped like a bird in the mornings. Not me. I crave silence.

And coffee.

I pulled on sweatpants, my mind flashing to my late-night reading. Bob Stewart's name, bio, and job title were on the school district's website. Principal/Superintendent. Both?

Had I dreamed it? How could that be possible? And his work experience. A teacher for a very short time—just a couple years—somewhere down south. Then back to school for certification and the rise to principal positions, but only for two or three years at each school. He'd been here at Barnes for four years. And also the superintendent? This was a step up for him—new power.

My computer was still open to a dissertation that described how it was legally possible to be both a principal and a superintendent at the same school. It was done at smaller, rural schools as a cost-saving measure, but often resulted in what was called "role conflict." The superintendent, after all, was the CEO of the district, responsible for fiscal management, public relations, facilities management, and human resources. The principal was supposed to be an instructional leader, building manager, curriculum expert, role model, and communicator. Someone whose main job was to supervise and evaluate teachers and staff; lead professional development; meet with parents, students, and community members; and coordinate events at the school. The dissertation concluded that these roles were often in conflict and were difficult to maintain in one person.

Well, that much was clear.

I hobbled out of bed and down the stairs with Piper talking a mile a minute, my mind still on this dual role. *I mean, how can you be your own supervisor? And what had the folks in all those other towns thought of Bob Stewart after two or three years?*

My body hadn't memorized the way to the kitchen yet, even though as a child I had spent time in this small Victorian. Back then, I thought it looked like a gingerbread house, packed with books and a few grouchy cats I spent hours chasing through the rooms. Now, in the early morning light, I could see all the work that needed to be done. Paint chipping off window trim. Rot at the bottom of the back door where snow piled up all winter.

The wood floor groaned beneath my socked feet. *This is all mine now. I'm the one who has to take care of it.* It still didn't seem possible.

In the kitchen, I reached up and grabbed a handmade mug off a hook. It was brown, with large, white 1970s-style flowers. I remembered my Aunt Esther loving that mug. I filled it with coffee. Esther was everywhere in this house—I still felt like I was simply house-sitting while she was away. Any day now, she'd come home, and Piper and I would be on our way somewhere else, with a hug and a tray of hot maple rolls.

No. She was really gone.

A pang of guilt shot through me. How had I missed the chance to say goodbye, to learn more about her life here?

"French toast, Mama. Didn't you hear me?" Piper stood there in her nightgown with big round Saturns across it, rainbow rings looping each one. She held Clyde the hedgehog in the crook of her elbow and hopped from one foot to the other.

I tried to focus on her. I held the warm mug and couldn't shake a feeling that Esther was with me, in that kitchen, wanting something. Maybe she was. Maybe the ghosts of the dead are all around us, every day.

I set down the coffee, went to the fridge for the eggs, opened the door, and felt a persistent pull at my attention, back to the computer, back to Bob Stewart.

On Monday morning, Piper and I pulled out to drive the few miles to school as the day broke. It was almost the end of daylight savings time, so the sun had barely risen, washing the neighborhood in pale gold. The old maples that lined the road shimmered yellow, the first rays of sun hitting their deep brown trunks.

Piper wasn't chirping this morning. Not at all.

As the truck crept closer to the school, more cars with parents and kids in them filled the narrow streets. I looked at Piper in the rearview mirror.

"How are you doing, honey?"

She said nothing, staring out the window, clearly miles away in her mind. Shoulders slumped, folded in on herself, she looked like a tiny, injured bird.

"Today is going to be a great day!" I cringed at my own voice even as I said it. There was that high pitch again. I paused at a stop sign, rotated my ring. Looked back at Piper. She just stared out into the world.

"So, I'll pick you up right here after school." I practically sang it as we approached.

She didn't move a muscle.

I reached over to undo her seat belt, then stepped out into the middle of the drop-off line.

In front of me and behind, kids flapped their arms, waving goodbye to their parents.

Well, their moms, to be exact. Well-dressed, well-coifed moms in minivans or giant SUVS or Saabs or Subarus. Their outfits were right out of the pages of a parenting magazine. Their kids had variations of the same style as their mom's, matching the color palette and theme, nothing too bright or too patterned. Lots of effort went into this curation. The kids walked up the sidewalk to school like all this was perfectly normal and expected.

Didn't any dads drop their children off in this town?

The woman in front of me gave me a long up-and-down

look: me in my old, hooded, cross-country sweatshirt and track pants, opening the back door of a pickup truck that needed a good wash.

I stared right back and forced a smile. *Everything is great!*

The woman, with her intricately highlighted hair, didn't smile back. Was that pity in her eyes? Disgust? I was clearly not up to the Mom Code around here.

I stood at the truck door, but Piper didn't budge. Her lack of movement was a silent challenge. If I wasn't stuck in this line, with people waiting behind us, I might have been proud of this little protester.

"It's okay, honey," I said. "You can do this. Let's get on out and head to school."

Piper ran her hand along the inseam of her worn leggings.

I crouched down to her level, waiting, like I'd learned to do.

Finally, she turned her head. Car doors opened and closed around us. The line grew behind us. So many cars. I could feel the impatience in the air.

"Can I go to recess today?" she said, her eyes pleading.

I paused. I honestly had no idea if all the testing was over. But I decided to be an optimist. Surely, she couldn't have missed recess last week, and still have more testing to do? "I think so, Piper, but I'm not sure."

"You promise?" Her big browns locked on me.

"I can't promise, sweetheart. I don't know the school that well yet." At least I was being honest now. I just couldn't fake that answer.

Piper looked away. Considered my answer. I held my breath. Her hair was pulled back into a low ponytail. She had on her favorite NASA T-shirt and star leggings. She looked nothing like the other girls in their jeans or skirts and designer shirts.

Cars continued to line up behind us. Parents called goodbye. Some pulled around, staring as they drove by, clearly irritated with the holdup.

I looked behind us at a cluster of moms on the sidewalk watching us, with their tight fitted pants or fresh Lululemon athletic outfits.

Piper moved in slow motion, the effort looked almost painful. She looked at me while she zipped her backpack like she was saying *Just try to hurry me.*

The slow pace galled me. Inside I was screaming *Come on!* My heart pounded with growing irritation, but I kept my face calm. The line of cars were stacked two deep now, there was no way they could pull around us anymore. I hate being late, hate making people wait.

Especially here. Where I was on stage and didn't know a single person.

Instantly, the air changed. The hair on my neck stood up.

I felt him before I saw him. Standing there outside the school doors. He scanned the line of cars, then his beady eyes settled on me.

"Piper," I pleaded. "Come on. We're holding everyone up."

When had this tone ever worked? Anytime my voice got the tiniest bit rushed and irritated, Piper noticed, caved into herself, or simply went limp.

But I felt Bob Stewart's eyes on us like a fist gripping my insides. We had to move.

I gritted my teeth, reached inside the truck, and pulled my daughter out. My little girl didn't resist, which almost broke my heart. I set her down on the sidewalk and she stood there, pint-sized and fragile.

I kissed her on the head, gave her a quick side hug goodbye. She didn't move. I walked around and got back in the truck before I changed my mind, stuffed Piper back in the cab, and headed for Boston that second.

I lowered the passenger-side window, leaned over, and said, with as much cheer as I could muster, "I love you! Have a great day!"

For a moment, Piper just stood there like she might stay there all day. Finally, she turned slowly toward the school, but she didn't step toward it as I pulled away. I looked in the rear-view, almost hitting the car in front of me as I watched my baby standing there, dejected.

Bob Stewart's snake eyes watched me pull away. Then he turned to Piper, stock still on the sidewalk.

The moment the school was behind me, my eyes filled. How could I just leave her there? What would they say to her? I wiped my eyes with one hand and gripped the steering wheel tightly with the other.

I cycled through my options.

Homeschool? But then how would I find time to study and pass the bar? How would I finally become a lawyer? Make the money we need? And Piper needed social interaction. She was so painfully shy, she might never interact with other kids if she didn't have to, especially when we knew so few people here.

Maybe a private, small Montessori-type school? I hadn't found one here, and even if I did, the tiny settlement from my last job gave us only a few months' worth of funds to live on.

We were still on Tom's health insurance, at least for the next six months. After that, we'd need COBRA, or some other insurance, and that was expensive. Burning through the money with private school tuition would be irresponsible. We might as well sell the house and move back to Boston—or maybe to central Vermont, my childhood home.

A tight fist of tension settled between my ribs as I made my way back to the house. I had planned to unpack a few more boxes. To start studying for the bar exam for real this time.

But I could still feel Bob Stewart's icy eyes on the back of my neck. And a sickening feeling that I had left the most important thing to me in the world right there, with him.

# CHAPTER THREE

I sat among boxes of books at the small desk in my new bedroom, staring at the practice questions on my laptop. They were organized into sections: Civil Procedure, Constitutional Law, Contracts, Criminal Law and Procedure, Property, and Torts. The words sat there on the screen. I didn't click on a section, didn't know which one to start with. With Piper at school, I had the whole day to study, and I needed to get going.

The aggressive cheerleader voice, the one that's followed me around my whole life, spoke up.

*Let's go. You have to do this. You have to finish.*

Still, I stared at the letters, the bold font, the link to my future. I twirled my aunt's ring.

And it came right on time: the other voice, shifting to a whisper, a male voice.

*You'll never finish.*

*You'll never be a lawyer.*

This frequent guest, the self-berating voice, followed me everywhere, constantly pressured me to do more, always more.

It was a heckling voice from a nonexistent audience, critiquing my every move and decision.

I inhaled slowly, trying strategies I had read about:

*Treat yourself like a friend!*

*Notice your feelings!*

It was hard to pinpoint the origin of the voice. Was it my sixth-grade teacher, who thought I talked too often and too loudly, who thought I'd never accomplish anything, never do higher-level math? Or maybe Brian, my high school boyfriend, who made fun of my courtroom dreams?

Certainly, it was my ex-husband. He only worked when he had to, and enjoyed his hobbies—ice hockey, brewing beer, and mountain biking. He thought I worked too hard, was too serious, and would never make it anyway, so why try?

*Lighten up!* he'd tellme.

He never believed I would finish this thing I had worked so many years for. This goal that I had to interrupt when Piper came along. And so far? He was right.

And now Bob Stewart.

These people were a constant chorus in my head, living rent-free and trashing the place, all of them.

I had to get away from them. I stood up and went to one of the boxes that held my athletic clothes. Whenever the voices got too loud, when I felt like crawling into bed and fading away, I ran.

In every place I ever lived, my feet gave me the best tour. The smells, sky, sidewalk, trees, houses, and neighborhoods were always better experienced on foot. In Vermont, it was hilly dirt roads, avoiding unleashed dogs; and then college, in Boston, it was building a map of the city that my body itself knew, running along the Charles River and by the Victory gardens.

Running grounded me, helped me manage the nagging

voices in my head, whatever they were yelling at the time. After running, sweaty, legs tingling, I was always able to focus on a task and manage my emotions better. I changed clothes and grabbed my bright blue running shoes. Aunt Esther's cat, Steinem, meowed in protest that I was leaving, watching me lace up in the foyer.

I stepped out and breathed in fresh fall air, the smell of soil and dried leaves. It had an instant clarifying effect. My feet pounded down the street, maples overhead providing a tunnel, their orange leaves scattering on the road.

Thankfully, I felt the voices move to the background. I pumped my arms up and down as I turned right on Main Street and headed into town. I ran by Donovan's bar, all the stools sitting up on tables, past the small bakery. I made it to the bridge over the slow-moving, soupy river. Leaves floated on the water's surface, making their way to the next part of the watershed, down into southern New Hampshire, and ultimately out to the Atlantic.

I turned up a hill alongside the river, climbing up to where the houses were more widely spaced. My lungs burned with the colder air, and the clap of my feet on the dirt was the only sound. I crested the hill, just about to turn around and head back when I noticed a small farmhouse and the words "Whitebridge School District" on a wooden sign by the road. There was a nice SUV in the dirt driveway, shiny and black.

*Huh. Just like in Vermont. Old houses, renovated into offices.*

I stopped, watching the building through the line of trees. No lights were on inside the building, which was strange, with that big, glossy car there. I turned around and headed back down the hill, across the river, and through town. The sun was higher now, showing more of itself, reflecting off the leaves.

Maybe I was overreacting. I'd always had a wild imagination.

My parents told me I'd kept them hostage with long, elaborate stories when I was little. This was just one of those. I took a deep breath and my brain settled, calmed.

*Go home. Study for the bar.*

Later, showered and seated at my desk, I read the same question about Constitutional Law over and over, trying to force my brain to process it, until my eyes blurred and burned. So much for a clarifying run.

Aimlessly staring out the window, I saw an older woman in what looked like plaid fleece pajamas. She was walking slowly up the driveway toward Aunt Esther's house—*my* house now. Her long hair was piled in a knot on her head, and she was holding something in her hand.

I ducked away from the window, didn't really feel like talking to anyone. I wanted to study for the bar exam, even if I was blankly reading and rereading the same question and getting nowhere.

The woman disappeared from view for a moment, but then I heard her at the front door. She apparently set down whatever she was carrying and started back across the street. I watched as she crossed the road, walking with a slight limp, toward the old Victorian house opposite our place. A white, fluffy cat that matched her hair exactly ran to greet her like a dog would, and together they walked under a large maple tree, up the stairs, and into her house, the screen door slapping closed behind them.

And even though I hadn't finished a single practice question—the one that took up most of the computer screen still stared angrily at me—I headed down the stairs to the front door and picked up a large casserole tray sitting just outside it. I peeled back the foil cover, and warm, sweet steam rose to my face.

Hot maple cinnamon rolls.

Just like Aunt Esther used to make.

Then I noticed the sticky note, bright yellow with shaky blue writing across it.

*Welcome to the neighborhood. I miss her too.*

A huge feeling of relief washed over me.

*Maybe we'll be okay here.*

I walked to the kitchen with Steinem circling my feet. The delicate tabby still seemed to be searching for Esther, wandering around the house, peering into spaces and around corners, in boxes and under beds.

I grabbed a fork, took a seat at the small kitchen table, and dived right in. Hot maple richness filled my senses as I took bite after bite. I remembered all the times I would sit in that exact spot as a child, while my mom and Esther talked and laughed and drank coffee, and we all ate rolls just like these.

What did they talk about? I wished I knew now, wished I'd paid more attention.

Esther had worked for twenty-eight years as the town librarian before she got sick. Just what had she loved about this place? I remembered her as a highly intelligent woman, with no husband or kids, but a house full of books and a job she loved. Now, being here as an adult, I wondered how my aunt managed life here in this small town. I imagined she faced a crushing pressure to be just like everyone else: Go to church, have a family, look nice, cheer on the high school sports team. Did Esther ever fit in and feel at home here?

I felt as if she was sitting there with me; Aunt Esther, in her colorful vintage dresses, as if she'd just come home from work. Dresses with books on them. Or planets. Or in fleece pants and a thick Patagonia sweater on weekends, with Steinem's hair stuck to it here and there. She always asked the best questions about my life, my friends, my interests. How did I not realize how unique and beautiful that was? She would lean forward, listen to my answers like nothing else in the world mattered to her. What a gift.

But I didn't ask any questions back. Oh, children—such sweet little narcissists. How I wished I could go back and ask my aunt about her life here. Was she happy? What fulfilled her, kept her here?

I stopped eating, even though they were *so* good. Had to save some for Piper. I rolled the foil back over the rolls and headed back to the computer, back to Constitutional Law.

After school, Piper sat at the same table, eating a few rolls that I'd microwaved for her. I'd learned not to ask too many questions about school, to let Piper talk about her day in her own time.

But it was hard. Painful, even. The silent spaces. The waiting.

Piper swung her legs back and forth as she chewed. A sticky piece of roll stuck to her cheek. Steinem brushed against the table by her feet. The heat clanked on.

I couldn't wait any longer.

"So, how was your day?"

Piper nodded, chewing.

I was rushing her. I felt like I was always rushing her. *Put on your shoes. Get to the car. Get ready for bed.*

I looked down into Piper's purple backpack on the floor by the table. A piece of paper with a brightly colored mandala on it poked out.

"What's that?"

"A design. I did it today."

Her little socked feet swung back and forth.

"Nice! Can I look at it?"

"Sure."

I pulled the design out. Written across the bottom in block lettering was the word *brave*, with a thick, black line drawn through it.

"Why is this crossed out?" I asked her.

Piper shrugged.

"Ms. Mitchell asked that too. Can I have another one?"

Ms. Mitchell was the school counselor. I remembered seeing her name and photo on the school website.

"Did you see her today?

"Yeah. She helped me. Can I have another one?"

"No, you'll ruin your dinner."

Piper squeezed her lips together in a pout.

"Piper, you *are* brave! Why did you cross it out?"

Piper stared at me, her face blank.

"Can I go to my room now?" she asked.

"Yes, sweetheart," I sighed.

As she lugged her backpack to her room, I picked at my cuticle, spun the ring. What did "helped me" mean, exactly? How much of the day had she spent with the school counselor?

And there was my own nasty voice in my head again. *I'm failing Piper. She's messed up because of me, the decision I made to pull up stakes and come here.*

I picked at the corner of a maple roll, my appetite suddenly gone.

On Sunday morning, I grabbed my travel mug full of coffee and headed out to Aunt Esther's pickup. It still smelled like her—a mix of old books and a light floral scent she must have used.

With Piper humming lightly from the back seat, I drove down the street and turned toward the grocery store.

The morning was a perfect, crisp October day. Glowing, vibrant maple leaves clung with their last effort to the old trees that lined the road.

I turned left from our little street, and almost instantly, the road was lined with cars.

The great white building with its brilliantly colored stained-glass windows loomed over the neighborhood. People were climbing out of cars, walking toward the wide oaken entrance. Entire families with tucked-in shirts, polished shoes, dresses, and perfectly coiffed hair. It was almost like a scene from the 1950s, except for a few grumpy teenagers following behind their parents in crop tops and jeans—but no rips, though I was sure there had been arguments about that.

Church. This was a church town.

I slowed down to make sure I didn't clip a door or a person.

"Look, Mama. It's Mr. Stewart."

The way she said it: her voice small, hollow, wavering.

Bob Stewart was walking away from his shiny, silver SUV. Beside him, a short woman in a basic navy blue dress and pearls. She walked slightly behind him, looking down, and two kids walked behind them, tweens or teenagers in khakis and sweaters.

As if on cue, Bob Stewart turned and looked at me driving by in the old red pickup with its dusting of road dirt and rust around the door. Several other families turned to look too. And their expressions said it all.

*You're not going to church.*

*You don't belong here.*

I set my face and focused in front of us.

"Mama. Why were they staring at us?" Piper asked from the back seat.

"Because we're different, sweetheart," I said, making eye contact in the rearview. "We aren't doing what everyone else is doing."

Piper stared out the window. She nodded. This was something she understood.

# CHAPTER FOUR

At the grocery store, I stopped the car, exhaled. I really needed my Boston friends. The ones Tom and I had been close with. But the divorce had rattled those relationships, and then, of course, I'd moved here.

I stared at my phone, considering sending a text to someone. Maybe Julie—we'd been friends since college, before Piper and all the couple friendships that now seemed shaky. I missed our regular coffees, the happy hours.

"Mama," Piper said. "Come on."

Inside the store, Piper was taking her sweet time deciding on breakfast cereal when Laura, the woman from under the moth-surrounded school lights, appeared in the aisle.

She didn't look like a member of the cult of stylish moms from school drop-off.

"Hey. Good to see you again," she said, halting her cart. "Cereal. So many choices," she said to Piper.

Piper didn't look away from the boxes.

"Sorry. She's really shy with new people."

Why was I always apologizing? For myself, for Piper. Always.

"No worries. How are you settling in?" Laura's voice went lower, like she was sharing a secret. "Did you recover from the board meeting?"

"Barely. That guy gives me the creeps." Might as well be honest.

Laura nodded and eyeballed some granola.

I pressed on. "I've found out a lot about him, and about that dual role he's got going."

She looked at me.

"Whoa, seriously? Okay. You gotta get out."

"What?"

"Out. Like not to the grocery store, or online. What are you doing tonight?"

"Oh, I can't. I have Piper."

"No worries. My oldest daughter can babysit. She's fourteen and very responsible."

I paused. I wasn't sure we were ready for this. I hadn't been away from Piper, except a few times when Tom had her, since . . . well, I couldn't remember. We had a babysitter once or twice in Boston, and that hadn't gone well. I turned slowly toward Laura in the grocery aisle, thinking.

"I'll drop my daughter by at six. Then we can go have a drink and snack at Donovan's."

And like that, she rolled her cart away.

"I know where you live," she called over her shoulder.

"This one." Piper tossed a box of Cocoa Krispies into the cart. Way too much sugar, but for once, I didn't care. Despite feeling uneasy about leaving her, I smiled at the thought of going out and possibly making a friend here.

"Let's go over it again. Laura's daughter, Niki, is coming over to play a board game with you and have some mac and cheese."

Piper nodded. She was drawing rows of trees beside tidy brick houses and apartment buildings, a picture of our old Boston neighborhood.

"This is our street," she said. "And here's our house."

She'd drawn a heart on the door of a brick duplex, and a wrought iron fence around the small yard surrounding a large oak tree.

I swallowed. "That is lovely. Yes, it looks just like it," I said. Then, "Piper, will you be okay? I'll only be gone for an hour or two."

She nodded her head slightly.

"Have Niki call or text me if you need anything."

She colored in the orange treetops. She didn't look up.

"Hey, Pipes. I love you."

She nodded, staring intently at the drawing, as if she were willing it to exist.

*Kids take time to transition*, I thought. *This is all normal.*

The bar was dark and cavernous, covered in wood paneling. Dart board in the back. Sports on the TV overhead, above the bar. Laura and I sat at a small table. There were only a few other customers spread out around us.

I smiled, felt my body relax, loosen. A night out. How long had it been?

"So, you did it. Made it out of the house." Laura smiled and tucked an errant curl behind her ear.

"You really didn't give me any other option."

She laughed, a joyful burst. Quite different from the worried mom in the parking lot of the school, but the same loud and unexpected laugh.

"Well, I can tell when a woman needs to get out. Especially in *this* town."

The bartender came over.

"Hey, Silas. Have you met Liv yet?"

A pair of the palest blue eyes met mine. They were framed by sandy brown hair, set in an open, friendly face. He was a broad-shouldered, classic New Englander. Looked ready to chop some wood.

"No. Hi, Liv, nice to meet you."

I lost my words for a second. Those damn eyes sent me off course. Laura should have warned me about them.

"Hi, yes, you too," I finally managed, then had to look down. It was too much.

"Silas teaches pre-K down at the school."

*Huh?* I looked up at him, arched an eyebrow, wondering how he got away with being both a pre-K teacher and a bartender in this town of all places.

"Scandalous, I know," he said, smiling, revealing a sweet dimple on his cheek. Oh, sweet Jesus. I could fall into that dimple and never return.

"But those student loans won't pay themselves back, will they? Anyway. What will it be, ladies?"

Later, sipping at my second drink, I felt warm inside. The hard cider was dry and crisp and tasted like fall. I'd learned about Laura's family, her fifth- and ninth-grade daughters, a husband who was away a lot.

"So, what about you? Single? I saw the way your eyes lingered on our dear Silas."

*Our dear Silas.* Like he was property of the town or something.

I looked down, felt heat rush to my ears. I'd been busted for sure.

"Don't worry. All the moms in this town, and some of the dads, whether they'd admit it or not, have looked a little too long at Silas. Plus, he's actually nice."

"Huh. How does he manage at that school then?"

"Luckily, the pre-K is cut off from a lot of things, and he has a bit of a different schedule from the rest of the school. For some reason, I think they take it less seriously, maybe because the kids are still babies. I do know that Principal Stewart doesn't approve of Silas working at a bar and has made several comments about it. Looks bad for the perfect, academic, morally upright environment he wants to portray."

As if he could hear us, Silas looked up from stacking glasses and smiled at me.

Maybe this town wouldn't be so bad after all.

After a long gaze, I returned to my senses and asked, "So, what's *really* happening at Barnes?" I tried to sound casual.

"I see how you dodged my question."

I smiled sheepishly.

"All right. We can save that one for later. The school? Man. It's rough. Seems like a military facility, honestly. The kids are little soldiers, ushered off to academic subjects in lines."

"Jesus."

"Yep. And the teachers keep their heads down, usually doing what they're told, keeping their doors shut."

"That's awful. How come they haven't tried to oust him?"

"Oh, they tried. A few years ago, one teacher, Lydia Brown—she was creative, funny, outspoken. She taught fourth grade, and she'd been here for about three years, I think. She was pretty progressive and started teaching her kids about managing their emotions, understanding their identities, using their voices for change, social justice, that kind of stuff. You'd see her class, they'd be smiling and free, and the other students looked like prisoners, totally envious. I couldn't wait for my daughters to be in her class."

"What happened?"

"The board happened. All I know is, she went from shiny and happy and engaged, to quiet, reserved. Then on leave. Then, gone. Midyear." Laura finished her Sam Adams in one final swallow.

"Gone?"

"Resigned. And she moved away, immediately."

"Wow."

Laura continued, signaling to Silas for another drink. "And anyone who supported her, or asked too many questions, got letters in their file, bad duties at school, teaching placement shifts they didn't want. All of it justified by being 'good for the kids.'" She made air quotes with her fingers.

I shook my head. *How was this possible? What was in it for them? Simply power and control?*

"This is what I mean. The board is run like a mafia. You get in line, or you get out. Simple as that."

My phone sounded, and I fished it out of my purse.

> Hi. It's Niki. Sorry to bother you.
> Everything's okay. But Piper is
> refusing to get ready for bed.
> She's wandering in the yard.

Wandering in the yard?

This had been my life since she was born. Piper wasn't like other kids. She'd walk out of parties, up the stairs, and under beds to read or color. While shopping, she'd hide under clothes racks, retreating to a soft, safer world, causing me downright terror that she'd been kidnapped.

Even when she was a baby, loud sounds, strangers, and crowds exhausted her.

Holding the phone, I grabbed my purse. "Sorry, Laura, I have to go."

"Everything okay?"

"Yes, it's just Piper being Piper." I sighed.

Laura stood and adjusted her low bun and glasses. We waved to Silas.

He nodded back, opened his mouth like he wanted to say something, but I was already walking to the door.

Laura drove us the short distance home in silence, and I tried to squelch my simultaneous guilt and frustration. Just one night. A few hours out. A possible new friend. That's all I'd wanted.

We pulled into the driveway, and I jumped out of the Subaru and through the door before realizing I'd left Laura to walk in on her own behind me.

"Piper? Niki?"

My voice echoed in the hallway. No answer.

My heart pounded in my throat.

"Wait, they aren't here?" Laura called.

Nope. Not there. Not anywhere to be seen. Maybe Piper was still wandering. Hopefully, she was still in the yard and not in town, or down near the river.

The back door was open and I ran out, scanning the small hill that ran down to the border of our property.

"We're over here!" Niki called.

I let out the breath I felt like I'd been holding since I got Niki's message. I realized my hands were shaking.

The grass needed mowing, even though it was late fall. The bottom of my jeans dampened as I walked across the yard toward a small maple tree. Piper stood under it in her constellation nightgown, looking up into the branches. She called out softly.

Niki walked over to me. Her hand clutched her phone tightly, her eyes wide, exasperated.

"I got her in her pj's, but then she saw this cat in the tree, and she came out, and I couldn't get her back in. No matter what I tried."

I was used to this, and I knew Niki would probably never babysit for us again.

"It's okay," I said. "Thank you." I opened my wallet and gave her two twenties.

Laura and Niki left, and I crouched down on the wet grass. It was dark, with only the light from the back door casting shadows on the grass.

"A cat is stuck up there," Piper said finally, pointing. "I saw it run up. It might need help." Her eyebrows pulled together in concern.

"It's okay, sweetheart. I think that's our neighbor's cat. I've seen it around her house. The nice neighbor who brought us the rolls, remember? Let's go inside. It's cold and late."

Piper was silent. Her eyes finally locked on the fluffy white cat sitting in the crook of a branch.

"I can see it. Come on, kitty, come on down!" she called to it. She paused, watching the cat turn its head toward her. "I didn't like Niki. She was on her phone the whole time."

The stab of guilt was quick and sudden. How could I have left her with someone she didn't know at all? Then again, didn't I deserve a night out once in a while?

We heard a voice from across the street.

"Snowflake! Come on, Snowflake!" The voice was low and raspy, like a small metal box with only one mint left.

The white cat jumped out of the tree and down to the

ground in a flash and trotted through the yard, tail straight up. Piper followed behind her.

"Piper, we need to go inside!"

But my daughter was off following Snowflake through the side yard and to the curb.

The maple-roll woman held her door open and Snowflake ran in. She waved at Piper, who smiled and said, "Goodbye, Snowflake!"

The woman called out, "Thank you!"

Piper smiled as she skipped back into the house, her nightgown flapping. I let out a huge sigh and tried to fight back another wave of exasperation.

*Why was parenting this child so hard?*

# CHAPTER FIVE

Once Piper was finally in bed, I replayed the night in my mind, lying in a bed that didn't feel like my own, even though we'd been in Whitebridge since September. I tried reading, but I couldn't stop thinking.

*Lydia Brown.*

I sat up and grabbed my computer. I searched online and found the name gone from all of the school websites. Gone from all Whitebridge sites except a mention on the town library page, where she was a regular. It was like Lydia Brown had never lived here at all.

Social media was limited too. I did find several people who could have been her but probably weren't. If she'd been active on social media, those accounts were deleted.

No mention of a Lydia Brown teaching at Barnes. No mention anywhere, nothing.

Disappeared.

I scrolled more. Finally, I found a short article in the *Weekly Voice*, a regional publication for several counties in central New Hampshire. A small Community Update article reported:

"Barnes teacher Lydia Brown leaves mid-school-year for personal reasons. She will be missed by our community."

Personal reasons.

What did they do to her?

My neck itched, tightened. I reached up and rubbed it.

Little kids marching in lines like prisoners. Lydia Brown sounded like a great teacher who did the opposite with her class. Why was she gone? What had happened?

I found the school board's web page on the district site and looked at documents linked to meetings from two years earlier, when Lydia still worked at Barnes.

*Agenda: Executive session. Personnel.*

*Agenda: Executive session.*

There were no minutes from several meetings listed. Was that even legal?

And why so many executive sessions?

I sat back against the pillows, looked up like I always do when thinking, and racked my brain. I remembered studying public governance and open meeting laws. Boards could go into executive session to discuss matters related to contracts, personnel, disciplinary actions, litigation, safety issues, arbitration, or mediation. All it took was one board member making a motion to go into executive session—two-thirds of the board had to second and agree to it. Personnel was listed in the notes for several meetings, spanning October to December. A few other business items, but nothing more.

Whatever they had pinned on her, however they had threatened her, they had done so quickly. And quietly.

I looked at the moonlight coming through the window beyond the lacy, pale curtains.

I knew what I had to do. I'd go through every single Lydia

Brown on the internet if I had to. Find the right one. Find out what happened to her.

I spun my ring, picked my cuticle, with Steinem curled up next to me. *I'll figure this out.* This was the kind of thing I'd done at the firm, and I was good at it. I loved researching, following leads, putting together a giant puzzle, seeing how it all connected.

I loved the work, even if I wasn't an actual lawyer. Not yet.

What happened to Lydia—and what was happening at the school—was bullshit. I couldn't leave this house right now, or this community, but I could investigate, and I could tell this story, somewhere, somehow. Try to make things better.

I started files for my research. A folder for Bob Stewart and one for Lydia Brown, to start. I downloaded the few press articles I could find and chronicled my search for the right Lydia. I made voice recordings on my phone with questions, leads, information. I recorded all the details from the conversation at the bar and the first board meeting.

I didn't feel the hours roll by, didn't notice the sun coming up, leaking light behind October clouds.

The house phone and my cell phone rang simultaneously, pulling me out of my stupor. It was Piper's school. I jumped up, my computer flying, papers falling to the floor. Steinem flew off in a blur.

"Shit! Shit! Shit!"

It was 8:30 a.m. School started at 8:10 a.m.

Piper was seated on her bedroom floor surrounded by Lego towers—red, blue, green.

"Why didn't you wake me up?" I nearly shouted, barreling into her room.

She was unperturbed. She slowly placed a small black block on the top of a high tower.

Steinem trotted in, walked around the towers, and rubbed against Piper.

My little girl shrugged her shoulders. "Piper, I need you to get ready for school *now*."

No answer.

Would it hurt to have a kid who would just answer me, do what I said, even part of the time? What was that like?

"Piper?"

Thankfully, she started moving. I ran back to my room, jumped into last night's pants, and pulled a sweatshirt off the floor.

I made for the door, grabbing an energy bar for her off the counter.

"Piper! Let's go!"

I pulled up to the school parking lot too fast, still trying to catch my breath. Only staff cars filled the lot, and a custodian was blowing leaves off the walkway. I got out of the truck and met Piper on the sidewalk. I took my daughter's hand and pulled her along.

"You look tired, Mommy," she said as we made our way toward the door.

*Great. I'm sure I do.*

I tried flattening any bumps in my ponytail with my free hand. Piper brushed a chocolate crumb from her cheek.

I pressed the button on a small beige box beside the school's front door. I noticed a round piece of glass in the center of the box. A camera. It looked like an eye. Because of course it was.

Through a nearby window, I saw a woman with short gray hair look up from her computer. She squinted at us. She looked at me first, with no apparent recognition, then at Piper.

Then she nodded.

The small box made a horrible buzzing noise, and I pulled the heavy door open.

The school entryway was eerily quiet. The classrooms were just beyond two glass double doors to our right. Ahead of me, behind the woman, were the administrative offices. Inside the office, I could see the board chair, the one with the ironed-straight hair, talking to Bob Stewart.

They turned to look at us.

I forced myself to stand tall. I would not shrink for these people. This kind of thing happens sometimes—people sleep through their alarms.

*I'm not a failure as a parent*, I insisted to myself. *I have my shit together.*

But I felt the opposite when Mrs. Patrick, according to the little sign on the desk, looked up at me.

"Good morning." She said this like she had to. Like it cost her money to say it. "I see you're running late."

*Do not apologize. Don't do it.*

"Yes. I have Piper Wilcox here, in third grade."

"Yes, I know Piper." There was little emotion there, even though a tiny pumpkin sat on her desk, for the season, the sole decoration.

"Do you have a reason for tardiness? A doctor's appointment?" Mrs. Patrick took in my bunched-up sweatshirt. My matted ponytail.

"No. Unfortunately, we just overslept." Modeling honesty.

Mrs. Patrick nodded. Typed something on the computer. I cringed inside. Maybe I wasn't the only one making a case file.

"Okay, send her down." She nodded toward the heavy double doors.

I felt Piper's small hand tighten around mine.

"Is it okay if I walk her to class?"

Mrs. Patrick looked back up at me. Her beige cardigan matched her hair and complexion, like it had all been washed in boiling hot water, drained of color.

She paused. Tapped her fingers on the desk.

"She's old enough to walk down to class, right?" Like Piper wasn't even there and couldn't possibly have her own agency. Her voice was falsely chipper. A forced high pitch.

Piper's hand now had a vice grip on mine. She wasn't letting go anytime soon.

"I'd like to walk her down there, please."

Mrs. Patrick tilted her head, gave a smile that wasn't even vaguely happy.

"Okay," she said finally. "Just be quick about it."

Then she picked up the phone.

The walls were white, and the floor was brightly polished, even though it all looked like it was built in the 1980s. The doors to the classrooms were closed. I peered in as we passed. The kids sat in rows in most of the rooms, looking down, little pencils moving across papers. Their faces, when I could see them, looked tired and expressionless.

"Is it always this quiet?" I whispered to Piper.

"Yeah, most of the time," she whispered back.

We walked slowly down the hallway, Piper taking small steps, delaying the inevitable. I resisted the urge to pick her up and run out of the building.

We got to the doorway of her classroom. The kids were sitting on the carpet in a circle, at least. Ms. McCallister was reading them a book.

*Okay, at least this looks normal,* I thought. I breathed a sigh of relief, then bent down to look at Piper.

Her small face was creased, a line between her eyes.

"Okay, little bird. Pipes. You can do this."

Piper nodded. Her own hair was matted, flat on one side.

I kissed her forehead, hugged her tiny frame, and sent her in.

"Good morning, Piper!" the teacher called as she sat down at the circle.

I stood up a little taller.

Maybe I was blowing everything out of proportion, like my ex always said.

Maybe my instincts were wrong.

Except they usually weren't.

Especially about the men at the firm. And I had ignored it then.

When I turned around to leave, I saw a little sign that said, *PRE-K, THIS WAY!* It was hand done, in colorful block letters. So different from the rest of the building, as if the sign itself was a form of creative resistance, there on lavender construction paper.

What harm would it do if I went down that hallway? Just snuck a quick peek at Silas in action? I had to see that. A bartender, a pre-K teacher, those eyes?

I followed the little sign down the hallway to a room at the far end of the school. Stood at the pre-K door. The students' names were written in bright, glittery letters, taped to the door.

*Violet! James! Holly! Raquel! Jack!*

I smiled and peered through the small rectangle of glass into the room. Books everywhere, bright construction paper, cute animals on the walls. On the floor, sitting on a safari animal carpet, was Silas. A book was open on his lap, and leaning on him, eyes glued to the pages, was a small boy.

Silas must have sensed me there at the door. At least that's what I told myself.

He looked up and nodded hello, but with confusion in his beautiful blues. Or maybe a warning, because I heard what was coming next, right behind me.

The precise sound of high heels on linoleum.

"Excuse me! Excuse me!"

I turned around and forced a smile.

"What are you doing here?"

There she was, right in my face. The woman I assumed was the board chair from the meeting. Brooke Bentworth. Pressed dark gray pantsuit, thick mascara, her mouth a thin red line. Her face had deep wrinkles but was made up to cover them. Like she wore makeup twenty-four hours a day, and slept in matching, ironed, creaseless pajamas.

Her eyes took me in from head to toe—old sweatshirt, workout pants, disheveled hair, probably thinking I looked like I might rob the place. Or steal a kid.

I thrust my shoulders back. I was a good three inches taller than this woman, even in her heels.

"I was just dropping off my daughter."

"Is your daughter in pre-K?" She held up a manicured finger, bright red, pointed toward the door.

"No. Ms. McCallister's class."

The woman's lip turned up in a slight smile. Like she was really going to enjoy what came next. Brooke clearly enjoyed her power and was ready to use it.

"Right. So, we don't let parents just roam the halls here. It's a security issue. I'll need you to leave. Now." She said this in a tone reserved for unruly children taking extra candy. Or a dog misbehaving.

I had dealt with women like this before. Too many times.

I squared my shoulders again.

"I was dropping off my daughter, and just took a quick look around."

Brooke shook her head slowly from side to side.

"Again, I'm going to have to ask you to leave, or I'm going to have to call security."

Not wanting the situation to escalate, I simply nodded and turned around, heading back toward the exit.

Just then, the little boy who had been reading with Silas opened the door to head to the bathroom across the hall.

"Ben, go back into the classroom! We have an issue out here," Brooke snapped. Ben backed up into the room, eyes wide and filling with tears.

*Jesus.* I rolled my eyes. *Apparently, I'm "an issue" now?*

I continued walking down the hall and realized the woman was escorting me out. She was right there behind me. Didn't trust me to make it to the front door on my own. She was so close, I could smell her perfume, a sickly sweet floral scent. I felt like she'd grab me by the elbow or tackle me if I veered off course.

One of the custodians appeared in the hallway. Flannel shirt tucked into Carhartt pants.

Thick neck, bushy eyebrows, salt-and-pepper hair.

*Ah. Security.*

"Is everything okay here, Ms. Bentworth?" he said, clearly seeing the look on her face, and the awkward way the two of us were walking. The gray woman in the main office must have called him.

"Yes, Nick. Everything's fine." My escort's tone was clipped and cold. "I was just showing Ms. Wilcox to the exit."

He nodded, looking at me like I was trash that needed taking out.

"I'll take it from here," he said.

And then he actually took me by the elbow. Like I was in pre-K myself. I felt his thick fingers gripping me through my sweatshirt.

The woman—Ms. Bentworth—stopped walking as the

custodian and I continued down the hall. I could feel her eyes on my back.

I shook my arm free of his grip, shrugging sideways.

"Don't *touch* me," I barked at him, and then walked out the front doors on my own. The woman at the front desk stood, phone in hand, mouth agape, as I burst out into the fall morning.

I stopped walking for a moment, halfway to my car, and took a deep breath. I looked down at myself in my dirty clothes, reached up and touched my matted hair.

*Am I the crazy one? Or is something seriously messed up at this school?*

I made it to the truck, got in, shut the door. Felt safer.

I looked at my watch. I had just enough time to drive to a little town on the border of Vermont and New Hampshire and get back by the end of the school day. My research had indicated that the Lydia Brown I wanted to meet might be working at a diner there.

I had matched some photos online, with references to the restaurant and the town itself. I was fairly certain that's where she'd be, and if I left right away, I could make it there and back in time to pick Piper up.

I started the truck, turned the radio up loud, and headed out into the morning.

*You people have no idea who you are messing with.*

# CHAPTER SIX

I sank my fingernail into the jagged cuticle on my thumb, picking at it as I pulled into a nearby gas station. I needed a giant coffee to fuel the drive to the border.

The bell on the door announced my entrance. I stepped into the mini-mart and filled the largest cup I could find with the darkest roast. This was no time for weak coffee.

"Hi there. How are you doing this morning?" the person behind the counter said.

The simple human kindness, after being tossed to the curb, stopped me. The pin on their chest said Star, they/them.

"Just came from school drop-off," I said, grabbing my credit card.

"They run a tight ship over there, don't they?"

"Sure do," I said, pressing buttons, rushing, not looking up.

"Hey," they said. "Take it easy, okay?"

I said thank you and headed for the door.

I retreated to my car with steaming coffee in hand, heart pounding. Made a note to come back when I had more time (when would that ever be?) and follow up with the kind lip-pierced gas station clerk.

It was like a big town secret, this militant school, and everyone knew it.

I drove on the back roads toward the highway, pushing the speed, Esther's truck rattling along, taking the bumps as best it could. I stared ahead, thinking about what I knew so far, listing all of it in my mind.

I knew that Bob Stewart was both superintendent and principal. This was allowed and tended to happen especially in smaller, rural areas. This dual position caused role conflict, with one person trying to both manage staff and be an educational leader, but also function as a financial and facility manager and overseer of the functioning of a school district. The board seemed under his power. On top of that, one board member had just kicked me out of the building. So, it certainly wasn't just Bob Stewart who was weirdly authoritarian. And the custodian seemed more than happy to participate as well.

I knew that Lydia Brown was a teacher who resigned two years earlier, in the middle of the year, for reasons that were unclear. Silas was working in that school in a way where he stood out. From what I could tell, this was not a good thing. Good for the students, but not for him. And at the school board meetings, parent and teacher input was not welcome. At all. Parents weren't welcome in the school building. Well, at least I wasn't. Maybe I just wasn't the "right" kind of parent. Last, the school had a reputation for "rigor" and "strict academics," and the town seemed to be afraid of it, for reasons that weren't obvious beyond general unfriendliness and hostility.

I spun Esther's ring as I pulled onto the highway. Patches of sun burst through dark clouds. The weather was unsure, changing. I picked up my coffee, pushed down on the gas, then turned on the radio.

My parents said when I was little, I always ran fast—so fast that I would bash into things, from the moment I could walk. Coffee tables. Chairs. It was how I earned my nickname, Boomer.

And when I wanted something, I ran toward it just as quickly. I pushed and pushed.

Ignored everything else. Had to finish.

So what exactly was the problem with the bar exam? Why couldn't I concentrate on studying and passing it?

I pressed harder on the gas pedal. Bright leaves flew by. The mountains were covered in patchy, shifting light.

Because motherhood. Caretaking. Making baby food. Trying to study. Worrying about the chemicals in plastic baby bottles. Fretting if Piper was developing okay because she talked late, didn't like engaging with people. Thinking that I had better get back to work at the office because Tom wasn't making enough in construction. Agonizing at the thought of leaving Piper with someone else. So many things to think about. They left no room in my life, no room in my brain.

I couldn't concentrate, could barely get four hours of sleep consecutively, was barely able to brush my teeth and answer the phone—how was I supposed to find time to study for this test?

And it made me angry all of a sudden. How was it that the world just expected moms to go back to work and be like they used to be? I felt like an entirely different person. My whole concept of life, my constellation of beliefs, feelings, and personality, had shifted when Piper was born. All the things that used to take up my time, used to occupy my mind, fell away.

Then there was the way Tom would mock me, for not changing out of the clothes that I slept in, for barely functioning, for not making dinner or doing anything other than caring for the baby. And the worst part: He had questioned how bad it really was for me at the office, as if I didn't even know my own experience, hadn't lived it myself.

I tightened my grip on the steering wheel, pulling myself back into the present. I'd find Lydia Brown, learn what there was to learn, then I'd study for that damn test and become a lawyer who would come for anyone who treated women the way the men at my last firm had treated me.

About an hour later, I pulled up to the Sunshine Café on Main Street in Rothsboro. I caught a glimpse of myself in the rearview mirror with the tiny newsprint book hanging off it.

Damn. I looked like I'd had a rough night.

I took my long brown hair out of its greasy ponytail and secured it in a bun, took a lipstick from my purse and glided it over my lips. I brushed cat hair and crumbs off my sweatshirt and pants. That was the best I could do for the moment.

Dense clouds were gathering, gray and heavy. They sat with flat bottoms, like they were sitting on glass, over the tops of the hills around the town. I stepped out of the truck and walked inside. A tiny bell sounded on the door, and I was engulfed in bright acoustic music, plants hanging and draped everywhere, walls painted a cheery yellow, with swirling beams of sunshine reaching out across the walls. It was all so bright and interesting, and so in contrast with the day, that I forgot for a moment why I was there. I hadn't slept in twenty-four hours, and I shook my head, trying to organize myself to meet Lydia Brown.

"Morning. Sit anywhere you want," a woman called to me as she walked by with a steaming pot of coffee in her hand. There were a handful of other people in the café. A college student with headphones and a coffee; a couple sharing a newspaper and a stack of pancakes; and a bearded man having an early lunch.

I picked a corner spot, settled in, and opened my laptop to take notes.

"Hi there," the waitress said, her brown-gray hair piled on top of her head with curls cascading down, and a big purple crystal necklace hanging from her neck. "Can I start you off with some coffee?"

"Yes, please."

She returned moments later with a handmade, 1970s-type mug a lot like the set at Aunt Esther's. "Thank you."

I decided to just come out and say it.

"I'm wondering if you could help me. I'm looking for a woman named Lydia Brown for a case I'm working on."

A case. I was working on a case. It was just that no one was paying me for it. I was working pro bono. The woman's jade green eyes flickered. She considered me—someone who didn't look like a lawyer in my sweatshirt and yoga pants.

"Depends who's asking," she said, the cheeriness replaced with a flat, protective tone.

"My name is Liv Wilcox, and I'm looking into the management of Barnes Elementary School, in Whitebridge, New Hampshire. I know that a Lydia Brown was employed there as a teacher, that she was highly regarded by many, and that she resigned midyear under unknown circumstances."

The woman nodded, considering me. I could see the wheels turning in her mind, calculating risk, deciding whether she should trust me.

Buying time, she said, "Let me take care of these few tables and I'll come back."

I concentrated on staying calm. I had another forty minutes before I had to be on the road back to school to pick up Piper.

The woman walked back with dirty dishes from other tables and didn't reemerge for at least twenty minutes. Was she calling

Lydia? Helping her sneak out the back? It wasn't like the place was that busy.

I walked to the bathroom, trying to peek around into the kitchen, to listen to any conversation. I heard some muffled voices from behind the counter but couldn't make out what was being said.

Back at my seat, the coffee was cold. The waitress finally emerged, walked over, sat down at my table. She held her crystal necklace in one hand.

I leaned forward, ready.

"There *is* a Lydia Brown who works here. She's bright and caring and creative, and that school nearly broke her. She's off today . . ."

"Can you tell me the next time she is working?" I interrupted. Rushed her.

Bad idea.

"Hold on," the woman said, holding her hand up. "I need to know why you're here."

"I'm concerned about the school, and the way Lydia was treated."

The woman nodded. "Okay. Well, lots of folks seemed 'concerned' but nobody did anything to actually help her. Everyone was protecting their own asses."

She stopped suddenly, looking away.

"Look, I can't imagine what she's been through. But I'm trying to figure out what's happening at that school."

The woman stared, looked at me long and hard. I squirmed inside but kept my eyes on hers. I wondered how many minutes I had before I needed to be back on the road to pick up Piper.

"Okay, but how do I know I can believe you?" She finally looked away, out the window, and then back at me. "Look, I'm not as naive as she was. I think this is all much bigger than

Lydia, much bigger than Barnes Elementary. I need you to show me that you're really in this to help people like her." She rotated the crystal in her hand, rolling it back and forth as she spoke. "Otherwise, I won't let you in this door again. She's been through too much."

I waited a long moment, then held up my phone. On my screensaver was a photo of Piper, coming down a slide into a pile of leaves, a smile of pure joy radiating from her face.

"This is my daughter, Piper. She's in third grade. She is my life, and she's in that school. I don't trust it, it feels off."

The woman looked long and hard at the phone, then back at me. She took a deep breath, like maybe she hadn't in several days.

"I'm also a lawyer," I added, "and I started working on this case to figure out what's really happening there."

It was a tiny lie. I wasn't a lawyer quite yet.

It felt like the air stopped moving as the woman considered me, holding my gaze long enough that I started squirming inside, but I didn't look away.

Finally, she nodded.

"Okay. Come back another day. We'll think about it."

*That's it?*

Frustrated, I wrote down my email address and phone number and gave it to the woman.

I looked at my watch and started fishing around in my purse for a few dollars for the coffee.

She stood up, her long dress settling around her.

"Don't worry about it." she said, gesturing to the table.

"Thank you," I said, standing up and pushing in my chair.

"Sure," she said, watching me. She picked up the mug and started walking back to the counter, then doubled back to me.

"You need to be careful. Your daughter matters the most. Don't forget it." She said this with her eyes wide, so I could see the tiny flecks of yellow in them, and a crazed urgency on her face. My heart skipped. That was a warning.

I pushed through the door, back out into the drizzle, and looked at my watch. I should have already left to get Piper. I ignored the rumbling in my stomach, and my scratchy, tired eyes, and ran to the truck. I peeled out in reverse, no time to spare.

I blasted the radio to keep me awake and driving fast. There was no room for error here, I had to get to pickup on time.

Otherwise I would be branded "that" parent. The one that brought her kid in late, picked her up late, stayed out drinking, never came to parent conferences, used their grocery money for booze . . .

I imagined the things they could pin on me. How they would try to make me seem unhinged. Unworthy. I set my jaw. Pressed on the gas. I wasn't that person. I'd always been on time. Focused on Piper.

I turned onto the highway and saw the flashing lights ahead, and the cars slowing to a stop.

# CHAPTER SEVEN

I felt my shoulders tighten. The brake lights blazed ahead, everyone coming to a stop. I pumped my brakes, coming to a dead stop like everyone else.

"Shit!"

I couldn't see the reason for the flashing lights up ahead. An accident, to be sure, but I couldn't think about that. I could only stare at the clock, and the minutes rolling by as I slowly crept forward.

I'd barely had enough time as it was. Now, I would be late.

And I hated being late for anything. I'd plan the minute-to-minute timing of meetings, errands, the route I drove to pickups and drop-offs, calculating time down to the second if possible. My parents were always late to everything. My races, parent conferences. They didn't care at all, smiled, apologized profusely. It was embarrassing and drove me crazy my entire childhood. I had sworn I would never be like that.

Each minute that went by was a violation. My skin itched, my body hot and inflamed. It was 2:33 p.m. I was at least thirty minutes from school, which got out at 2:53 p.m.

I called the school, waited through the robo-message, then heard the voice of the same woman, the gray ice queen.

"Hi, it's Olivia Wilcox. I'm stuck in traffic. I'll probably be late to pick up Piper."

"Okay," she said with forced politeness. "I'll let them know."

And she hung up.

I could see it in my mind. The gray ice queen rolling her eyes, saying, "That crazy mom from this morning? She's going to be late for pickup. Figures."

I rolled on slowly, picturing them gossiping about me in the office. Creeping forward as time inched by. My breathing shallow. My fingers tightened on the steering wheel, my forearms like twisting rope.

The voice inside my head arrived, like an uninvited guest at a party.

*You're not a good parent. And you'll never be a real lawyer.*

That same voice had told me after I'd walked away from a dissolving marriage: *You'll will never find anyone else to love you. He wasn't that bad.*

And at the office: *No one will believe you. You're overreacting.*

And probably the very worst comment that voice made, in a list of awful comments: *You're a bad mother. You shouldn't have left her there. A better mom would homeschool her. Or put her in the Montessori school. You've no idea what you are doing.*

I shook my head trying to clear it, but the words kept repeating. That voice was an asshole.

After what felt like hours, I crept by a car on its side, a tow truck and an ambulance nearby, lights still flashing. The traffic finally eased beyond the wreck.

I had twenty minutes to travel what usually took around forty-five. I pushed air through my teeth, hit the gas, and said, "Piper, I'm coming."

My phone buzzed. A text from my ex.

> Where are you? The school is calling me.

Another buzz.

> Why are you late to get her? If you hadn't moved I could have picked her up!

Another message appeared. A voicemail from Piper's school. The call must have come in when I lost service for a minute. I cursed under my breath, pushed forward even faster.

The rain was coming down sideways as I splashed through the puddles in the parking lot.

It was 3:17 p.m. No parent or caregiver cars were there.

I pushed open the truck door, pulled my hood up against the rain, and ran toward the school entrance where only a few hours ago I'd been shoved out.

Piper sat in the lobby in her shiny yellow raincoat. All the air and energy were drained from her small frame. Her eyes looked up at me as she opened the door, eyes that broke me into a thousand pieces. Big round eyes filled with tears. She ran over, hugged me tightly. I breathed for what felt like the first time in hours, holding my baby girl, right there in the doorway.

It was only then that I noticed the woman who was standing to the side, awkwardly waiting.

Ms. Mitchell. The guidance counselor. Had to be.

Thank God it was her and not the other bullying, horrid people at that school. Her expression was pulled into worry, a crease between her brows. She wore a plain dress that looked a bit rumpled. "Ms. Mitchell?"

She nodded.

"I'm so sorry," I started. "There was an accident, and I got stuck in traffic."

Ms. Mitchell nodded. She looked like she was good at listening.

"Thanks for waiting with her," I continued, my shoulders dropping a bit. "It's nice to finally meet you."

Everything would be okay. I was just a little late for pickup. It happens all the time.

Ms. Mitchell nodded, trying to force a smile that didn't come, like she was already exhausted from the effort.

"You too. But I must ask, are you okay?" She took a step forward, her face opening into a question mark.

I stopped. "Yes, of course. Just a little rushed and worried about Piper."

Ms. Mitchell nodded again, her gaze steady, inquiring, observing me in yesterday's clothes, wet and matted, in the doorway.

Did Ms. Mitchell think I was on drugs or something? Drunk? I could feel her analyzing me, looking for signs of dysfunction with her guidance counselor brain.

"Well, you must be ready to go home," I said. "Thanks again for waiting."

I turned to go, taking Piper by the hand.

"Olivia," Ms. Mitchell said. "I heard what happened this morning. And now you're late this afternoon. People are talking and worrying about Piper. I'm here if you want to talk." She paused, tilted her head, looked at me with soft brown eyes, and said, "It's okay to need help." Her face looked pale, washed out, like she carried the worries of the world.

Then she pushed back from the door and was gone.

*People are worrying about Piper. The safety of Piper. Because I am unstable. Untrustworthy.*

The words were like scalding hot water.

I led Piper back to the truck.

We were both soaked by now. The day had been forty-seven days long. We drove the wet and shiny streets back to the house, silent.

"I'm sorry, little bird," I said as we pulled into the driveway.

It was all I could get out. Piper nodded. She was all talked out, it seemed.

While Piper took a bath, I stirred some pasta, stared at my phone.

Of course they had called Tom. He was listed as a co-parent on all the forms. But how was he going to help all the way from Boston? And of course he hadn't even said hi. Asked how I was doing. Then again, he was always sparse with his words, even more spare with his emotions. Anything that disrupted the things he loved to do was a major inconvenience.

I remembered how much I needed him to be a dad so I could deal with the situation at work. Or how I needed him to go to the grocery store while I finished my online classes.

All of it had been just too damn inconvenient for him.

I tapped out on my phone: *We're fine, I was just stuck in traffic.*

Three dots. Then nothing.

That act alone described him well. The effort to type back was just too much.

Piper was silent in the tub and hadn't said a word since we got home. I'd apologized several times. She'd just headed to the bath, her feet heavy on the floorboards.

Finally, she emerged, her dark hair shiny, in her fleece pajamas with bright red snowflakes. It was a fleece kind of night.

She came out to the couch, Steinem following her. I handed her a warm bowl of mac and cheese.

"We can eat on the couch tonight," I told her.

The steam rose from the warm, cheesy noodles. We sat down. Steinem jumped up, settled between us. Everything seemed okay for a minute.

We ate, and I asked her that great big question that usually never worked for parents.

"How was your day?" I finally ventured. "I mean, other than my being late."

Piper looked at me, chewing, like, *Really, Mom*?

"I miss Daddy," she said, picking at a loose seam in her fleece top.

I sat, unmoving, smoothing my face. "I bet you do, sweetie. You know he loves you. And you'll see him soon. Next weekend, in fact."

Piper nodded, leaning back into the couch.

"It was a lot easier in Boston."

"What was easier?"

"Everything," Piper sighed. Just the act of speaking seemed to take up all her remaining energy. Like she was pushing a boulder up a hill.

I nodded, didn't know what to say about that. I wanted to make it better for her. Make everything easier.

"It'll get better," I managed.

Piper looked up at me, her long eyelashes framing deep brown pools. She looked like she was trying to believe me, trying to make those words true. A few moments passed. The mac and cheese was gone. Piper put the bowl on the small table in front of us, then leaned back, pulled Steinem into her lap.

"They asked me questions about you today, and we walked

around the garden, even though it was raining," she said, absent-mindedly petting Steinem.

*What?* I took in a quick breath. *They interviewed her about me?*

"What kind of questions?"

*Don't freak out.*

"Like, if you ever left me alone anywhere or acted weird. If you took care of me."

My body froze. I stopped breathing. Cozy moment over.

I sat up. "Who asked you this?"

"Mr. Stewart. Ms. Mitchell took a lot of notes."

*Bob Stewart interviewed Piper at school, asking questions about me? Dear God.*

I felt my breath growing shallow, the buzz of anger in my ears.

*Keep it calm for Piper. Don't scare her.*

"Okay. First of all, I love you and would never do anything to hurt you. Today was a bad day. We overslept and then I got stuck in traffic. Things like this happen."

"I know," Piper said, "I told them you were a good mom, that you were just tired sometimes."

Steinem rolled over. Exposed her bright white belly.

The sky outside darkened, the color slipping away from the trees.

I remembered to breathe. Felt the impact of what Piper had just said.

*A good mom. Just tired. Doesn't that describe almost every single mom in the world?*

But I had bigger problems now. The school was trying to make a case about me. An irresponsible mother, one who couldn't be trusted to take care of a child. After one day of late pickups, drop-offs. One damn day. After walking down the hall in the school to a different classroom. I'd been on time, cared for her, driven her all over Boston, Vermont, and in between, for snacks, violin and swim lessons, endless errands, every single day since she was born, and all it took was one day to undo it. I had a target on my back. Just like Laura said—what felt like years ago, but was only a few days. They had bullied Lydia Brown, and likely many others into silence.

Maybe it was too much. Maybe it would've been best to just keep my head down. Recover from this, ask questions later, in a few months. It was hard enough to co-parent with Tom as it was. I certainly didn't need more stress in my life.

The anger drained from my limbs, like a deflating tire. It was all too much—the rushing, the worry. I'd set it aside for now, focus on Piper.

"Let's get you ready for bed," I said.

Piper fell asleep during read-aloud time, curling into me like a baby kitten, snoring softly while I finished the story.

I wished we could stay like this forever.

No judgment. No school. No having to prove myself. Warm covers, warm cat at our feet. Before I knew it, I'd slipped into a deep sleep as well.

I still hadn't checked that message from school on my phone.

# CHAPTER EIGHT

It was around four a.m. when I snapped awake, realizing I was in Piper's room, her arm draped over my chest. I'd been asleep since seven, a deep slumber that I'd needed for days. The idea that I had let it all go—the investigation, the striving—had released something in me. Let me finally relax clenched muscles, unwind my neck. Settle into the coziness of Piper and the bed.

Coffee.

The only thing that fueled my rolling out of bed and rolling to the small, star carpet was the idea of a steaming mug of the dark blend downstairs.

I walked down the steps and into the small kitchen, clicked the coffee on, grabbed my favorite mug from the cabinet, and waited. Looked out the window over the sink. The clouds had moved on overnight, and a few stars twinkled at me from between the branches of reaching trees.

Maybe I was overreacting. Maybe I could settle in here. Study for the bar exam quietly. Go out with Laura every so often. Shuttle Piper around. Find an art class for her to take somewhere. I could ignore what was happening at the school.

And if it got worse, I could just pull Piper, and have her go to an online school, or homeschool her, though that would certainly wreck the "study for the bar and finally become a lawyer" thing.

Steinem had come down from Piper's bed, hollered a meow at me.

I fed her, and the coffee beeped that it was done.

Thank goodness. Deep, bitter brew coming my way.

I wandered with my warm cup into the small room that was Esther's office. I clicked on the small desk light and looked around. It looked the same as it had when Esther was alive, except for a few of my boxes on the floor. Any computer work I'd done had been on the couch, in bed, or at the tiny desk in my bedroom. I just couldn't bear to bring my own work stuff into this sacred space.

The bookshelf, floor to ceiling, was a work of art. The books were clustered by color, not by subject or author. The shelves were a tour of the rainbow, starting with orange and yellows at the bottom, traveling up into reds, then beige and brown, and moving to various shades of green, and a row of blue books at the top. I wondered if Esther had been forced to be so organized at the library, with the number system for finding books, that this bookshelf provided her with some creative freedom, some joy.

I smiled before taking a slow sip, ran my fingers along the spines.

*The Handmaid's Tale* by Margaret Atwood.

*On Intersectionality: Essential Writings* by Kimberlé Crenshaw.

*The Beauty Myth* by Naomi Wolfe.

*The Rose Code* by Kate Quinn.

*Feminist Theory, From Margin to Center* by bell hooks.

Esther had a rainbow of revolutionary books in here. A bookshelf that was a paragon of female intelligence, bravery, perseverance, love. I smiled. It was an invitation.

I'd read some of these books, but it had been too long. I

promised myself I would read them, each one, in honor of Esther and to know her better.

After I passed the bar.

My eye caught on a small clay trinket on the shelf, in front of bell hooks and Kate Quinn.

A small ceramic cheetah, sitting up, its chin jutting outward, looking out. It was orange on its back, with muscular legs, splashes of black dots across its body. The striped tail curved around itself. But her small painted face was fierce. Mouth slightly open.

I reached out, afraid I would break it, this precious thing my aunt had kept. I laughed a bit to myself. Why did Aunt Esther have a cheetah on her bookshelf? She didn't seem to be a leopard print, wild print, or safari type of person. She was the town librarian after all.

But these books, this cheetah. They told a different story. Maybe I hadn't known Esther. Not really. Yes, I knew she loved books and helping people find them. I knew she never married and loved me fiercely. She was always focused on me, my life, my education, my dreams. Maybe there was a message from her here, among the books and her other belongings. I sat there, cheetah perched on the shelf near me, with the words of dozens of women around me, as the sun came up.

That morning, we were on time. Both showered, dressed. I felt in control of myself as I pulled up in the drop-off line. The fall day was bright and blue, the small yellow birch leaves the last to hang on, and winter was on the wind, tossing the rest of the leaves around the horseshoe parking lot.

Piper was chatty, which was a welcome relief. Like she had

let me off the hook for the day before. Or that she, in that enviable childhood way, had completely forgotten about it.

Either way, Piper was describing a dream where she was swimming in a magical ocean with dolphins who led her speeding through the water like a torpedo. She chirped on.

I smiled and stepped out to help Piper out of the car. That's when I could feel the air change around us.

Bob Stewart was standing in a navy sweater vest over a stiff shirt, hands in pockets, under the awning. Next to him stood Nick, the custodian. His arms were crossed over his barrel chest. Both men stared at me, their eyes carving into my body. I sucked in a quick breath, started fumbling over the straps.

"Mommy, what's wrong?" This child didn't miss a thing.

"Nothing, sweetheart." I answered, not looking back at the two men. "You ready?"

Piper stared at me, her brown eyes checking to see if I was okay. She finally nodded and hopped down. I kissed her cheek, patted her head, and watched her go. The two men didn't take their eyes off us. Other moms looked from them to me. I wished the ground would swallow me, make me disappear.

I felt dirty and guilty—a familiar feeling. Just like they wanted. To put me in my place. Make me feel small and weak.

I walked back to the car, pulled away. My hands were shaking again. All the showering, matching clothes, being on time—it hadn't mattered. Not one bit. Numb and barely aware of the car, I drove the short distance home.

My phone buzzed. A text from Laura.

> Jesus, what happened? I saw Mr. Snake Eyes and his henchman giving u the evil eye. U okay?

I sat in Esther's truck, trying to figure out how to respond. Then I remembered the voicemail I'd never checked from school. I hit the button, put it on speakerphone, held my breath.

"Mrs. Wilcox, this is Superintendent Bob Stewart. Your behavior today was unacceptable. We do not let parents roam the halls whenever they want. And now, you're late to pick up your child. We're concerned about Piper. If you are not here in fifteen minutes, I'm afraid I will have to report you to Child and Family Protective Services for negligent parenting."

He didn't sound afraid at all.

I tried to get out but couldn't leave the car. My whole body shook, a cry starting at the base of my spine, traveling up, consuming me right there in the driver's seat.

*You are not a good parent. You might as well give up now.*

I hiccuped. I just had to outlast this feeling, not let it swallow me.

This was a warning, a threat. They weren't going to take Piper away from me just for being late. The system didn't work that way. But now I had to keep my head down. Be on time. Not ask questions. I wiped my eyes with my hands, stepped out of the truck, and walked toward the house.

I saw the woman with the white hair across the street watering the mums on her small porch. Bathed in morning light, she waved.

I raised my hand slightly in response and headed inside. Walked to my room, got back into bed fully dressed.

I remembered another day I had done the same thing. Had felt that same suffocating shame, the feeling that I was doing it all wrong.

I had just left the HR office. I wore a black suit that day, a string of pearls. Classic lawyer look. My hair pulled back. The woman interviewing me had been kind, factual, patient. Her short hair cropped against her head, her fingers tapping out notes.

So many questions.

*How long have you worked at Floss, Deegal & Alter?*

*How long have you known Andrew Floss and David Alter?*

*What is your role at Floss, Deegal & Alter?*

*What were your interactions like there?*

*Did you ever hear uncomfortable, unwanted sexual comments, or jokes?*

*Did you ever feel that one of your male colleagues placed a hand on your body in a way that was unwelcome?*

I had sat there. Had said *No, no, no, none of that ever happened.*

Because I wanted to graduate from law school, wanted a good recommendation.

Because I felt I needed them. They had the power, and I wanted it. The women who had reported them, my colleagues, my friends, would have to wait. I was one of the many women who made that trade-off. I denied what was happening for my own benefit. I was a traitor.

The interview had lasted only forty minutes, but it felt like forty years—sitting there, telling lie after lie after lie. I held my back ramrod straight. My mouth moved as if I were pulling tight strings. It took every bit of my energy to contain myself as if my entire body was about to crack open.

That day, about a year ago, was like this one. Sunny, brisk, and change was on the wind. Nature moving on. I had crawled back into bed at home in Boston after the interview, shedding only the black suit jacket before wrapping myself in blankets.

Tom had asked if I was okay. He was the one who had encouraged me to lie. To think about what I had to lose before anything else.

What he didn't realize was that I had already lost everything. My integrity. My dignity.

Like Piper often did, I didn't respond to his words. I stared at the wall, until my mind went blank. And here, back in bed, I had that same feeling.

*Be quiet. Sit down. Shut up. Swallow your pain. Your feelings. Your experiences.*

I stared at the wall. I didn't know if I could do this all again. Just pretend everything was fine, like back then. It had cost me so much.

I got out my phone. Tapped out a message to Laura.

I'm okay. Just had a rough day yesterday.

She responded almost immediately.

Yeah, I heard. Everyone is talking about it.

I sat up in bed.

Everyone??

Again with a lightning-fast response:

Well mostly Silas and some of the teachers. That u took on ice lady. Brooke Bentworth, little ms perfect woman. I need to hear what happened. And that ur okay.

I paused. Was Laura really a friend? Or did she just want gossip to brighten up her life?

What did it matter?

*Okay*, I typed.

*Coffee and walk?* appeared moments later. And even though I didn't think I could get out of bed, I said yes.

Laura appeared exactly twenty minutes later with two coffees in hand. I stepped out of the house, wondering if this really was a good idea. The bed was warm, Piper was at school, and I could have just stayed there, doing nothing.

So much of my life was running around.

"Hey," I said to her.

"You look like you need this," she responded, handing me the coffee.

I managed a small smile.

"Okay, so, tell me everything."

I told her about being late for drop-off, and stopping by to see Silas's classroom, and being forced out.

We walked down the leaf-lined street. They crunched under our feet.

"Man," Laura said, "that's horrible."

I nodded. I didn't have a lot of emotion to spare. We turned down another side street lined with old Victorian houses, small, neat yards, and big trees.

"I knew Brooke was horrible, but you'd think after what she'd been through, she'd have more empathy."

"What do you mean?" I shoved my hands deeper into my pockets. Tried not to be curious but couldn't help it.

"Well, her older son has struggled with all sorts of issues in school, and she's had to work to get him support and resources. She said that was the main reason she ran for the board. But once she got in . . . well, it's been nothing but business, procedure, silence."

I nodded as we made our way down the sidewalk. I

understood the silence. I'd been there myself. The old neighborhood smelled like laundry detergent and decomposing leaves.

"And you stood up to her."

I stared at the sidewalk. Mumbled, "I guess."

"You *did*! I've been here for fourteen years, the last four or so with this militant prick for a principal, and his minions running the board, and you stood up for yourself."

"Well, it doesn't really matter now."

"Of course it does! Every time you stand up to someone in power, it makes it easier for everyone else to. Isn't that some sort of quote? I bet your aunt would have known."

I looked up quickly. Sometimes I forgot that Aunt Esther had lived a life here. Even if a quiet life. Everyone would have known her, or of her.

Which raised the question: What else didn't I know about Laura?

We came to the end of a row of houses, where it opened into a field that looked out on the town below. I paused, looking out at the burnt yellow meadow, a fall carpet. Struggled to find the words, and then finally just said them.

"They threatened to report me to Child Protective Services."

All the color drained from Laura's face.

"*What?* They can't do that. No way. You were only in the building."

"And then I was late for pickup."

"So what? I've been late before. More than once. This is the real world. We're parents, doing the best we can." Laura's hands went up in front of her to punctuate this point, a small burst of motion.

"Yeah. Well. I can't risk it. She's everything to me. And I'm on my own."

We walked in silence, starting down a side of the field. Grass stuck to my shoes as they dampened from the dew. Laura listened.

"There's been talk of securing bids on a project to upgrade the elementary school. You just know all of them are in cahoots with each other to make a profit. Everyone knows everyone and does little favors. It's gross."

*Everyone knows everyone. Everyone does "favors."*

*What kind of favors?*

The woman with the crystals at the Sunshine Café had hinted at a bigger scheme at the school. I wondered if anyone believed her.

Laura paused, looked out over the yellowing field.

"And what about Lydia Brown? Did you find her?"

I looked at her profile. Laura had been nothing but kind to me since I got here. But were we at the level where I should be telling her everything?

But she was my only possible friend here. So I told her about the visit to Vermont, and the owner of the restaurant. We continued walking as I explained everything I'd learned. The field led to the parking lot behind the big bank on Main Street.

"I swear to you, Liv. That waitress is right. Something big is happening here. And it's hurting people." Laura turned. "I haven't reported bullying of my kid for fear of retaliation. And I see it on the teacher's faces. They can't do their best work, or even try any new ideas, because he has a lock on all of them, on all their daily movements, actions, curriculum. Makes me worry and want to move, even though my entire family is here."

Yes. I knew all about the limitations of finances and moving. Two crows flew above our heads, black blurs, and I heard the thumping of their wings as they passed.

"I'm sorry to hear about the bullying," I said. "When you're ready, I'd like to hear what happened."

She nodded, her mouth pulled in a tight line. The wind picked up and pulled part of the hair out of her characteristic bun.

"They can't take Piper. That's just an empty threat. But you. I think you're smarter than them. You've got to keep going. Figure out what's happening at that school."

How did she believe in me already? Was this all fake, or did she see something in me I couldn't see myself?

I kicked around some leaves at my feet.

"Not if it means Piper will pay a price,"

Laura paused, looked at me. I never noticed her brown eyes were almost black, like Piper's. "What would she think if you did nothing? And let them bully everyone?"

Laura had a point. And she didn't mince words.

"What kind of example of a woman do you want her to see?"

I felt this wash over me. Was inaction really an option? I had already done that once and could still feel the sting of shame. Who did I want to be, what did I want to show Piper about injustice?

I felt the school ring on my finger. It was one of the first things I found in Esther's house after she died. It sat on her dresser, like she had planned to put it back on at any moment. I'd seen it on her hand over the years. It was my grandmother's high school ring, thick and golden with Saint Mary's High School initials engraved across it. She had wanted to go to college to become a teacher, but instead got married soon after high school and had two girls in quick succession. Her husband, Elmer, worked in the electronic factory for minimum wage in town and drank too much each night. He died in his reclining chair one night when his daughters were still young. My grandmother had to raise two girls, all in a dingy, cramped apartment they had to move to, with only her salary from the Sears department store to support them.

I straightened my spine, pushed my shoulders back. I could do hard things. I was built for this. I nodded, and Laura did too, both of us confirming the fight.

"So, let's go over this again," she said, "and I can tell you more about what happened the other night at the board meeting."

I recorded more voice memos while Laura talked. As we made our way back to the house, my phone pinged.

A text from an unknown number.

I'm ready to talk —Lydia

# CHAPTER NINE

I looked at my watch. It was 6:05 p.m., and it was already pitch-black outside. Nothing like fall in New England to make you think you need to eat dinner by four thirty and be in bed by seven. I sat under the bright lights in the lot of Marshfield's convenience mart, where Tom had agreed to meet. I drove south forty minutes and he drove north from Boston about forty minutes, and the convenience store was right in the middle, somewhere between the highway, dirt roads, farms, and towns. Local construction workers came and left with six packs in paper bags, a sandwich or snack under their arms.

"I'm going to miss you, little bird," I said to Piper, who was holding her hedgehog, staring into the parking lot.

"Where's everyone going?" she said.

"Heading home, probably."

Piper watched.

"I wish we could go home too."

It struck me in the chest, every time.

"You are! You get to visit Daddy and our old house this weekend!" I chirped.

"I mean with you," she said.

I nodded. Kids sure knew how to break your heart.

"Yeah, sweetheart, I'm sorry about that," I said, apologizing yet again. "But I know Daddy will be happy to see you."

Piper nodded, the shadows making deep pools and pockets on her sweet face. Just then, Tom pulled up right next to us. He jumped out immediately and opened the small extra cab door of my truck.

"Piper-bird! There you are!" He swept her up in a full-body hug in a single, smooth move.

"Daddy!" It was the loudest she had spoken in weeks.

I watched. The joy Piper brought to his face, his scruffy exterior all cracked open.

"Hey, Liv," he said. So much less excitement for me.

I gave him the rundown of when she'd last eaten, how she'd been wandering off a bit, and when pickup would be on Sunday. He listened, then helped her into his car, an old SUV. "Thanks," he said. "What are you gonna do this weekend?"

I paused, unsure of how to respond.

"You know what? Never mind," he said. "Have a good one."

He walked away, hopped in the car, and was pulling back, leaving me standing there, waving to my precious baby, driving away from me.

I hated leaving. Was not used to it at all. I didn't know how other parents did this—like leaving your arm behind. It was physically painful. I craved one last hug for the weekend.

I had to distract myself. This "school case" was certainly good for that. So many avenues to follow. Back in the car, I went over in my mind what I had learned recently, and what I had gathered on my phone.

The board had been meeting about building a new school wing, a suite of offices—including a large office for the principal and administrative staff—a large conference room for the board meetings, and a large garden shed. Apparently, the small library wasn't cutting it for meetings. They were calling for requests for proposals from several construction companies, including one owned by a member of the board.

Apparently, no one thought that the last part was a big deal. It boggled the mind.

Laura had been outraged that the improvements had nothing to do with instructional spaces for kids. At the board meeting, she'd wanted to say something, but there had been no opportunity.

And how were they securing the finances? I recorded a note to look up who the financial director for the district was and to look up the process that schools used to fund new construction projects.

The double yellow lines wound down the dark country two-lane back to the village of Whitebridge while I considered my meeting the next day with Lydia Brown. We had planned to get together at the Sunshine Bakery, and Lydia hadn't said much other than she would like to talk. I ran through questions in my head:

*What happened before you resigned?*

*What was your relationship like with Bob Stewart?*

*What were your interactions with the school board like?*

When I knew more, I could consider my next steps. For now, I had to get as much information as possible, collect it, and see how it connected with what I already had.

And how about Brooke Bentworth? What was her story? After I got back from Lydia, I promised myself to research her and find out how she'd become so awful.

Laura was right. I owed it to Piper to expose the truth. I wanted Piper not to cross out the word *brave* when describing herself, or me. The truth was that working on this case had made me feel alive again for the first time since the divorce. Like I could finally think, use my skills for something good, a problem that needed solving.

I made the final turn toward Whitebridge and pulled onto Main Street. I passed Donovan's, saw a handful of cars in front, and turned around.

*Why not?*

I walked in, and Silas looked up from the bar, smiled.

Damn. This was a dangerous idea. Warmth spread throughout me even though the fall night was cold. He could take me completely off course in so many ways. And what fun it would be.

"Well, look who it is," Silas said as I walked over and took a seat at the bar. "You meeting Laura?"

"No, I just stopped by on my way home," I said, and his lips turned up slightly as he dried a glass, taking this in.

"Cool," he said, and then bit down on his lip for a moment, his eyes scrunching up like he was trying to figure out what to say next. "Also, I wanted to tell you . . . I was really upset about what happened at school the other day," he said. "I didn't know what to do. I tried to warn you with my eyes that you had better go."

"I noticed. But a bit too late."

Silas winced. "Ugh, yeah. But you handled yourself well with Ms. Bentworth. I saw you stand up to her."

"Sure. Until she had the custodian toss me outside."

"I'm sorry about that. *So* not okay." He stopped drying and stacking glasses to look at me straight in the eyes.

There they were. Little pale gems. Maybe a little too young for me, but also . . . maybe not.

"Can I get something to drink around here?"

Silas laughed and served me my favorite hard cider.

The bell on the door rang, and a group of guys came in—

American flag shirts, bandannas, scruffy beards. Silas looked up and sighed.

"Great, this group again, and Gina is out tonight. I'll be right back."

"No problem," I said, and Silas walked over to them, back by the pool table. After bringing them a couple pitchers of beer, he settled back in on a stool next to me.

"What's it like to work there?"

"Honestly? Not great. I've been there for five years, started right after I got my master's in early education at the University of New Hampshire. The first year, the principal was Charlie Watkins—kind of a Santa Claus type. You know . . . happy and round, made kids laugh, even the ones in trouble, and gave teachers breaks by subbing in their class for an hour here or there, covering lunch or recess duties. Brought us cookies and coffee. He was supportive, a great listener, and part of the reason I started at the school. But he wasn't 'rigorous' enough for this one group of parents. They wanted better test scores. Better data. It was data, data, data. Academic achievements only. They fought for a new principal—one super focused on old-school academics. My whole first year there were all these meetings with parents and the board, and some of the teachers went and stood up for Charlie at meetings, saying how they felt supported by him and how the school was a fun, safe place to be.

"I mean, don't get me wrong. He wasn't perfect. He was soft on students, especially those who misbehaved, but he tried, and he loved all of the kids. And wasn't that what they needed? But my entire first year got consumed by this drama—meetings, rumors, so many emails. Finally, several of the board members quit—were chased out, really—and within a few weeks, that group of parents who had been complaining all ran for the open positions, and got on, and they made Charlie's life miserable. In the spring of that year he resigned, and they hired Bob Stewart, who was committed to their strict vision for the school."

I took this all in. Sipped my cider. The crew in the back got louder.

"And once he was there, everything changed. All the colorful kid-created murals got painted over. The teachers had to keep their heads down, especially those who spoke up. Most did. Except Lydia Brown. She just couldn't do it.

"After a bit, Stewart started observing her teaching. So did board members. They would just come in and watch her lessons any time, unannounced. And they didn't like what they saw."

I leaned in. Silas lowered his voice and got closer to me too.

"Lydia taught the real history of the United States. She taught her fourth graders about how the founders of this nation never lived up to the ideals they wrote about, how they enslaved people. She taught about gender roles and stereotypes, racism and LGBTQ+ rights, all in age-appropriate, creative ways. She used picture books, art, and music. I learned so much from her." He shook his head.

I imagined how incredible this must have been for her students, and how hard it was to be this way in a school like Barnes.

"Did you say school board members observed her class?"

He nodded. "Mostly Brooke, but others too."

I turned my ring, scanning my mind about what I'd read in law school. I had never seen anything about board members being part of the teacher observation or evaluation process, or even just observing classes at all. Didn't seem right, especially if the board members had such an axe to grind. My thoughts were interrupted by a loud cheer from the men by the pool table.

"So, what happened after those observations?"

"Letters in her file, saying her teaching was radical, political, divisive. The union rep tried to help. First, Lydia started writing letters in response to the file, rebutting them with facts and logic. Because those have to be allowed in there too. But they kept after it. They showed up, constantly critiquing her, looking for mistakes. Then the board started asking to review her lesson plans in advance each week."

"They can do that?" This was definitely not normal.

"Yep. I guess," Silas said, exasperated.

I wondered why Lydia hadn't lawyered up. *Can teachers even afford to lawyer up? What else could she have done?*

Silas continued, staring out over the bar. "She lost weight. Stopped sleeping. Started retreating into herself. And the board? They saw blood in the water. They knew they had won. They kept after her, even following her personal life, making sure everyone knew about it."

"Knew about what?"

But Silas's eyes grew wide as a man in a camo jacket came and plopped down next to me, too close, so that his jacket flopped open and touched my leg. His hair was covered with a bandanna, with gray-and-black curls popping out at the sides.

"Hey, Silas, we need more beer," he said while staring at me.

I looked down at the bar.

"You, young lady, are new in town, but we know who you are," he said, his voice gravelly like he'd swallowed a bag of rocks. He leaned in closer. He was in that nebulous zone between forty and sixty, and clearly lived hard; deep lines were set into his forehead and on the sides of his mouth.

I lifted one brow, an expression that said, *So what?*

"The guys and I are wondering . . . you got a boyfriend? Like maybe pretty boy Silas here?" He looked like he might fall off his chair and into me.

"Okay, Frank, that's enough," Silas said, holding up a hand.

"No," he said. "I don't think so," and a few shouts came from behind him.

"Go Frank!" and some loud laughs.

"What I really want to know . . ." He placed his thick, grubby hand on my thigh, and I froze. "Are you on our team, or are you all feminazi like your aunt was?"

I erupted at once and swung my hand hard toward his face. But that gruff bastard, even three pints in, ducked out of my strike zone, bobbing to the left.

"Feisty little thing! You're just too slow. I could teach you a few things." He came closer to me. His breath was hot and smelled like stale beer.

But then Silas had Frank by one of his arms, and started pulling him toward the front door.

"Hey, man, I was just playing! So, she *is* your girlfriend, huh? At least someone is getting some of that!"

The men yelled from the back, "Hey! Let him go!" but didn't come to his assistance. Too much effort, especially after a few pitchers of cheap beer.

Silas heaved the heavy wooden door open and tossed Frank out onto Main Street.

Something about the way he did it told me that this wasn't the first time.

My whole body pulsed—I could barely catch my breath. Fear and adrenaline stuck in my throat and I felt frozen to my chair. Through the still-open door, I could see Frank on the street in front of the bar, near my car. There was no way I was going out there.

Sitting there, I thought of all the times I'd escaped. Near misses.

The times in college when boys had followed me and my friends around, supplying drink after drink, trying to get us alone on porches, in bedrooms, dark hallways. We always had an exit plan, a strategy, and we'd look out for other girls. All of them, friends or not. But this would get fuzzy as the night wore on, details would blur, and desires would run high. Girls would disappear with boys, laughing, stumbling. And what happened next wasn't always clear.

The more recent times when I would walk the other way around the long meeting table, avoiding my boss's chair, eyes, hands. Or how I would open the door "to get fresh air" and prop it open, giving myself an exit.

Like a trapped animal. Always having to look for a way out.

Silas returned, walking briskly to the back table and summarily chewing them out. Saying they all would be kicked out if they acted like that to anyone again. There were some grumbles, some *Come on! We were just playing!* comments, but then they settled back into the game and the half-full pitcher before them, apparently not missing Frank.

Silas then walked over to me, in front of the bar.

"Liv, I'm so sorry that happened. Are you okay?"

It took all my energy to stand up. I took a step toward him and melted. I found the perfect crook in his arm and chest, a spot that I needed, and fell into it, hugging him tightly. A few of the guys from the back looked over, raising an eyebrow, one whistled.

"I hate this town," Silas said. He brushed my hair off my face with his hand with such gentleness. We stood there, like that, for a moment.

"So why do you stay?" I asked.

He blew air out from his lips, shook his head. "Well, this is my parent's place. They couldn't run it without me. And they're getting older."

It looked like there was more he wanted to say. I waited, his face inches from mine. But he said nothing more about it.

"I wish I could take you home," he said, then inhaled quickly. "I mean, to make sure you get in the door safely," he recovered. His cheeks flushed an instant fuchsia. I smiled as I forced myself to step back from him, from the sturdy warm place I wanted to stay all night.

My whole body was cold now, especially in the spaces that had been touching him. I deflated, the burst of adrenaline draining from my limbs. Suddenly, I could barely stand.

"Let me walk you to your car. Make sure that dirtbag is gone," Silas said.

I grabbed my purse, and we headed for the door.

"How did that guy know my aunt?"

"Everyone knew your aunt. She helped everyone at some point find what they needed. Someone in the family was sick? She'd find a book about the condition. Looking up some family history, or new hobby of beekeeping? She could find the information you needed. And she was whip-smart and didn't take shit from anyone,"

"Even in this town?"

"Especially in this town."

As if I could like him more.

He opened the door and tiny bits of white floated down around him. The first snow of the season fell like miniature, glittering jewels.

"Will you look at that," Silas said. "Here we go. Winter is on."

Snow curled around us, sticking on Silas's hair like a winter crown of fairy dust.

He walked right behind me, close enough that I could feel him there. The sidewalk was a little slippery from the fresh snowflakes.

"You better drive carefully," he said as he opened the door to my truck. He paused, looking in, probably remembering Esther for a moment.

"I grew up in Vermont, you know," I said, smiling for the first time since Frank had sat next to me. "Thank you," I said to Silas, risking a look at his eyes, now with snowflakes stuck in those thick, glorious eyelashes.

"No problem," he said. "I'm just sorry it ended like that."

I said, "Me too," and shut the door. It seemed sudden, loud, final. Empty.

I paused.

*Go home. Go home. You have work to do.*

Silas stood there and watched me pull out, then heaved open the heavy wooden bar door, as snow swirled around his head.

What he didn't see was another car pulling out right behind my truck.

# CHAPTER TEN

My thoughts were still with Silas, the comfort of his hug, how he had walked me out and stayed close. Even so, the evening had left every limb heavy and tired. I drove slowly down Main Street toward my neighborhood, leaves skittering across the road in front of the truck like fast-running small animals, snow coming at my windshield in white, blurry lines—trippy and surreal.

In a flash, a car came up behind me, following too closely, its headlights aggressively beaming through my back windshield. I squinted and looked at the time on the dashboard. It was 10:53 p.m. Who was out in Whitebridge this late? Maybe it was a group of teenagers, driving around. Or just someone with a tailgating problem.

But as I turned into my neighborhood, so did the car. My body shook awake, a chill that had nothing to do with the weather running through me. I looked in the rearview, but all I could see were the high beams.

Was it Frank? Hammered and angry that I'd denied him? He certainly shouldn't be driving. Or someone else? A stab of fear jolted through me.

Maybe it was just one of my neighbors, on their way home, driving like an idiot because of the weather.

*Stop being so uptight. People tailgate. People live here.*

I turned right onto my street, scanning and noticing that most of the lights of the houses around mine were turned off, occupants already retired for the evening. The vehicle stayed just inches from my bumper. If I braked suddenly, it would rear-end me. My heart thudded in my chest, my mouth instantly dry.

With Piper at her dad's, I was going to be home alone. If it was a drunk Frank, I could probably get in the house before he could get to me.

Maybe.

If it was someone else? Maybe not.

*Why were women always having to figure out their escape routes, the distance to the door, the dangerous math of "could I make it there"?*

I started sweating. Drove right by Aunt Esther's house, and so did the car. I pulled into my neighbor's driveway across the street, suddenly, without signaling, risking the car smashing into me. The driveway was right next to her small porch. The tailgating car slowed to a stop but stayed on the road. Gusts of wind moved the branches of the giant maple trees around us, dropping sticks and leaves as they bobbed.

I hadn't planned on pulling in there; I just knew I needed to be somewhere, anywhere, not alone. I didn't know if I should get out of the car or just wait until the person left. I turned and looked. The car sat, unmoving, a dark shape inside, unidentifiable.

Then the porch light flipped on and out came the white-haired woman, a big black down jacket covering her pj's, and Snowflake the cat right behind her. She looked at the truck, and then to the car, through the wind and snow and leaves.

She took a few steps forward and waved at me to come inside.

She didn't have to ask twice. I jumped out and ran to the porch, the wind pelting me sideways in a violent burst.

As I reached the porch, I said in one breath, "That car, it's following me."

The woman held her hand over her eyes, and squinted at the car, looking carefully.

"Get inside," the woman said, and I shamelessly ducked behind her and pushed through the screen door. The car screeched away, suddenly peeling out across the quiet neighborhood road.

I stood just inside the doorway, in front of the woman now coming back in, my body shaking again, a bone-rattling shiver starting at the base of my spine.

"You poor thing," the woman said. "Go sit on the couch and we'll get you warmed up."

I followed that order and found a worn, cushy olive-green couch, and sat. The woman placed a hand-crocheted afghan across my shoulders. The weight of it, the feel, was just what I needed.

"Let me make us some tea," she said, like this situation was the most natural thing in the world.

"I'm so sorry to wake you up. To disturb you," I managed.

"Don't be silly. Neighbors look out for each other. Your little girl was certainly looking out for my Snowflake the other night."

I leaned back, giving in to the warmth of the blanket, the softness of the couch. I looked around through half-open eyes.

In the small living room, across from me, there was a fireplace and a mantle. On the mantel sat a row of pictures—a family of five, kids in various stages of growing up, then looking all grown up, pictures of young adults, graduating from college, getting married. Snowflake came in and jumped up next to me, his long white fur framing his large, round body. He curled up like a heat log next to me. I noticed pill bottles and a few paperbacks on the coffee table, and some peppermint patty wrappers.

The woman appeared back in the room with two mugs of steaming tea. She sat in a striped, puffy chair next to the couch, and set the cups down on the coffee table, sweeping the wrappers and pills away with one hand.

"I see Snowflake found you. Sorry, it's a bit messy."

I nodded and smiled, placing a light hand on the purring cat's back.

"Thanks for being awake, and for letting me in."

"The car looks to be gone. I'm sorry that happened. Must have given you quite a fright."

I nodded again, trying to find words.

"I can't believe we haven't officially met. I realize I didn't even sign my name on the maple rolls."

I finally remembered my manners.

"Oh! Those were amazing. Thank you *so* much. Piper and I devoured them."

The woman smiled. "I'm glad. You know, I loved that aunt of yours. She was so smart and kind. She would bring me those rolls and we would talk and talk. She checked on me all the time."

Of course she did.

"I'm glad to hear that," I said, enjoying the warm glow of the living room.

"Well, I'm Matilda, if you haven't already figured that out. My husband used to call me Tilly, but now, most people just call me Till."

"It's so nice to meet you, Till. I'm sorry to drop in on you like this. Piper's with her dad, so I'm all alone tonight."

She took a sip from her tea, the steam coming up over her eyes.

"It can be hard to live alone," she said simply.

I nodded, a lump in my throat. Based on the way she spoke about her husband in the past tense, it was clear that she knew more about that than I did, for sure.

"Moments like that, when you're feeling unsafe, are terrible. So, tell me. What happened?" she asked.

I told her about the bar, about Frank, but not exactly what he had said about my aunt. I wasn't sure Till would be ready for that, or if I even wanted to repeat it.

"Oh, ugh, Frank. He's a town blowhard. Usually drinking, usually loud, and almost always inappropriate. But following you home? That seems like a step too far, even for him."

I sipped my tea, though my insides were still cold. If it wasn't Frank, then who? Till watched me as wind pelted the window across the room, rattling the pane.

"Why don't you just stay here tonight?" she said. "I have so many rooms I don't use. You look like you could just fade into that couch right there. That way, I'm right here with you, in case that person decides to come back."

I wasn't sure why, but the woman's kindness started to chip away at the fear that had laced itself around my spine.

I wouldn't be alone. Till would be right there. And she did look like she could handle herself. She might be old, but she lived alone through New England winters and looked tough as nails.

I nodded, and curled up, right there, on the couch, right next to Snowflake.

"Okay then. My bedroom is right upstairs, first door on the right," she said, like she was talking to a child that might have nightmares.

But my eyes were already closed.

I woke up with a sore neck and Snowflake curled up against my stomach, making tiny snoring sounds. It took me a minute to remember where I was. The night before flashed back fuzzy in my mind. Silas's light blues, Frank's hot beer breath on my face, his sweaty hand on my thigh. The bright lights pushing ever closer on my way home. The pull and comfort of Till's company, and the couch.

I heard the older woman padding around in the kitchen. She must have heard me stirring because moments later, a big mug of coffee was placed on the table in front of me.

"Good morning," I said, and stretched. It instantly felt like we were old friends. And maybe because of Aunt Esther, we were. Till went back into the kitchen for a moment, then returned with her own mug and sat down.

"Did you sleep okay?"

"Yes, thank you so much. You really saved me last night."

Till took a sip of coffee. Her hair was pulled up into a high bun on her head, tiny wisps of hair curling out of it, and she wore red plaid flannel pj's and white sock slippers. Her eyes were still puffy from sleep, or maybe a lack of it, and she sat with one foot pulled under her.

"You know, Esther really helped me out. When Charlie died, I couldn't leave the house. I didn't want to see anyone. She understood that. She brought me those rolls, soup, anything I needed. For longer than you can imagine. That first Christmas, which I dreaded, she brought me down to the town square, in front of the library, to see when they turned the lights on the giant tree. We didn't stay long. But it gave me hope that things wouldn't always be that way. And since she lived alone, we spent some time together—like one Thanksgiving when all our families were snowed in. We shoveled a path between our houses, and ate all the food we had bought for our families who were going to visit. We could barely walk that path at the end of the night, we were so full."

Till laughed to herself. She looked up at me, her eyes a bit weepy.

"She loved you so much. You were like her daughter, you know."

I nodded. Felt a pang of guilt that I hadn't visited Aunt Esther enough those last few years, when the firm was absorbing my life and Piper demanding any other time I had. The transition to kindergarten had not been smooth.

"I should have visited her more. Especially at the end."

Till nodded. I held my breath.

"We do the best we can," she said, her eyes warm, the lines around them delicate. Her words were generous and kind, and I knew it.

"How was it, you know, at the end . . . before she died?"

Till's eyes squinted, like she was looking into a mirror, into the past, seeing Esther there.

"She was mostly at home, with the hospice nurses, and folks visiting off and on. I stopped over a few times to sit with her while she slept, or watched TV. She was quiet, but still reading, and still writing, I think."

"Writing?" I knew my aunt had been a voracious reader, but I didn't know she wrote.

"Yes," Till said, draining her cup. "I think she wrote to keep track of her reading, mostly."

I smiled again. "She was always telling me about some new book or idea. I only read a novel every once in a while, and she was trying to get me to branch out. A true librarian at heart."

I emptied the coffee cup, the hot liquid warming me, thinking of my aunt. Till and I sat in silence as the morning light came through the living room windows.

"You know, you can come over here anytime," she said after a long moment. "Really. It's hard to live alone sometimes. And if you're ever stuck and need a place for Piper to be, I'm happy to have her here. She would liven things up for me."

"Thank you," I said. "That's very kind of you."

Till nodded. "I used to be so focused on things staying organized and predictable. So much time on the house, on decorating and meals and details, and when Charlie died, I realized that all of that didn't matter. I didn't feel like doing any of it anymore. All that energy left me. Now I like being in my garden, taking walks along the river, watching shows, talking to my daughters and son on the phone."

"And eating peppermint patties?" I said and smiled.

"Yes, I just love those," she said. "Can't get enough."

Snowflake uncurled in a dramatic, body-shaking stretch.

In an instant, my brain jumped back to what had happened last night.

It must have been Frank. He had waited in his car to follow me home from the bar. That made the most sense. I shivered to think what he would have done if I had pulled into my driveway.

"Till. Did you see what kind of car it was last night? I know it was blowing pretty hard,"

"From what I could make out, it was a smaller sport-type car, like a Honda Civic or something. I think it was black because I could only see it shining, no color. But it was so dark, it was hard to tell."

"Okay, thank you." I stood up. I had to get ready to go see Lydia Brown. "I can't thank you enough."

We walked to the door and Till placed her hand on my shoulder, gave it a gentle squeeze but said nothing.

As I left, the spot on my shoulder felt empty where her hand had been. I stepped out onto the frozen, shining grass, which crunched under my feet as I headed home.

An hour later, I'd finally changed out of the clothes I'd slept in, showered, and was on my way to Vermont. The cloud-filtered sun tried to melt the ice on the sides of the road, which was taking its sweet time to recede. I thought back to the puzzle pieces swirling in my mind, tried to pin them down.

A small gray or black car had followed me. So, I would drive around looking for that kind of car.

Esther wrote. So, I would search the house, high and low, for her writings.

Lydia Brown had been forced to resign. I was about to speak with her.

Despite the clues, despite my action items, nothing was connecting. I'd found no criminal activity. But my gut told me there was more to this story. I would keep digging, keep pulling on every thread.

I went through what I was going to ask Lydia again and again in my mind as I drove the hour to Vermont. I'd be ready.

I opened the door to the Sunshine Café with the sun barely lighting the scene. The older woman with the crystal necklace said good morning and took me to a small booth near the back of the restaurant, then headed off to get coffee.

Moments passed and I wondered if Lydia was going to show up at all. I spun my ring, sipped my coffee, fiddled with a crack in my cuticle.

And then in a flurry, a girl with a purple crew cut came pushing out of the swinging doors from the kitchen and walked toward the table. She hunched forward, her spine curled in a C, eyes scanning the room like she was searching for something that would harm her. The woman with the crystal was right behind her, gaze locked on the girl, a mug of tea in her hand.

"Lydia, I'll be right in the kitchen if you need me." She looked at me and nodded, giving me a *You better not upset her, or I will kick you out of here* look. Crystal or not, this woman meant business. It occurred to me that this might be her mother, the way their eyes were the same shape and distance apart, the way she hovered protectively, and walked with the same rounded spine.

Lydia slid into the booth and kept her eyes down on the deeply lined wooden table. She looked like a stiff wind might knock her over; she was rail thin. Her cheeks curved in, and her skin was a pale gray.

"Hi," I said as gently as possible. "Thanks so much for meeting with me."

Lydia glanced up for a brief second and then back down. Her eyes darted around. She looked like she might run.

She was like Piper, only even more amped up. This was going to be harder than I thought. And this was not how I'd pictured her. I'd pictured a vivacious, enthusiastic teacher, one who made students laugh, challenged them, someone full of creativity and life.

Not this empty, skittering shell before me.

What had they done to her?

# CHAPTER ELEVEN

We sat there for a moment, Lydia looking behind me, and around like a jumpy cat.

"Are you expecting someone else?" I asked.

"Nope. No. Just looking around to see if anyone's with you. Following you. Are you recording this?"

All the words came out in a quick jumble.

"No, I'm not recording this, and I'm alone."

"And no one followed you? Are you sure?"

I flashed to last night. There was no way she could know that less than twenty-four hours ago I was followed home, but still.

"No, no one is following me," I responded, keeping my voice steady.

"Yeah, well, you just wait. Keep asking questions and they *will* be." She rocked back and forth slightly as she spoke.

I nodded, took a breath. This young woman was not okay. I needed to keep her calm, but also keep her talking.

"Who do you think might follow me?"

She looked up at me finally. Her eyes were electric.

"You haven't figured it out yet," she said, her brows shooting up.

My heart started pounding.

"No, I guess not." I felt stupid, unprepared.

Lydia broke her stare, rolled her eyes. "Did you think my firing was a single incident?" Her voice rose as she spoke, and her mom looked up in alarm from the coffee machine.

I wanted to run away. Hide under the table. Forget about all of this. I had no idea what she was talking about.

*That's because you aren't really a lawyer*, the voice inside my head said.

I took a breath. Remembered my questions.

*Keep the interviewee calm. Make them the expert.*

"Can you tell me what it was like to teach at Barnes?"

"What was it like to teach there?" She looked around like her memories were flittering around her head. "Everything changed when they hired Mr. Stewart and took over the board. It used to be a place kids loved, a place of fun and curiosity."

Lydia looked up into the air, remembering, her face easing a bit, and I could see a version of her that had existed before all of this.

"And then what happened?"

"What happened?" Lydia seemed incredulous. "It started with something all teachers experience, really, just a parent complaining about something to a principal. Happens every day. But this time? It was the start of a campaign to get rid of me."

"What was the complaint about?"

"A book I was reading to the class. It was about a Chinese immigrant main character living and working with her family in a hotel and facing challenges like poverty and discrimination. Nothing revolutionary, and a great story. It's what teachers should be reading, and what kids should be talking about. But apparently the fourth graders were too precious and fragile to learn about it." Her voice dripped with bitter sarcasm. "And the handful of kids of color at Barnes we should just ignore, and pretend racism wasn't an issue for them."

I shook my head even though none of this was much of a surprise based on what I'd seen of Bob Stewart and his lackeys.

"Then I was brought up as a 'problem' and 'political' at the school board meetings. Parents started showing up, saying they were 'concerned' that I was making their kids feel uncomfortable, or guilty. They posted about me on social media, got lots of attention. They yelled at board members at meetings. Before I knew it, I was being observed all the time, even by board members. I had no idea that was even allowed! They reviewed all the books I had in the classroom, took some of the best ones away. And my budget for books, for field trips, was completely cut. Nothing. They might as well have put a muzzle on me."

"What did the other teachers do?"

"They got in line." Lydia looked like she had swallowed tacks. "After a few teachers tried to stand up for me, the board started watching them too. Noticing what time they came in, what time they left. If and how they used their personal days, sick time. Filing reports on them if they were one or two minutes late. Or leaving for appointments. Publishing their standardized test results. Making them compete against each other, focus on keeping a job, keeping health benefits for their families, instead of standing up for me. And eventually they all backed down. They felt bad, for sure, but they needed those jobs. At that point, I knew it was over for me."

"That must have been awful."

Lydia ran her hands through her purple hair, nodded.

"What about the union? Couldn't they help you?"

"They did, but by the time they really got involved, the

writing was on the wall. I couldn't take it anymore. The constant surveillance. The daily school climate was unbearable. I stopped eating and sleeping." Lydia stopped squirming for a moment and looked me straight in the eye. "Your aunt helped me out the most."

My face must have registered shock before I could stop it.

"You don't think I did my research on you? I knew about you way before you knew about me."

I couldn't find words at first but finally managed to get out: "What did my aunt do?"

"She helped me see the bigger picture about my work. Took care of me. And for a while, before she got really sick, I thought we might win." She shook her head and let out a gentle sigh.

"Damn, she was smart," she murmured.

"What was the bigger picture?"

"Have you been to Reynolds out on 302?"

"What? No, what is that?" I asked.

"The start of the bigger picture. But be careful. Once you know, you're dangerous to them."

As if her own words had startled her, Lydia jumped up. She stood next to the table, hugging herself, retreating inward.

"Wait, what do you mean?" I said, standing up as well.

Lydia locked eyes with me again. "I've said enough already. They shut me up, destroyed my life. But you . . . maybe you can do this for all of us. For me, for all of the teachers working there, for the kids at the school. And especially for Esther."

And with that, she was rushing back, behind the counter and into the kitchen again. She left me there, my brain spinning.

"Lydia!" I called. "Can I text you sometime?"

She didn't appear again, and I wasn't sure she'd even heard me. I sat back down, deflated. Tried to decide what to do next.

But then my phone pinged, and her contact info appeared on the screen.

Okay. Do the work. Reynold's on 302.

I opened the Maps app on my phone. It was a small country steak house on Route 302, about twenty minutes outside of Whitebridge.

Strange. I was going to have to go there, but first, I needed to see what Esther knew.

I pushed back from the seat and quickly headed to the truck. I only had twenty-four hours before I had to pick up Piper.

Out on the sidewalk, the sun was out but held little warmth. A stiff breeze hit me and I pulled my jacket closed. It was becoming clear that none of the answers I wanted were going to come easy.

I walked into the house and fought the urge to take a nap. Part of me wanted to just give up, climb under the covers, sail away to dreamland, and forget all of this.

But Lydia was counting on me. And the kids were too. Even Piper.

And I had a feeling, deep inside, that this was only the beginning.

I made some coffee, added an extra scoop of the grounds into the cylinder. I needed all the help I could get. I'd been missing things.

Maybe I had been distracted by Silas. Maybe I wasn't cut out for this. Maybe I really just wasn't smart enough. I filled the water and waited, doing what I did best, letting that awful voice beat me up inside.

My mug full of coffee, I walked into the small study filled with a rainbow of revolutionary books. Steinem followed at my heels. I sat down at the tiny desk facing the window and clicked the mouse on the desktop computer, feeling like I was sneaking into my aunt's private things. Like she would come around the corner at any second, and I would hold my hands up, apologize, feeling like a teenager caught doing something illegal.

The screen asked for a password.

I imagined Esther would have left it there, or maybe it would be in one of the boxes Mom had sent. Then again, my mother didn't keep the best track of files, or passwords, or anything really. I wasn't sure where to look.

Steinem rubbed against my ankles. Of course.

I typed: *Steinem.*

Nothing. I knew I only had three tries but couldn't resist trying one more time: *gloriasteinem*.

The screen blinked and Esther's home page appeared. I searched around for different folders, wondering how my aunt had organized her files, where she might have kept information about the school.

She was a librarian after all. There must have been a clear, organized system.

I was shocked to discover a folder with my name on it. After hesitating for a second, I double-clicked on it. Inside were dozens of photos my mom must have sent Esther, or ones she had taken herself over the years.

There was a photo of me holding a just-born Piper. She had a shock of black hair and was so tiny, smaller than my upper arm. There I was, younger, awash in exhaustion, love, and peace, my face puffy and pale. I clicked through other photos of Piper, or

Piper and me. Esther was organized, and Esther loved me, that much was clear—even if there was so much that I didn't know about her life. So much that I had missed, stuck in my own world.

I kept clicking around, searching through countless files. PDFs of articles, one after the other—why we need diverse texts, how diverse texts help kids, how to counter misinformation, how to do a library audit. And screenshots of quotes and book covers.

Nothing about Barnes, Bob Stewart, or the school board. Even in the places it took work to find. Not in the seemingly random folders, though Esther didn't have a lot of those, and not in the deleted files.

My eyes burned. My leg was asleep. I didn't even know how long I'd been sitting there. But I had to keep working, even though I was exhausted. The sun was inching lower in the sky and I thought about stopping until morning. But . . . no. Every other night I would need to be home with Piper. I couldn't afford to waste this opportunity.

*I need to see the school under the cover of darkness, to get a sense of the space and what was happening there, without the militia breathing down my neck.* The restaurant would have to wait until later.

I left the office—inadvertently startling Steinem, who had been curled up by my feet—and headed into the kitchen, grabbed my keys, and stepped out into the October evening. I felt the breeze on my skin. It was significantly warmer than the previous night. I made my way to the truck and hopped in. Across the street, through the thin curtain, I could see Till's TV on, shining a light in her living room.

Just seeing it, knowing she was there, provided a bit of comfort.

As I drove down the tree-lined street, a crescent moon

peeked out, delicate and arched. First, I drove the well-worn path to school. Just a mile or two through the neighborhood and on to Main Street. The two streetlights cast a glow on the small downtown. There was Donovan's on the right, next to a sweet little bakery and the hardware store. I wondered if Silas was working, and if Frank and his posse were there. It was so tempting to just walk in there, home in on Silas. Get him to take me home. Forget everything else.

I shook my head. *Focus.*

On the right, across the street, set back a bit, was the post office and then a large, modern bank building. It seemed out of place on the quaint Main Street. Whoever designed it clearly hadn't gotten the memo about buildings needing to fit into historical downtowns. And then there was the small-town square, a bit of land in front of the library, with benches, and great big oak and maple trees, now mostly devoid of leaves. I tried to imagine Esther sitting on one of those benches during her lunch break, feeling the sun on her face, a book in her hands.

I took the left on the side street that went straight to the school. I wondered if there were cameras as I pulled in and saw the beige building with two circular columns in front. There were no cars in the front lot or the pickup circle. The bright security light, still surrounded by moths, cast deep shadows. I saw a small dirt driveway leading to the back of the building that I hadn't noticed before.

Were there cameras recording me? I scanned the building but under the darkness of the sky and the crescent moon, I couldn't see any. I crept the truck up until I had to stop in a small dirt lot. My way was blocked by a massive garden that was surrounded by chicken wire wrapped around tall, wooden posts—probably to keep deer out.

I studied the scene in front of me, tried to make sense of

the dichotomy. Gardens were creative, messy, dynamic places. Surely, cultivating a garden didn't count as the "rigor" that the group of parents, the school board, and Bob Stewart wanted to project. Lydia said the whole school had shifted with the new principal and board.

Maybe the garden was just a leftover from the previous regime.

It was hard to see, but the garden still looked slightly active, like the last of the fall plants were being harvested—though the previous night's snow and temperatures could have done them all in. I could see at least three rows of plants at various heights. And next to the garden, there was a large gray shed with a lock on it.

Bob Stewart didn't strike me as a gardener. Though maybe he gardened like he led the school: everything in rows, everything organized, orderly, doing exactly what it was supposed to be doing. He probably used a lot of pesticides on any unruly weeds.

I'd been in the front of the school before, but never this back area, had only seen it from a distance. There was another entrance to the school building. I figured this must be where the custodians parked, because tucked under a small awning was a snowblower and some other big, new-looking equipment. I creaked open my truck door as fast as possible, like doing so quickly wouldn't alert the authorities. I knew this was risky. Someone, maybe the police, might come after me for being on school grounds when school was closed.

I jumped out, ran to the back entrance to the school, and peeked through the glass window set into the thick metal door.

It was a storage room, or a workroom/office, for the custodial staff. For such a small school, it was surprisingly spacious. The space was packed with power tools and equipment, more than would be needed for a school that size. There were coat hooks and a few living room chairs in one corner. A door looked like it led to the main part of the school. On the back of the door, I could just make out a sign.

*What happens in the Man Cave stays in the Man Cave*, it proclaimed in burnt orange letters, surrounded by a border of the same color, like a street sign.

Ugh. I hated that whole concept. Like weren't most spaces designed for and by men? Like they didn't already have easy access to the pleasures of the world? I remembered Nick, the custodian who was more than happy to grab my elbow and throw me out of the school.

I looked closely, paying attention to the details, building a map in my mind. The layout of the school. The massive garden and shed. The custodial room, stacked with what looked like brand-new hardware. There was a shining table saw and rows and rows of other tools.

As I took it all in, I suddenly realized that I'd lost track of time. Realized also that I was no longer alone.

The crunch of tires on gravel snapped me back to reality.

# CHAPTER TWELVE

I bolted toward the door of the truck, threw it open, and jumped in. I knew the car would be coming around the back of the building just like I had. In front of the truck was the garden, but by the backside of the school was a dirt walking path that led to the front of the school. There was no time to think. I gunned the engine, swerved around the massive garden, and drove on the trail. The truck lurched up and down on the rocky path made for children's feet, not vehicles. I pressed on the gas. I couldn't get stuck there, trespassing at my kid's school at night. My head almost hit the roof of the truck and the engine made a grinding sound, chewing up the dirt and grass as I climbed up a small hill and flew back down the other side. Now I could see it, the road up ahead, not far now, just a straightaway. But around the other side of the school, a gray, beat-up truck appeared on the back entrance driveway, coming toward me.

I pushed down harder on the gas pedal, felt the wild acceleration lift the truck up into the air on the final lip to the road, and then I landed with a thump, setting down as I yanked the steering wheel to the left, pulling hard to make the turn onto the street. I skidded right, then left, tires spinning, burning rubber, until I righted the wheel, and turned on my lights, heading toward Main Street, before I dared to look back. No one was behind me—for now.

Was it Nick, the thick-necked custodian? I didn't want to be found on the road, but I also didn't want him to look for me at the house, so I slowed when I got to Donovan's, stuck my truck right between two others, and ran for the door.

As I pushed inside, the gray pickup crept by. I hoped he didn't see my truck, and the chunks of mud and grass likely stuck in the wheel well. I made a mental note to wash it off before school drop-off.

I was a live wire, limbs burning with adrenaline as I pulled up a chair at the bar. My breathing was rapid and I tried to slow it down, waiting for Silas to look up. Not that his eyes would help me calm down, exactly.

As if he heard my thoughts, he looked up from stacking glasses.

"Well, hello there. Glad to see you here again. I wasn't sure if you'd be back—considering last time." He looked around, and I did too. No Frank. Just a few older folks in the back. "You okay? You look . . . flushed."

"Yeah. Just needed a place to be for a minute."

I kept an eye on the door to see if Nick barged through. Maybe I could duck behind the bar. I scanned the path that I would take to get there.

Silas noticed. "Liv. What's going on?"

I tried to figure out how much to tell him. "I'm just . . . trying to figure out what's happening at that school. It isn't right."

"Is someone following you? Liv, this is crazy." His eyes darted around.

I smiled at him. This man, who was at least ten years younger than me, cared. His eyebrows pushed together with worry.

I reached across the bar. Took his hand. He looked at it. His skin was warm, soft, inviting.

"I'm fine. Really. I just need to stay here for a bit."

Silas nodded. "You're welcome here anytime. And please, Liv, when you're ready, tell me what's going on so I can help."

It would be so easy to fall into him and never look back.

But not yet. I still had work to do.

"Okay," I said. "I appreciate that. I'll let you know."

After a few more moments of chatting, I figured it was safe to head out. Nick, or whoever it was, had already passed, and hopefully had given up looking for me. My heart rate slowed. I was in the clear.

I pulled back from the spell that was Silas and headed for the door, alone. This was how it had to be.

In the dark I woke with a start and knew instantly what to do. I sat bolt upright in bed and threw back the covers, sending Steinem scurrying away. It was still the middle of the night.

Of course. Of course Esther wouldn't have made it easy.

Her password might have been easy. But she wouldn't just leave everything out there for them to find.

She must have had a web backup or a memory stick. And it would probably be password protected. If Lydia and Ester had been working together, there had to be evidence of it.

Esther was, after all, a thorough librarian, researcher, and curator.

I made my way downstairs to the office, turned on the small desk lamp, and logged in to the computer. I rubbed my eyes and began the search. I looked for folders named with aliases, for patterns, number codes, clues. Time crept by. My initial burst of energy started draining from my mind.

There was nothing but inky blackness outside. I wondered how Till was, hoped she was sleeping. Being alone because your partner died was quite different from being alone after a divorce. I was exhausted, and my bed was calling to me.

I looked at the screen one last time before giving up for the night. Noticed a small, green circle in the upper right corner for the first time.

*Huh.*

I clicked on it. And a portal for web backup sprang to life.

*Yes.* She had paid for an auto web backup.

Because she was Esther, she had a backup system. Of course she did. If someone had cleared her computer, or if she had an external one that she plugged into this computer, there was likely a backup here, and it would have been easily missed, if anyone was looking.

Another username, another password.

I tried Esther's email and variations of Steinem.

Nothing.

I tapped my fingers on the desk. This one was going to be harder. I looked around. Esther didn't seem like someone who would have an old-school paper list of passwords, but then again, maybe she would. She was of that generation where folks wrote passwords down. I looked in the small desk drawer. Pens, sticky notes, paper clips. Nothing written on. No bits of evidence, clues I could use.

I looked at the time. It was 3:17 a.m.

Lydia. Maybe since they were working on the case together, Lydia was a backup to the backup.

I texted her.

Sorry to text so late. I'm in Esther's computer, looking to get access to the web backup. Do you know the password?

Several moments passed. I stared out at the dark sky beyond the window, feeling my own systems shutting down. I slid into semiconsciousness.

The phone vibrated several minutes later—something I heard from what felt like a great distance. Lydia must have been a light sleeper, or a hopeless insomniac.

I surfaced from my half slumber and checked my phone.

You got in the first gateway. Finally. At least you know one of her feminist heroes.

Of course Lydia had to get a dig in there.

Also, her cat.

I inserted a cat emoji.

Lydia laughed at the text. At least I had made her smile—that was something. Three more dots flashed.

It is a simple code. Each letter a number, starting with one and A.

Okay. What do I do with that?

What did Esther value above all?

Books, reading, truth.

Getting closer.

I felt like I was failing a test.

Then my eyes fell on the enormous bookshelf. Scholars and poets, philosophers and scientists, curious souls of all kinds.

KNOWLEDGE

Exactly, yes. Good. What does it equal?

Of course. *Power.*

So the numbers, then =, then power!

Thank you.

Make her proud.

Then she was gone.

Fully awake now, I jumped up. Grabbed a piece of paper from the printer, wrote out the alphabet, with increasing numbers underneath.

Such a simple code. But effective.

I checked over the code twice. The number stood for Esther, and hopefully, it would give me access to all of her hidden work. I typed in the long number, the equals sign, the word "power," and an exclamation point, and blessedly, thankfully, it accepted the password and allowed me in. My arms pulsed with excitement as I clicked into the computer backup, a new screen lighting up with secret files on a green and white background. I scanned them.

And there it was.

A file labeled Barnes Elementary. And inside that, a file on the board. And one for Lydia Brown.

*Damn, Esther. Okay. You did some work.*

My eyes itched. *Nope, no sleep yet. Come on.* I jumped up and ran to the kitchen.

Steinem trotted after me. Clearly, we were on a mission. Time for strong coffee.

Back in the office with a dark brew in my hand, I clicked the Barnes Elementary School file. It popped open and I started going through the documents.

First, an architectural map of the inside of the building, showing the front and back entrances, and all the classrooms. I studied this, made myself familiar with the hallways, doors, closets, and storage rooms, especially the large one I had peered into earlier that night.

I moved on to the budget from the last several years. It was a complex spreadsheet full of all the purchases, services, and programs it took to run the small school. I scanned the sections, finally getting to the maintenance section. It was short, had categories like tools and equipment, but the numbers were extremely high. Hundreds of thousands of dollars spread across a few of these categories. *Strange.*

I rubbed my face, took a big swig of coffee, then clicked on the Lydia Brown file and saw several things. First, a document with notes and lists of names. One file: *Meetings with Ms. Dominique Stevens.* And then, several downloaded PDFs: the campaign to get rid of Lydia.

There were letters to the editor in that weekly paper—an especially biting one from Brooke Bentworth—and copied emails of a special parent meeting to discuss the "radical and indoctrinating" teaching methods of Lydia Brown.

While this information was all known to me, to see it there in black and white, was horrifying. I imagined Lydia's devastation, her heartbreak.

I googled Dominique Stevens, who popped up as the New Hampshire National Teachers Association union legal representative. She'd been practicing for fifteen years and had plenty of credentials. The kind of person you'd want on your case.

*Well done, Esther. You helped Lydia fight back.*

But it hadn't been enough.

There was only one documentation of a meeting with Dominique. It read: "Dominique thinks we have a case. We're going to take this all the way."

But that was it. Their work had apparently stopped after that. And then Lydia resigned, left town. What had happened? Maybe I could find this Dominique. But then again, even if I did, client-attorney privileges meant she wouldn't talk to me.

My head slipped forward. The coffee wasn't cutting it. I had to get some sleep.

*Just take a quick look at the board file.*

I had to.

Esther had copied all the available board notes from each meeting for several years. I knew I had to go back and read these carefully, the ones I could access, because so many of them were labeled "executive session"—in other words, hidden from the public. I read a few, my eyes starting to close, my brain shutting down. It was almost 4 a.m.

I decided to click on one last file before calling it quits.

It was a photo, a receipt from that steak house Lydia had told me about. It was a bill for $480, signed by Bob Stewart.

This place had to be important, had to be a part of this puzzle. And damn, that was a lot to spend at a restaurant.

There was a second receipt, this one from a local jewelry shop, Moyer's.

This was odd. I could see a restaurant receipt, but a jeweler? How had Esther gotten these? Just how deep into this was she?

The receipt was hard to make out. But I could see the purchase was $10,871.

The item description only said *necklace*. The signature? None other than Bob Stewart.

All the details, files, and notes swirled in my head as I rested it on the table, just for a minute. Sleep finally swallowed me.

# CHAPTER THIRTEEN

At some point I must have stumbled from the computer up to bed.

The sun had risen, the last of the river fog starting to burn off to reveal bright blue patches of sky. Days like this were numbered in the fall in the northeast, and could make you forget that a brutal winter was coming.

I woke and instantly thought of Piper. How was she doing with Tom? He had always been a pretty good dad. Silly, funny, and caring most of the time. Grumpy only when he didn't have time to do what he loved for a few days in a row. And then, he was short. Short with her, and with everyone else too. I wondered if he would get like that with Piper at the end of their time together.

With the separation, then divorce, that shortness multiplied, and that was all I saw out of him. But maybe not Piper. Maybe he saved the good for her.

How had I not thought much of Piper in the last twenty-four hours? I'd been completely consumed by Lydia and the files—and if I was being honest, I felt alive, had been swept away with this case, and hadn't even texted to check in.

Not that he had either.

I rolled over. Tried to clear my mind, sink back into sleep. I'd only slept a few hours, needed a lot more.

My brain continued its churn. Clearly, Tom didn't think I had it in me. He thought he could just coast in our marriage, nit-picking away at me, minimizing my struggles, my work, my constant labor—all of it. But the realization that I had to leave Tom and also finally speak up about what had been happening at the office all but hit me in the face on the same day.

I looked at the clock on the nightstand. It was almost eight in the morning. I rubbed my eyes. I had until five before I had to meet Tom and Piper.

I could study for the bar. Finally.

Or . . .

I could finally go to that steak house, continue the research. See what Lydia and Esther were talking about.

Maybe Lydia was a bit delusional. She certainly seemed to be unstable when we met. Maybe this was just a case of one teacher getting bullied out of her job. Surely awful, but it probably happened all the time across the country.

There probably wasn't some grand conspiracy. What was that concept I'd learned about in law school?

Confirmation bias.

I had memorized so many definitions, and this one floated to the surface of my mind like it was written on a note card and handed to me.

Confirmation bias. The tendency to seek out, interpret, judge, and remember information that supports one's preexisting beliefs and values.

Maybe there was nothing bigger going on. I was just late to drop-off, late to pickup. The board and Bob Stewart were overly focused on "rigor" and academic achievement and lacked joy and creativity. Not a crime, just a culture. A rotten, toxic, horrible culture. But not illegal.

And I was an outsider.

I rolled over, pulled the comforter up around my shoulders, trying to fall back to sleep.

Steinem woke up, stretched her four paws in opposite directions.

But Esther. Esther is why this was about more than one teacher.

She built files, a case, and she was shining a flashlight for me. I looked around the bedroom. Across from the bed was Esther's dark wood dresser, with a big mirror attached. On it sat a photo of Esther and me, from when I was in college. I wore a pink hippie dress, a braided yarn necklace from the summer camp I was working at around my neck. Esther wore a brightly patterned button-up dress, the print looking like it was from Kenya or South Africa. Her head was turned toward me, and she was smiling, hugging me sideways.

I remembered that day. I had come up from Boston to have lunch with her—not for any specific reason, just wanted to see her. I hadn't even told my mom I was coming. Not that it would have mattered anyway. My mom wouldn't leave the homestead for such a short visit. We'd eaten tomato soup and grilled cheese, the best thing in the world, right in the kitchen downstairs. Esther had asked all about my classes, my professors, my roommate. She smiled and listened and nodded.

I pushed back the covers. It was time to give up on sleep. I was going to get back at it, do some more reading on Esther's old desktop.

A few hours later, I stepped out of the old house and pulled the door closed, locking it. The bright sun greeted me, the fog gone and the sky a brilliant blue. I stood for a minute, feeling the warmth on my face.

"Liv! Hello!" And there was Till, in a red tracksuit, coming back from her walk by the river. Her long gray hair was pulled back into a tight ponytail, and her limp was less noticeable.

She moved toward me at a slow, steady pace.

"How have you been?" she said.

"I've been pretty good, Till, how about you?" I hoped she couldn't see the puffiness of my eyes.

"Oh, just fine. Today's absolutely stunning. What a beauty." I nodded. I could feel the time ticking by, but didn't want to be rude.

"You been mudding somewhere?" Till asked playfully.

And I remembered the truck. It sat there, streaked with red-brown mud caked on the doors and the sides.

I didn't know what to say.

"You know what? You don't need to tell me. But I did have trouble sleeping last night, and at about 4 a.m. I got up and sat in the living room."

I was trying not to look at my watch. I could feel my last minutes of freedom for the next few weeks slipping away.

"And I saw a gray truck in front of your house, just sitting there. For quite a bit." She paused, shook her head. "I didn't like it."

My brain pulled back in to focus on Till's words.

"What?"

"Not the same car that followed you the other night. A different one. I got worried."

I imagined Nick, sitting in his truck, watching my house.

"Did anyone get out?" I shuddered. I'd locked all the doors. Wait. Even the basement? I hoped I had locked the basement.

"I don't know if they did before I got up, but not while I was watching. Liv, are you involved in something dangerous?"

The creases between her eyes deepened, and she tilted her head.

"Just this town," I said.

"Honestly, I don't know what's going on with this town, but this is not how to greet a newcomer."

"You got that right," I said, picturing Nick walking toward my basement door in the middle of the night.

We stood there in the late morning light.

"Okay, well, remember I'm right across the street. One more thing: Do you and Piper like homemade mac 'n' cheese?"

I smiled and nodded.

"Well, good! I'll make some today, so you and she have a big pan of it for this week." She was a godsend.

"Till?" I called as she started to walk away. She stopped, looked back, a slight rounding of her back as she moved.

"Yes?"

"How long did the truck stay?"

"Well, after I got my wits about me, I turned on all my lights and stood in the window, watching, letting him know that I saw him there, until he pulled away."

If he was coming for me, or going to do anything, surely this light parade, and this fierce woman, had made him move on.

Not just a godsend. Till was also a badass.

I finally pulled out on to 302, hearing chunks of dirt fall off my truck. I really had to get it washed—this was like a big sign announcing that I'd been the one to leave those deep tire marks all over the property of Barnes Elementary.

But there was no time now.

I drove just outside of the town limits, where the speed limit of the rural highway goes up to fifty and the houses were fewer and farther apart, most of them trailers or cabins tucked up into the woods. The grass and the leaves were all that late October yellow, the last holdouts before stick season, the time between bright leaves and snow, came in, their color an act of defiance, of resilience. They almost sparkled in the sun, set against the blue sky like a vibrant painting.

I thought through my options. If no one was at the steak house, I could look in the windows, take pictures, see what information I could glean from the outside. Which was probably not much. But if someone was there, I could go in and ask a few questions.

I pulled up and saw an old station wagon tucked into the back of the brown building. A large model of a cow, looking a bit startled, stood on a pole in front of the restaurant in case customers needed a visual image of what they were about to eat. The station wagon looked to be the vintage of Esther's truck, at least twenty years old, running on a wish and a prayer.

Probably a waiter setting up for the dinner shift.

I parked out front to give them a chance to see me—no surprises, especially in a place like this, far from other businesses or people.

I walked slowly up to the front double doors, which sat under a smaller cow sign. They were locked. I looked into the large windows, which were dirty around the edges.

Inside, I could see a woman wiping down tables. She was dressed in a black T-shirt, skirt, and tights, her hair dyed blond, dark brown roots showing from her slick, hair-sprayed ponytail. She looked like someone who had been on her feet working since the day she was born.

The woman glanced up at me. I waved, pointed to the door.

The woman shook her head. Mouthed "Not open yet."

I knocked on the glass.

The woman, irritated, turned around quickly, whipped the cloth down by her side, came to the door, and pushed it open. Her face was thick with makeup, covering the blue tint and puff under her eyes.

"We're not open yet," she repeated, her voice gravelly.

"I'm so sorry. I'm a local reporter working on a story about the history of this place."

I went with "reporter" at the last minute because it sounded less scary than "lawyer."

"You know, a feel-good piece," I continued.

"Who do you work for?"

I paused. Remembered the weekly I saw at the grocery store that was filled with town news, usually upbeat takes—no investigation, no hit pieces.

"The Whitebridge Weekly," I said brightly.

"You know, I'm busy. I have to get this place ready all by myself." The waitress turned, walking back in, and I followed her.

"It'll just take a minute, I promise."

I took in the place. The lobby had a small section of coat hooks, surrounded by wood-paneled walls lined by photos and articles with the same faded orange-brown hue.

The waitress looked me up and down. "You can follow me around if you want, ask some questions, but I gotta get ready for opening."

We entered the main part of the restaurant, where the wood paneling sporting the same spray-tan orange continued. There were neatly arranged, half-set tables covered in white tablecloths. More photos appeared along the walls.

I followed the woman to the tables, where she checked the

ketchup levels and used another bottle to refill the others. I absently wondered how many years she had been doing this, and how long the ketchup at the bottom of the bottles had been there—ancient ketchup.

"So, how long has this restaurant been here?"

"Last spring, we celebrated one hundred years of business. A hundred years of veal and chicken parm with your choice of starch. You know, you should talk to the owners, Bill and Lisa Stedworth, though they're super busy. I'm really not the one to talk to."

"Okay. I'll do that too. So, who does this restaurant mostly serve?"

The woman, who put on a name tag that read *Gloria*, said, "Workers, business folks, and sometimes families from the surrounding rural towns. Not just Whitebridge, but Danforth, Riverdale, and Devlin too. Some of those towns don't have a restaurant, or they live on the side closer to us, so they come here."

"A regional hub of steak."

"Something like that."

"Does the restaurant ever get used for special events?"

"Sure, all the time. We have all sorts of clubs and groups meeting here. Trout club, Rod and Gun club, political groups, you know."

Gloria walked up to the host station, stacking menus. She was quite small and looked like she might vanish behind the podium.

I considered what to say next. I could see that Gloria was getting a bit impatient.

"How long have you been working here?"

She shook her head. "Seventeen years." Said it as if every year had cost her. Like she couldn't believe she had spent that much time in this place.

"Wow. That's a long time. What's the hardest part of your job?"

Gloria raised an eyebrow.

"Well now, that won't be for any paper. No way."

Gloria looked done with me.

I persisted. Tried again.

"Seventeen years. You must have seen a lot."

"Oh, sure have. This place is an old boys' club. At least now they don't grab my butt anymore or say the rudest things most of the time."

I pivoted. "Does the school board meet here ever?"

She wiped down the host station. "No, not really, but there is a group that used to meet here that had some school board members in it. They were always working on something, and drinking a lot."

There it was.

Who was meeting, and why? But I knew Gloria wouldn't know this.

"What did they talk about?"

A back door groaned open.

"Oh. Sounds like Mark is here, our cook. He's really grumpy. You should get going."

"Do you mind if I use your bathroom first?"

"Sure."

"Thank you, Gloria."

"No problem." She was already off. Another day, another dollar.

"Have a good shift," I called.

I walked toward the bathrooms. The hallway between the men's and women's was lined with photos of groups of people who had been there. I scanned them quickly.

What were the chances that the board would be there?

I pulled out my phone and took photos of some of the

groups, searching. It looked like it started in the '80s, from the clothes and conditions of the photos, and moved forward in time as I looked from left to right. Mostly men, drinking, having meetings, and Gloria, or other women like her, serving them.

Nothing.

I gave up and headed toward the women's room, when one of the more recent shots caught my eye. I spotted Bob Stewart's bald head right away. And the rest of a crew of about eight people. I quickly recognized a few of them, snapped a few photos, and turned to go.

I headed to the truck. A few clouds had moved in, and I knew I had to hustle to pick up Piper at the halfway spot. I walked briskly across the gravel lot, and heard a familiar clunking sound as the gray pickup pulled in.

I covered the last few steps in bounds as it pulled in right next to me. I had never washed the truck. The evidence was all over it.

Nick, who looked like he ate rocks for breakfast, stepped out of his truck as I ducked into mine. I quickly locked the door. My hands shook on the steering wheel.

He leaned against his truck. Watched me as I pulled out, gravel spinning, onto 302. He stood there as I turned and headed out of town, and into the forest-lined country highway with spotty cell service.

Would he follow me? This guy was everywhere.

I looked in my rearview, but nothing was there except increasing clouds and a darkening sky.

# CHAPTER FOURTEEN

I pulled into the brightly lit halfway point gas station under layered, purple clouds, the color of a deep bruise. I was a few minutes early.

Nick had left me shaken.

So many times, it wasn't a physical grab or a brushing up against that made me feel uncomfortable, though those were certainly awful. It was the persistent stares from men—the look that said you were made only for his consumption, top to bottom, and that he had a right to every piece of you whenever he wanted. It was that kind of look that made me want to run and hide and disappear. I'd experienced it with my first high school boyfriend, the way he would make me feel that my only job was to look pretty and act like his prize, his property, and to perform for him sexually. To meet his needs whenever he wanted.

It took me years after that to realize that my existence was not based on pleasing everyone, especially boyfriends. So much to undo. When I had a boyfriend in college who gently paid attention to my needs, asked little of me, and encouraged me to be free, it was a revelation.

But Nick? His stare made me feel cheap and used, disposable. Just like Richard at the firm, especially once I'd finally told the truth. Then, what use was I? He said I wasn't smart enough—yet he used all my background work on cases. He made it seem like he did all the work, stealing my labor. Just like I remembered in fifth grade, when a kid named Stevie shared an idea for a group project I had just come up with like it was his own, and the teacher beamed at him. Some things never change.

I flipped through the photos on my phone. It was hard to see, a bit dark and grainy, but there they were, a group of folks meeting at the steak house. I could see Bob Stewart, and there was Nick, all cleaned up in a dress shirt. Brooke Bentworth was there, too, ramrod straight spine and ironed hair, in tight pants and a matching cardigan, one woman among men. I saw the two male board members, and another man who looked familiar but I couldn't place.

I'd have to figure that out. Maybe in Esther's files—I had to get back to check. I was so engrossed that I didn't hear Tom pull up next to me. He was suddenly knocking on my window. I jumped.

"Hey! Anybody home?"

"Mama!" Piper came around his car and jumped into my arms as I got out of the truck. I held her tightly, smelled her hair and felt her warmth surrounding me. My entire body relaxed.

"Did you have fun?" I asked. Piper nodded, jumped down.

"Bye, Daddy," she said, hugging him around the waist.

"Bye, Peanut. I love you." He tousled her hair, looked pained to leave her. He looked back at me like this was all my fault. We stood there for a minute, the silence oppressive.

Finally, Piper walked around the other side of the truck to get in.

I went to open Tom's trunk and get her bag. He came around beside me.

"I'll get it." He snatched the bag, and I grabbed the pillow and hedgehog.

We stood shoulder to shoulder. Bodies that once knew each other.

"How's studying for the bar going?" What a loaded question.

We stood there with Piper's things.

I shrugged. I really didn't know what to say, was done having to explain myself to him.

He stepped back. "Right. Okay." We stood there, by the open trunk of his car, while people pulled in and out of the gas station. Tom stared at my profile. He clearly wasn't done. "So, Piper told me about that school she's going to. Sounds like a hellhole. Why exactly are you doing this, Liv? For the free house? You could sell it, move back to Boston, put Piper back with her friends, and get your own place. Or even in Vermont, near your parents. It's not like you're loving it, right? It's a way different kind of town than you're used to."

Well, at least he had one thing right.

"And what exactly are you doing there? You aren't working yet, right? Sounds like you aren't studying, so . . . ?"

The temperature had started dropping, cooling around us. I shivered standing there, holding Piper's soft things.

"You know what, Tom? I'm taking a little break. I'm going to figure things out."

"Sure. Sure you are," he said with his usual smug, sarcastic tone. I wanted to rip the smirk off his face.

"What's that supposed to mean?"

"I mean, while you figure your shit out, our kid is suffering! She doesn't like it there!"

His voice was getting louder and I tried to keep from matching his volume. Tried and failed.

"Oh, that's just great. Great. Of course, it's all my fault, all of it, and you're the perfect fucking dad." My heart thumped, I felt fire in my chest. I couldn't resist. I barreled on. "How many beers did you have last night? Huh? While Piper was in your care? Probably 'just a few,' which we both know really means like six. So I don't want to hear it."

I'd gone for the jugular. The drinking. I opened the door to the truck too hard. It flew open. I threw in the pillow and hedgehog.

"Hedgehog!" Piper called from the back.

I tossed it to her, climbed in, shouted, "Bye, Tom," and slammed my door shut.

I pulled out and left him standing there in the light of the gas station, his arms held up in silent exasperation.

We drove in silence for a while, me trying to get my breathing under control.

Everyone was always telling me what to do, in one way or another. Teachers, friends, parents, professors, husband, boss.

I squeezed the steering wheel.

So sick of it. When did what *I* want ever become a consideration? When would I be able to call the shots? I named the game at the firm, finally, but it had taken too long. I had named the game in ending my marriage, which was the right thing for me, but clearly not for Piper. At least in the short term. But short term is where kids live. Which made all of this so much harder.

I stared at the yellow lines on the highway, stretching out below me.

It was time for me to take control.

Later, after tucking Piper in, I stepped into Esther's small office. I just wanted to be around her books, her things. I leaned against the doorframe, looking in.

There was a small chair and a standing lamp. I could imagine Esther sitting there, feet curled under her, reading one of these books. I sat in the chair, trying to feel her.

My body was heavy with the weight of exhaustion, of the adrenaline that had coursed through my body and then drained away.

I'd checked the locks on all the doors.

I'd looked out the window a few times.

Till was right across the street.

The chair rocked a bit, comforting me. My hand brushed a small table by the chair, tucked into the wall, that I hadn't noticed before. On the shelf near the floor, there was a stack of a half dozen or so small, black-covered artist's journals.

I reached down. The first one was covered in thick dust. I brushed it off with my sweatshirt sleeve and opened it up.

My aunt's handwriting was revealed, like an old friend. The way her letters ran together, like she had no time to separate them, couldn't slow down her ideas, her thoughts.

How had I missed this?

The whole book was filled with her words, her world. Maybe now, reading this, I could really know her, could really see what her life was like here, if she was happy. Maybe, Esther could show me how to be happy here. I flipped to the last entry, the last pages Esther would have written.

*The sun still comes up. The maples on my street keep growing leaves. It is an absolute miracle that all of this continues, while our small, human lives end, begin, or fall apart. Here we are, these humans thinking that all the details of our lives are everything, that we are in control. We control nothing. The only things that stay are the way the sun turns the night sky a deep blue, a purple before orange appears behind the mountains and trees, then lights them up pink, with arching branches in silhouette. How that orange will grow and grow until the whole scene is awash in color and newness. What a miracle that this happens every day.*

*I don't know if I have done enough here. I have tried to learn as much as I can. To be of help to anyone in search of information, resources, ideas.*

*And I have loved, oh, I have loved. So many kinds of love, really. The focus on romantic love is limiting. While I have had it, I have had so many other kinds as well. The love of my sister, my first friend, my backyard adventurer, my secret keeper. My niece Olivia Grace, who was like my very own baby, a deep love I had never known. And dearest Lydia. Lydia who was braver than I could be. Who went in each day, seeking truth and justice and liberation and wanted it for her students' futures. Who woke up thinking of her students and went to bed thinking of them. Who was dragged through the mud and the worst firestorm this town had ever created.*

*I tried to help her. We were almost there.*

*Lydia, the way her lanky body moved through space, the way a laugh would move through her entire being like a wave. But that stopped months ago.*

*The curve of her delicate cheeks. How they came in like snow drifting on a hillside, and back, to her lips.*

*Oh, I am such a sappy romantic. What did I say about romantic love not mattering as much? It sure took me a lifetime to find it. While I had some friendships that were close, this one is different. I feel more myself, more free and seen than ever in my life.*

I looked up around the room, which had shifted with these words. Everything I thought I knew about my aunt had been tossed up into the air.

I had in no way imagined my aunt, in her sixties, was in love with a young teacher, likely thirty years her junior. Was this real? Was the love reciprocated? In this town, what a scandal.

What a delight.

*And now here I am. Finding this beautiful thing, but at an ugly time. We fought, my dear, we battled them for your students, for us.*

*We lost.*

*I told you to keep fighting. That you could do it. But you said you couldn't do it without me. And that broke my heart more than any cancer did. Because the good guys are supposed to win. Love and truth and justice wins.*

*Not this time.*

That was the end of the entry.

I squeezed my eyelids shut. Felt the hot prickling pain behind them. How could this be how their story ended?

How had I not known?

My own aunt. I hadn't been able to visit at the end. I was too busy with Piper. Why hadn't I just pulled her from school and come anyway?

Sometimes just showing up is more important than anything else. No matter what.

And I hadn't. I'd missed it.

I could have met Lydia then. Could have eased Esther's pain as she lay dying. Reminded her that her work did matter, that she did have an impact.

Instead, I sent flowers.

I sat in her chair, her journal smooth and cool in my lap. Felt hot tears come. Then the rage like boiling water in my veins. If there had ever been motivation to keep looking into what was really happening at that school, this was it. My investigation was for Esther. For Lydia. For love. To make up for what I'd missed before.

I gently closed the journal, this piece of Esther uncovered before me. There was so much I didn't know, couldn't understand. But I knew I couldn't rest until we won. Whatever that meant.

I vowed to come back to this office, to read all these journals one by one, to know my aunt more fully.

I climbed up the stairs and got into bed, Steinem jumping up next to me, ready to settle in.

I knew what I had to do. Studying for the bar could wait. Esther's story wasn't over, and it was time to tell it.

I slept deeply and well. My bones settled, and my body and mind focused.

The next day after school drop-off, I didn't head back home.

The morning was cold and a fog had settled on Whitebridge, cloaking it in an eerie, ethereal glow. I'd had to scrape my windshield for the first time this season, cursing as I chipped away the thin ice, blasting the defrost while pulling my jacket over my frozen hand.

Everyone in New England should be gifted a garage because they endure this shit.

Now, the ice was gone, but wisps of fog remained, like woodstove smoke stuck low in the sky. I decided to search the neighborhood where I'd seen Bob Stewart go to church. The brick houses on this side of Main Street were made to look old, but they were clearly new on closer inspection. The yards were bigger and immaculately kept, barely any leaves in sight. There were bright mums on doorsteps, gourds in various shapes, dried corn stalks gathered. The mailboxes were orderly in front of neat and tidy yards.

I drove around, thinking about these people's lives. Were they as put together as their houses and yards appeared? Esther's neighborhood seemed downright quaint, its old homes with fading paint, leaning porches, wild old trees. This one seemed like it was trying too hard to be perfect. A manufactured version of the American dream.

After about fifteen minutes of cruising around, sipping coffee from my travel mug, I thought about leaving, thinking someone might notice me driving so slowly. This was a small town after all, and I was sure rumors about me were already flying all over the place.

As I started to speed up, I noticed the woman who had been walking just behind Bob Stewart on the way to church. She was carrying a cloth bag of groceries from her car toward her house, a large, brick colonial with two white columns by the fancy entrance. Two-car garage.

Classic black shutters, a perfectly raked and mowed lawn.

She walked slowly, staring out into space, looking lost in thought. She looked like any wealthy, small-town mom: cropped mom-bob haircut, plain Keds, and a nice, clean, basic aesthetic, located somewhere in that fuzzy age between thirty-five and forty-five, with a full, round face and body.

I watched her. There she was, married to that snake-man. I wondered if he controlled her every move, the same way he controlled every aspect of the school.

She must have felt me there, watching. Her head swiveled

toward me driving by in my truck, a slow, puppetlike head turn. Our eyes locked.

This was no evil stare. It looked almost as if the woman was underwater, sinking deeper, and looking up and reaching out to me. Trying to surface. Or maybe she was unwell, on a medication that had her senses dulled.

I shivered, broke the stare, then sped up and away.

If the woman wanted to, she could tell Bob Stewart that I'd been stalking her, and the police would have another reason to come by.

But something told me that she wouldn't do that.

Something made me want to tell the woman to hold on. That things would get better. But maybe I was assuming too much. Maybe she liked her fancy house, her stay-at-home mom role, her power by proximity.

I decided to look again at those articles and board meeting minutes for any mention of her that I might have missed even though I suspected she wouldn't have been at any of them.

I wondered about this woman's life. I twirled my ring, thinking, spinning the thick silver.

The silver. Then I thought.

*Ring.*

The jewelry receipt.

That woman certainly wasn't wearing a five-figure piece of jewelry, or at least in that very quick look it didn't seem that way—like that would be way out of character, something so flashy. Maybe it was in her bedroom, a peace offering, or an anniversary present.

But why would Esther be interested in that?

Maybe the jewelry was for someone else.

I sat at my computer, social media stalking Beth Stewart. She had a very limited online presence as far as I could tell. It seemed pretty locked down. From what I could find, she grew up in Connecticut and had met Bob in college in New Hampshire. Her cover image was a photo of her kids, both with preppy matching outfits, looking tidy and well-groomed, posed in their yard. Clearly professionally taken.

One girl. One boy. They looked to be somewhere around eleven to fourteen. The boy had dirty blond hair that was combed into control, with little lines from the comb holding back the curls that wanted to pop out. The girl, a splash of freckles across her face, looked a bit younger and had two braids pulled tight on either side of her head. The site had nothing else I could see. I searched the sidebar, drinking . . . what, my fourth cup of coffee? I had lost count.

The overload of caffeine made it feel like there was a little bird fluttering around in my chest, banging its wings on my ribs. The woman had just over three hundred friends, which considering the scope of the site, and her age, wasn't many. The page had the feeling of being a placeholder, a show, not a site she really engaged in. Who knew what this woman did, liked, felt, or read?

Beth was a mystery.

A voice whispered to me. *Maybe she's silenced. Maybe she wants to be free.*

I decided to head to the jewelry store next, when it opened—even though I wasn't sure how I could find out who that purchase was for.

And really, why did it matter? It wasn't a crime to cheat on someone.

But it really did look bad if you were both the principal and superintendent and a good churchgoing, family-values kind of man that he was obviously trying to be known as. I remembered the stares when Piper and I passed the church. Lots of judgment there. So if the big, responsible man was having an affair, wouldn't that conflict with his image? Or would that just make him more popular in this alpha dog, patriarchal town? I tapped my fingers on the computer. I had to be missing something.

I looked up and noticed a small print on the wall of Esther's office, one I had seen so many times since I was a kid. It had a beautiful butterfly made with bright, rainbow colors in a 1970s-type graphic design. I examined the small type on the bottom, really seeing it for the first time. It was a Maya Angelou quote: "We delight in the beauty of the butterfly, but rarely admit the changes it has gone through to achieve that beauty."

The words struck home with me. I felt alive following these leads, in a new way I had only felt in brief bursts at the law firm; I was never really free there. They had their thumb, or their hands, on me, every day, in one way or another.

When I would make a discovery, it became theirs. When I would voice an angle to pursue, they would take it, and pursue it like it was theirs. Nothing was ever my own.

This case, these people, and figuring out how it was all connected, was mine. I was free and focused in a way I had never felt—but also terrified because the stakes were so high.

Piper. I had to remind myself that she wasn't truly free in this situation. I had someone I loved deeply stuck right in the middle of this mess.

The fog had burned off and revealed a crisp, bright blue day. The fall had a way of breaking up with summer in spurts. It was horrible, messy, cold rain, then bright blue sweater days that made it seem like things would be okay, that winter wouldn't be so bad. Lighthearted even. The human spirit, constantly duped.

I got back in the truck and headed toward Main Street. I drove through town, over the bridge, and up the hill to the district office, located in the small white cape I had seen before while running. It was an unassuming building—quaint even. A few cars were parked in the lot, and lights were on inside.

I turned down the short driveway and parked as far away from the entrance as possible. I could see that the structure, white with classic black shutters, had been redesigned inside to house offices. Behind it was a field that had dried and turned yellow, its color in defiance of the gray winter to come. There were also a few paths leading back to Barnes Elementary School.

I tapped the steering wheel. Bob had offices here, and an office at the elementary school.

Board meetings were usually at the school. So why did they need this whole other setup? Most of what Bob touched seemed fancy and fresh, but not this place. It seemed tight and tidy, very New England. Functional. Not flashy or extravagant, just another low-profile building to taxpayers so they kept supporting the schools. It had also likely been the district office for decades.

If I could only get in there. I had an idea of the district budget, had some questions, and wondered what I could find inside. Maybe there was a way. As I sat there, considering, I saw movement inside the office, a blind being pulled up. An unidentifiable person peering out.

Nobody misses anything here.

I pulled out and away, adding this office to my list of places I might research, return to. Turning back toward Main Street, the tiny town bathed in midday sunlight, my phone vibrated on the seat next to me. It was the school.

"Shit," I whispered.

# CHAPTER FIFTEEN

I pulled over on Main Street, just by the hardware store.

"Hello, Ms. Wilcox. We're going to need you to come to Barnes to pick up Piper."

My mouth went dry.

"Is everything okay?" I managed to push out.

"She's refusing to come inside after an activity. This is unsafe. Because of our discipline policy, she'll need to go home for the day."

"So, she's suspended?" I practically yelled into the phone.

"Ms. Wilcox, just come to the school."

I hung up.

What kind of piece of shit place would suspend a third grader for staying in the woods for an extra minute?

I slammed the truck into reverse, and headed back, trying to cover the distance as fast as I could. Aunt Esther's truck hummed loudly while I pressed hard on the gas.

When I pulled into the small lot, I could see Ms. McCallister leading the class inside, in a line. I scanned the kids' faces. No Piper. I then noticed Bob Stewart and Ms. Mitchell standing by the entrance to a small patch of woods, behind the playground.

I jumped out of the truck, my feet flying underneath me.

What the fuck was going on? Where was my baby?

I sprinted up the small hill and to them.

"Where's Piper?"

Ms. Mitchell came over to me. Her face was creased deeply in the center, like she had been negotiating a world peace treaty and everything depended on her.

Bob stood there, beady eyes, impatient, arms crossed. Mouth clamped shut. Judgment poured off him like waves of radiation.

Ms. Mitchell used her best calm guidance counselor voice.

"Hello, Liv. So, the class came out here to do an activity. They were searching for natural habitats. It's a beautiful day."

I didn't want to talk about the weather.

"They were in the woods looking for animals and their habitats. From what I can tell, Piper had found something pretty special. Some kind of salamander in a log."

"Okay," I said, impatient to see my kid.

"And then another student took it and . . . *hurt* it."

I winced. That wouldn't have gone over well with Piper at all.

"Piper pushed the boy, picked it up, and now won't come out from under that downed tree over there."

She pointed to an upturned tree, its web of roots exposed and reaching upward, and a pocket of empty and loose soil, enough room for a bear den—or a hiding child. I could see the blue of Piper's sweatshirt, the rest of her tiny body hidden.

"Everyone's tried to make her come out. We finally had to send the rest of the class to lunch and call you. She's very upset."

Bob Stewart actually sighed. As if annoyed by the display of human emotion that he was being forced to endure. He clearly had more important things to be doing than standing outside with some guidance counselor and sad child.

I started walking away from them toward the woods. Bob Stewart caught me by the elbow.

What was it with these people touching me?

"You're going to have to bring her home. We can't have students here being violent with others and just running off into the woods."

His eyes met mine. Emptiness. No emotion, no understanding. Just seeking compliance. I shook off his touch. Scoffed.

"Yeah. Well, thanks for caring. It's really obvious how much you love kids. I'm going to make sure she's all right. And the little shit who hurt the salamander deserved to be shoved."

Ms. Mitchell's mouth fell open.

I turned on my heel and jogged into the woods, toward the upturned tree. Twigs cracked under my feet as I pushed my way through branches and bushes. This was not for adult travel—little bodies only. A branch grabbed at my hair, pulled, and I grabbed it back, snapping it off and tossing it away.

I saw my baby there, curled up under the tree hollow, in the leaves and dirt. She laid on her side, knees tucked in under her, black hair fanned out on the ground. Her face was streaked red from crying.

I knelt down next to her.

"Hi, little bird."

Piper's eyes were squeezed shut. She didn't move a muscle but pushed air from her lungs, a long exhale.

"I am *so* sorry about what happened, sweetie."

Piper kept her eyes closed. "He took it, Mama. He took it from me and threw it against a tree."

I got down on my knees next to her. The mossy dirt moved under me.

"It was tiny and beautiful and had little moving eyes and a stripe on its back."

Piper's face was in anguish at describing the beauty.

"It all happened so fast."

Male rage always did.

I noticed a little pile near where Piper was resting her head. There was a small, neat collection of leaves with a circle of small stones around it. Piper had clearly been here awhile, under the massive, intricate root system—a perfect spot, really.

For a tiny grave.

"Is that where you put the salamander, Piper?"

Piper nodded with a quivering chin. A tear slid sideways down her cheek.

Piper felt so much. All the emotions of the world were big in Piper's body. She was a stunning, elegant butterfly, flitting around in the pollution of daily life. I wondered how she would get on in the world. How she would deal with the endless parade of bad news. With losing the people you love. With heartbreak. Would the world harden her?

"How about we go home?"

"Principal Stewart said I was in trouble."

I grimaced. I could still see the outline of Bob standing there with Ms. Mitchell. They made an uncomfortable pair. I wondered again how she could work with him.

Trouble.

Weren't women always in trouble? Trouble for being too much, too little. For saying too much, too little. For weighing too much, too little.

"It's okay, Piper."

I laid down next to her, right there on the soil and leaf bed. Screw it. Tucked in so that my side touched Piper's back. I looked up, could see the trunks of trees heading straight up toward the blue sky, the reaching branches. It was beautiful. This was an angle I hadn't ever seen before. The world, so expansive and gorgeous.

"He said if I didn't come now, I'd be suspended." Her mouth struggled with forming the word, so it came out *sus-end-ed*.

"That's okay, Piper. Really."

"Mama, he tried to pull me out of here. But I was tucked in too far. He couldn't get a good grip on me." He had touched my baby. Blood pounded in my ears. I was going to kill him. "I don't like him, Mom. He scares me."

"Me either. But Piper, we have to stand up to scary people." *And people who tell you to be silent, just go with the flow, don't cause problems, don't make noise.* "We can walk right by them together, to the truck."

Piper opened her eyes. Slowly sat up. Took my hand. We ducked together through the trees and bushes on the edge of the forest.

Bob Stewart and Ms. Mitchell watched us.

As we got closer, I pointed to the truck in the lot and said to Piper, "Start walking that way. I'll catch up in a minute."

She didn't argue and kept going. I set my jaw, and walked right up to Bob, whose hands were shoved into the pockets of his wrinkle-free khaki pants. His wife Beth probably ironed them.

*Don't punch him. Don't get arrested.*

"Don't. You. *Ever.* Touch my child," I said, pointing at his chest, daring to look up at his beady eyes.

A shot of surprise and fear changed quickly into a smirk.

"How about you make your kid follow directions? She clearly doesn't have a good example of that." He took his hands out of his pockets, trying to look bigger.

"Okay!" Ms. Mitchell interjected, jumping between us. "Thanks for coming, Liv."

"She's suspended," Bob Stewart continued, ignoring her, a small thread of white spit at the corner of his mouth. "She can only come back once she apologizes to her teacher, and to me, and makes a plan so she won't run away again."

He was high on his power. His drug of choice.

"She didn't run away. She was lying under a tree after a classmate assaulted her."

"Assaulted her! Typical. Here we go." He rolled his eyes, another smirk growing across his face. "A kid grabbed a salamander out of her hand. Big deal. She's the one who pushed him to the ground. She can come back when she apologizes and has a plan."

*Apologize.*

*Apologize for having feelings. For having a body that did not want to be touched. For the actions of another.*

Being female was exhausting.

My skin felt like it was on fire and my heart thumped in my chest. I turned and started walking away before I lost control and punched him. That would be assault for sure, no matter how justified.

"Ms. Wilcox?" he called after me. "Don't come on school property again. That seems to be a problem for you."

Ah. There it was. He knew I'd been on the school grounds a few nights earlier. Nick must have been whispering in his boss's ear.

Ms. Mitchell ran to catch up with me.

"Call me if you want to talk," she said quietly, then stopped. I kept walking, staring straight ahead, and finally made it to the truck, seething.

*I will get that man. I will catch him in whatever scheme he has going on if it's the last thing I do.*

Piper sat curled up in the truck.

"Mama, are you okay?"

Of course Piper would ask that. She could probably see the waves of anger coursing off me.

"Yes, little bird. I'm fine," I said, and backed up and out of the parking lot. Another lie.

Piper needed hours to decompress, to bring her nervous system back to a state of calm. She sat in her room drawing. I started pacing, back and forth, across the kitchen. Suddenly, the house felt too small for my chaotic thoughts. I headed outside, into the afternoon sun, and stepped into the front yard. The air was cool, refreshing, and my mind cleared slightly.

*I have to fix this.*

Till, in her L.L.Bean fleece and khakis, like a New England uniform, walked across the street, breaking my trance. Her long gray hair was pulled back in a low ponytail.

"You two are home early. Is everything okay?"

I looked at her. My face must have told the story for me.

"Oh dear. Can I come in for a bit?"

I grabbed the old mugs and filled them with hot tea. I told her everything, and that blessed soul listened. She sat with me, shared my outrage, and I felt a little lighter, a little better, and justified in my anger. In fact, I had to calm Till down at the end of it. She knew people in town government, she said, knew people she could report him to. I told her to wait until I had more. Then we could make a plan.

Till gave me a squeeze on the shoulder as she left.

Piper was in bed with a book. She stayed that way all afternoon, her small body exhausted from the drama. After eating a large bowl of macaroni and cheese, she headed back to bed and fell asleep quickly. Moments later, Till crossed the road holding a large cup of tea and a book.

"Go out," she said. "Go see Silas. I'll read here and watch Piper."

I reached over and kissed Till on the cheek. It was warm, and she smelled like rose water.

The sun was down and it was midnight blue-black, but it was only 6 p.m. I found myself back at Donovan's on a bar stool, looking into those eyes that I was starting to think I wanted to look at forever. I delighted in knowing that he was a caring, creative teacher, not limited by the way gender had tried to box him into male roles and limitations.

"I heard you gave snake-man a talking to," he said, reaching over the bar to give me a quick hug. He smelled like pine trees. My body craved this, being held. I wanted to stay right there. Instead, I pulled back.

"Yeah. The whole thing was awful. He tried to drag Piper out of the woods."

Silas shook his head and began pouring me a pint of hard cider.

"I'm so sorry," he said. "Is she okay?"

"I think so. She was just really sad and needed the space to be sad. She was under a tree, it's not like she was running away or anything."

Silas nodded while I took a sip.

"And now she's suspended. A third grader. Suspended. For burying a salamander under a tree."

"Unreal."

"She just needs to feel safe. Have room for her feelings. And for folks to treat her gently. It's not too much to ask."

Silas shook his head. He exhaled like he was trying to push out his anger.

"I want to do something to help you," he said.

I shrugged. What was there to do? Silence sat between us.

"So, what's the deal with Stewart's wife?" I ventured.

"I'm . . . not sure," he answered, his face twisting up slightly as he considered the question. "She seems really sweet. I know she does all of the child-rearing, cooking, cleaning, and driving. It's hard to imagine Bob appreciating it very much. She always seems to be baking for the board meetings—gorgeous stuff. Like maybe she's pouring her frustration with him into baking." He laughed darkly to himself. "They sure don't deserve it."

I remembered her carrying the grocery bag, staring off into the distance.

"I haven't seen her much," Silas continued. "She seems kind of like a hermit. It's not like she comes to Donovan's. I'm sure she wouldn't even be 'allowed.' Wouldn't look good for him." He rolled his eyes.

"Yeah. I guess she doesn't have a lot of options. Go with the role he's given her, try to gain power somehow, or just hide away."

Silas nodded. "I'd want to escape."

The jewelry receipt flashed in my mind. "Do you think he's cheating on her?"

Silas looked out over the bar, thinking.

"I suppose he could be," he finally said, lowering his voice, leaning toward me. He glanced at two customers sitting by the window, but they were engrossed in their own conversation. He turned his shining eyes back to me. "But I can't imagine it. The danger, the passion—he just doesn't seem to be up for it. He likes everything in order, predictable. An affair certainly wouldn't be that."

I found myself wanting something that wasn't in order, wasn't predictable. Silas, on the bar, behind the bar, pressed against me, in all ways possible. I shook my head, took a big sip from the cider to help push the feeling back.

"Right. If he was having an affair, it would throw him," I managed to say.

"Completely. Like the way *you're* throwing him. No one talks back to him. Not after what happened with Lydia and the clean sweep of the board."

Liv thought about the jewelry receipt. Thought about Bob's wife.

The bell at the top of the bar door sounded.

"Yes! You're out!" Laura came in, shaking off her down jacket and grabbing a stool next to me.

Silas nodded at her and grabbed a bottle of Sam Adams from the fridge.

"So, what are we talking about?"

"Bob Stewart. His wife. A possible affair," Silas said as he opened the beer and placed it in front of Laura.

"Oh lord. That poor woman," she said and took a big sip. "He certainly keeps her busy running that household like a navy ship. I think she eats all the leftover baked goods she makes for the board. I mean, she's gotta have *something* to cope with all that nonsense."

I imagined Bob's wife staring blankly outside, eating a massive chocolate chip muffin at the kitchen island. It was all about control. If she had no control in her life, she would try to get it somewhere. Maybe it was with food.

I understood this. When my world at the firm started spinning, I sought control where I could get it. I ran. Pounded the pavement, mile after mile. Felt relief from the cage I was in when I was outside, running, free.

I looked up at Laura. "Maybe she just likes dessert. And if so, good for her."

Laura laughed to herself, then looked at her phone.

"Shit! I gotta go. Driving my kid around, it's all I'm good for, apparently." She chugged the last of her beer in an impressive and slightly disturbing display, and then set the still-sweating bottle down on the bar. "Okay, you two. Have a good night. Don't get in any trouble."

And I'll be damned if she didn't wink at me.

I flushed, the heat spreading across my body. I knew I should get home, that it must be getting close to Till's bedtime. I hoped Piper was still sleeping peacefully. Healing, resting from earlier that day.

How would we deal with the school and this suspension? Apologize? That place had harmed her. And what about the other kids like her? The ones who were different. Who didn't follow the strict and narrow set of expectations that the school's compliance culture demanded.

I had to get her out of there.

But how?

"Want another one?" Silas said, smiling. I really did. I imagined what would happen after that. My response took all of my self-control.

"Sorry, I have to get home."

Silas frowned. Leaned on his elbows toward me over the bar, his eyes lingering on mine. An offering.

*Where could we go, even just for a little while?*

At the end of the bar, the bathroom door burst open, and a man emerged, walking toward us, breaking the sweet tension. Silas stood up, and I let out a long sigh, watched the guy approach.

*Here we go again.*

He was wearing a navy blue mechanic's uniform and had a thick five-o'clock shadow all over his face. His eyes were soft, though, harmless.

He walked over, a little sideways.

"Hey, Peter," Silas said "I'm thinking maybe you've had enough for today."

The man ignored him. Silas's kind demeanor drained from his face.

"I heard you all talking about that man, and that school," Peter slurred. He reached out to hold the bar to steady himself. His voice was like chewed-up sandpaper.

I looked at Silas, eyes wide, as if to say, *We need to be more careful!*

Peter leaned toward us. His breath smelled like old potato chips and stale beer.

"They're running a business out of there, I swear it." He rubbed his chin. "Making shitloads of money, but that ain't the half of it."

He seemed to notice me sitting there for the first time.

"Oh, sorry, sweetheart, I didn't mean to swear," he laughed. "But what someone really oughta look into is that guy who sniffed around, where did he go?"

I lost my voice. Just sat there, watching Peter, his name printed on the uniform in a red oval.

"Who?" Silas asked.

But Peter had already decided to make the long walk toward the door, bumping into a few chairs on the way.

He turned and looked back at us, his eyes wide and distant. "Gone, gone, gone," he called, his voice floating around the front of the bar. He shook his head, turned, pulled open the door, and vanished out onto Main Street.

Silas looked at me. "I wouldn't worry about him. He's harmless, and pretty drunk."

But I shivered, the word *gone* echoing in my ears.

# CHAPTER SIXTEEN

I got home, thanked Till for watching Piper, and said goodnight. Apparently, the two of them had been happy as peas in a pod. Piper had gotten up and was glad to see Till, who promptly offered her some apple pie. Then they played Connect Four and Uno for a bit before Till read to her and tucked her back in. Till looked tired and happy as she gathered her jacket.

She turned back to look at me at the door.

"I'll watch her anytime, Liv, really."

I smiled. "Thank you."

"She really is something special."

I nodded. "Yeah, I agree. Thanks again. I appreciate it more than I can really say. Goodnight, Till."

Another reason to love Till forever.

Later, in bed, I started my night-time research routine. Pillows behind me. Tea on the nightstand. Deep web searching was about to commence.

I scanned news articles and missing persons postings, and found a man from about an hour south, who went missing six months ago.

This had to be him.

His name was Roger Shepard. He seemed to be a large, balding man, working for the state as a financial analyst in the Agency of Education. His bio was listed on the agency's website.

I kept scrolling.

I found a PDF from the New Hampshire Information and Analysis Center. On top of the document in big bold letters, it read *New Hampshire, Missing Person Alert.* It looked like the information was updated every month.

And it was a heartbreaking document.

At the top, it listed how many missing persons there were in New Hampshire, the total for that month. I was looking at a report from August, a few years ago. Apparently, there were seventy missing persons that month in the state, several carrying over from other months. Below that, all their small photos and descriptions came next. Men and women, teenagers, all adrift in this cruel world. Many looked like runaways. I got lost in their faces, imagining their stories. So many fifteen-to-seventeen-year-old girls. Missing, vanished.

I scrolled to the bottom of the document, and there he was. Roger Shepard. He smiled in the small photo, his round face friendly, with glasses, taking up most of the square. I scanned the entry:

| | |
|---|---|
| **Name:** | Roger Shepard |
| **Hair:** | Brown |
| **Current Age:** | 52 |
| **Eyes:** | Brown |
| **Missing From:** | Manchester, NH |

| | |
|---|---|
| **Height:** | 5'11" |
| **Weight:** | 200 lbs |
| **Investigating Agency:** | Manchester Police |
| **Race:** | White |
| **Clothing Description:** | White button-up shirt, khaki pants |
| **Gender:** | Male |
| **Brief Synopsis:** | Left for work at the New Hampshire Agency of Education, did not return home. |

A sense of cold dread crept up my spine as I sat there, the small lamp on the nightstand giving off a faint glow against the surrounding pitch-black darkness. The house clanged and rattled every so often, noises I was slowly getting used to.

Roger wasn't like the others I'd seen on the list.

Sure, I knew there were other reasons someone could go missing, like mental illness or addiction. That very well could be what had happened here—maybe Roger was fighting something or lost to drugs. Maybe. But an uneasiness roped around me, my insides saying that wasn't the case.

Later, I tried to sleep. Tried to erase the list of missing persons, beloved by families, out in the world, in places unknown. But their faces floated in my subconscious like ghosts. Some of them had been missing for years. How did families continue after that? Always looking. Always wondering. The concept of lost people—it chilled me. I pulled the covers up higher, under my chin, tucked myself in.

And what about Roger? *Gone, gone, gone.*

A guy who sniffed around.

A *financial analyst* who sniffed around.

The pieces fell together in my brain, like a puzzle clicking together. Of course.

I threw back the covers, stepped out onto the wood floor that creaked under me. I practically ran down to Esther's office, clicked on the small lamp. Pulled up the budgets Esther had saved. I found other budgets from nearby school districts to compare, the ones I could find online.

Roger was a financial analyst for the state. Surely, they did audits about how schools were spending their money every year. Manchester was about an hour south of Whitebridge. This could have been in his coverage area.

I kept researching, found that schools must have a financial report that detailed every single purchase or sale by the school. One of Roger's jobs, and the job of the agency, was to "collect and analyze school expenditures." Money in. Money out. Every bit of it.

Maybe he had found out something he wasn't supposed to.

Dear God.

I shivered. I knew that Bob Stewart was a narcissistic bully. But was he capable of murder? How could that be? I mean, he was a superintendent after all. He wasn't some shifty criminal.

I shook my head. What did a criminal look like anyway? Unhoused, addicted, a certain age?

*Nope. Nope. Nope.* That was bias talking.

Some of the worst criminals were wealthy men who wanted more power. And that certainly fit the description of Bob Stewart.

I started a new file on Roger Shepard. Wrote and screenshotted everything I could find about him and saved it on Aunt Esther's computer, where all the other budgets and documents about the school were.

*Where are you, Roger? What do you know?*

And most importantly:

*I hope you're alive.*

Piper didn't get out of bed the next morning. She lay there, a little ball, Steinem loving the opportunity to feel her nearby, curled up next to her.

I rubbed the sleep out of my eyes. The morning didn't help. The sun was barely out under thick clouds.

"Piper. Time to get up for school."

It was a little later than usual. Ms. Mitchell had emailed, had said that we could come in and make a plan for Piper's and everyone's "safety" and reentry into school. We had a meeting booked for 9:30 a.m.

Piper didn't move, but I could see her pushing her eyelids closed like a vice grip.

"I am NOT GOING."

I took a deep breath. My brain was foggy like it was filled with a thick haze. And the image of Roger. My limbs were heavy, and I didn't know if I had the fight in me to get Piper to school.

I knew what I *should* do. What a good parent would do. Pull her immediately, find a different school. Or spend the day together, exploring the woods and drawing and reading.

Restorative.

Or, sheepishly, take her to that meeting, start over at the school, try again.

But in my mind, I already had a plan for the day. Drive down to Roger's office and see what I could find out from co-workers, the setting. Make it back in time to pick up Piper.

My thoughts piled up like a traffic jam. *Shoulds. Want tos. Have tos.*

I knew Till had a doctor's appointment today.

There were no other options.

"Piper. I know yesterday was awful. But we can go in and meet with Ms. Mitchell, talk about it, then head to class. It won't be that bad."

I was lying.

It would be that bad.

I put on my practiced smile, leaned against the doorframe.

Piper rolled on to her back. Balled her small hands into fists.

"Noah threw a tiny salamander against a tree. And I'm the one who has to say sorry?"

She had a very good point. I sighed. Piper was starting to figure out how the world worked. How heartbreaking it could be. It wasn't built for sensitive souls like Piper. It was a take what-you-can-get world. Every-man-for-himself world.

I'd had to learn that the hard way. At an age much older than Piper's.

I moved over to the edge of her bed. Perched there like a bird, barely seated.

"I know. It doesn't seem right. But those are the school rules."

Piper shook her head.

"You told me that when rules are wrong, you have to break them."

*Damn.*

She was one smart cookie.

And I was never going to win this one.

So, Piper was coming to Manchester. She could just wait in the car while I did my investigating. Not a big deal.

"Okay," I said, standing up.

Piper sat up instantly, eyes opening.

"Really?"

I knew this was a very bad parenting move.

*Kid throws a fit and I give in?*

But it was all I could do. I had no energy for the fight, and honestly, that place was unsafe anyway. Piper was better with me.

Always better with me.

I could solve this thing. For Piper, for all the kids. I stood up taller.

"Yep," I said. "Get dressed. Get your things. We are going on a little road trip."

Piper practically bounced out of bed. All that tight resistance, gone. She knew she had won.

"Can we get Dunkin'?" she said, standing up, stretching. We used to make regular visits to Dunkin' in Boston, with one down the street we could walk to. Many cups of hot chocolate, steaming, discoveries on the sidewalk like worms and caterpillars on the way home.

"Don't push your luck," I said, smiling.

I called the school, left a message for Ms. Mitchell.

*We are not going to make it in today.*

I didn't say why, or:

*We are not going to apologize.*

*She didn't do anything wrong.*

I breathed slowly, keeping focused as we turned down Main Street. Passed Donovan's, Star Bakery, the post office. I came to the end of town, and started across the long, white bridge that gave Whitebridge its name. It was constructed of marble dug at a nearby quarry. The bridge was white, glittery when it was sunny out, and streaked with gray. Today, it looked ominous, unmoving under thick cloud cover, almost like it could connect directly to the sky. The railings were made of marble too, tidy uniform white columns, extending out along the sidewalk across the bridge, as the Otter River flowed steadily underneath. The greenish-brown water licked at the shore, where brown leaves swirled in circles before heading downstream.

It was a bit before nine, and little was happening in Whitebridge. But then I noticed a man walking across the bridge. I thought I recognized his gait, his back.

It was Frank, who had grabbed my thigh that night in Donovan's. The same man who might have followed me home.

I drove by, and willed him to keep walking forward. To not turn around.

But he did. He turned as if he felt me there. Turned and looked at my truck, his yellow teeth showing in a wide, disgusting smirk.

Almost as if he was saying: *I haven't had you yet. But I will.*

I stepped on the gas.

"Mommy, who was that man looking at us?" Piper said from the back. She noticed every single thing.

"No one, sweetie. No one at all."

I turned south on the highway, trying to leave that filthy smirk behind. It imprinted on me, like so many before. I tried to focus my thoughts on Roger. On finding this sweet-looking, round-faced, bespectacled man, who had family that loved him, who might have gotten in the way of Bob Stewart and his scheme for control of all of Whitebridge.

The mountains were covered by low clouds, so it looked like the tops had been cut off, and a line of gray perched like a low ceiling. I gripped the steering wheel. Piper seemed content, Clyde the hedgehog next to her, coloring pages on her lap. The world was in her control, at least for the moment. No demands. No expectations. No apologies or rules or social norms. Or salamander killers.

I circled the red brick building, taking in its bureaucratic design, the hard, colonial exterior. *New Hampshire Department of Education*, a blue sign declared, white letters a little faded, like a highway sign. Piper hummed as I looked for a place to park in the lot. The thick clouds had started breaking up, bits of sunshine streaming through the heavy blanket of gray. "Okay, babe, I'm going to visit some people in this building for a minute, okay?"

Piper nodded, not looking up from her drawing.

"Don't get out of the car, okay?"

"Okay, Mama," she said.

I felt a twinge of guilt in my heart for leaving her there. Ever since she was a baby, I had refused to leave her in the car alone for one single minute. But she was older now, and perfectly happy to stay in the car.

*She'll be fine. This is New Hampshire. A small town. Everything is okay.*

I grabbed the manila envelope I had prepared and headed for the entrance. There was a set of thick, black double doors. I opened those, then was faced with a lobby with all sorts of signs and numbers. I scanned the list, looking for the office of school finance.

Third floor.

I turned toward the stairwell and headed up, thinking this is probably how Roger made his way to work every day. Before he was gone, gone, gone.

I rounded the corner, walked down a hallway full of office doors, down to 315. The fluorescent rectangles of light overhead reminded me of that first meeting in the Barnes Elementary library. The one where they silenced and mocked me. I pushed my shoulders back. Stood taller. I had even worn more professional clothes today. I had on my black peacoat jacket, black pants, short boots, silver hoops, a classic New England garnet-colored scarf around my neck.

I pushed open the door and walked into the small office, where I was greeted by a woman at a desk, holding a paper plate with two large doughnuts. Next to her was a Styrofoam cup of coffee.

She was chewing and looked up at me from behind her glasses.

“How may I help you?” A small crumb sat on her lip, poised there, unmoving.

“Can I please speak with Roger Shepard?”

The woman immediately started coughing. Apparently, the doughnut she had just taken a large bite out of had lodged in her throat. Perhaps it was the mention of Roger.

She held up a finger as she reached for her cup of coffee. I wondered if she would burn herself with it as she took a big gulp, trying to wash the food down. Office coffee though—probably already cold. And mild. Brown water, really.

“I’m sorry,” she squeaked, like a hoarse frog. “He isn’t here right now.”

I watched her eyes, looking me up and down.

“Do you know when he’ll be back?”

What a question. I almost felt bad for her.

The woman’s gaze skittered around like a mouse being chased. She shook her head no.

I just stood there. The woman took another sip, trying to clear her airway.

“Is there someone else I can talk to?”

The woman slowly blinked, the wheels turning behind her eyes.

“Let me see.” She stood up, setting down the plate of goodies, and headed back behind the desk, into the other offices.

I stood holding the envelope, looking around. Typical small office. School-type fluorescent lighting. Cold, standard-issue metal desks. Photos on the desks. Trays of papers, inbox and outbox. Pens and notepads. I looked for anything related to Roger. Nothing.

"Hello. You are?" a tall thin man in a sweater vest and tie asked, extending a hand. He had a small, tidy mustache and purple-framed glasses.

"Olivia Wilcox," I saw no reason to lie. Yet.

"I'm Stan Bolduc. Why don't you come into my office?"

His tone was light, but the lightness was forced. The woman stepped aside, sizing me up like I was either another doughnut or the reason Roger was gone.

I walked back along the many desks in the main area. Another woman, seated back toward the kitchenette, looked up from her computer as I walked by. We passed an office with a gold nameplate on its open door.

*Roger Shepard.*

I walked slower, peering inside.

It looked like he was out for lunch. Desk, bookshelves, computer.

"This way," Stan said.

I walked through the next office door, and he shut it behind us.

"So, are you with another TV show? Newspaper? Because every time you guys come in here, it's traumatic for my staff."

"I'm not from a TV show or newspaper," I responded, keeping my eyes steady on his.

The man sat down at his desk with a thud.

I stood awkwardly in front of him.

As I continued to stare, he looked significantly older than I had thought before, by twenty years or so, his cheeks sagging, like he was carrying the weight of the world.

"Okay. Then who are you, and what do you want?"

"I'm a lawyer working on finding Roger Shepard. I wanted to know what he was looking into in Whitebridge School District before he went missing."

Stan blinked, a shocked look appearing on his face for a second and then vanishing.

"Who are you working for?" he asked quietly.

"Myself. I've taken an interest in the case."

"Okay, right. You don't think I have hobby detectives showing up here all the time? This isn't a game."

Reaching into my pocket, I took a step forward and placed a business card down on his desk.

"You can call my office," I said.

"Oh, okay, sure," he scoffed. He picked up the phone and called the number under the name *Olivia Wilcox, Attorney at Law.*

I heard a woman pick up, answer: "Olivia Wilcox's office, how may I help you?"

Till—amazing, as always.

Stan hung up.

"Okay, so you're a lawyer. I've talked to dozens of people already. There are no leads. Roger left to go to Whitebridge to talk to their financial manager with some questions, and he never returned. Absolutely no evidence of foul play, and no history of mental illness or anything else, really. He was friendly, beloved around here. We miss him, and I don't know what else to say about it."

Stan held up his hands.

"I'm really sorry," I said. "I can imagine how hard this is. But did you know the nature of his questions about Whitebridge?"

"Roger was a genius with numbers. He was constantly poring over the state's school board budgets, looking for irregularities.

He had found something there, I think. That's why he went up there—to ask a few questions, get clarity. Nothing crazy. I told the police all of this already, gave them his files." He caught himself and took a deep breath, as if talking about this was causing him physical pain. I felt bad, but I wasn't about to stop. "But like I said, no evidence of any crimes or foul play."

"Where was he supposed to stay in Whitebridge?"

"Look, no offense, but I've been through all of this with the police. Honestly, every single detail. And nothing happened. I don't have the time or energy to go through it again."

I wasn't sure what to do next. So, I went for it.

"Okay, well, I have the budgets for the last few years printed out in here, and I've highlighted some areas I have questions about. If you could possibly look at them and let me know if you think those were the same areas Roger was exploring, I would really appreciate it."

"I can't promise anything," he said, glancing down, looking deflated.

"I know. That's okay. Here." I handed him the envelope. He took it, set it down in front of him.

"Maybe he's still out there," I offered.

"Maybe," he said, looking down at the file. "But I don't think so. Roger wasn't the type to walk away from his family and his coworkers. He just wasn't."

I felt the weight of this.

His family.

"Please be in touch if you see anything there."

He nodded, still looking down.

I turned to leave as he continued sitting at his desk, spine curved downward, silent. I paused in the doorway of Roger's office.

I looked in, saw parts of Roger's life there, suspended in time. Everything remained as it was when he went missing four months earlier. What photos were on his desk? What small mementos were in his desk drawer? I desperately wanted to look, but knew I couldn't, especially when I heard someone clearing their throat behind me.

I noticed a small poster on Roger's wall.

*Keep Calm, I have a spreadsheet for that.*

Accounting humor.

Another cough sounded.

*Okay,* I thought, *I definitely won't go in.* My thoughts flashed to Piper in the car. I turned to leave.

"We all miss him, you know," the woman at the desk next to the kitchenette said. "He was a good man. Warm, funny. Worked hard."

I nodded to her. "I'm so sorry."

"Go find him," she said, a half whisper.

My eyes met hers. Dark, serious. She held my stare.

"I'll do my best," I said as I headed toward the exit. The woman at the entrance said, "Bye-bye now," in a softer tone than when I had arrived, and I walked down the hall, glad to escape the thick, grieving air of that place.

I stepped into the stairwell, looked down at the cars below, where I had left Piper in our truck. And parked right next to it was the old gray pickup.

*What was he doing there?*

Fear spiked in my heart like an ice pick. My baby.

# CHAPTER SEVENTEEN

I took the stairs two at a time, bounding down, boot heels clapping, echoing. Sprinting down the two flights in seconds, pushing the big black doors open, and bolting across the wet lawn to the parking lot.

There they were, the two vehicles next to each other, both empty.

I ran to my truck, looked in. No Piper, but sitting there was Clyde the hedgehog, on his side, her still-open book next to him.

*Shit, shit, shit. My baby.* My heart iced over, the breath caught in my lungs.

The other truck was that same gray truck of Nick's, the burly custodian, or an exact copy.

The judging voice screamed in my mind:

*Where is she? Where is she? Look, Look, Look.*

I scanned her door for signs of struggle. Her hair, a dropped pencil, anything.

But there was nothing. My heart hammered against my chest, my mouth bone dry.

*Maybe she just had to go to the bathroom? Maybe everything was okay?*

"Piper!" I screamed. "Piper!"

I turned a 360, scanning the grounds. Brick and cement government buildings, yellowing grass. I saw empty benches, picnic tables.

No Piper.

The road in front of the Department of Education trickled with traffic, a car now and then. There was a crosswalk. Was there a similar law in New Hampshire, that you had to stop for pedestrians? I ran across it, thinking Piper had done the same.

Trees.

There were large, old trees in front of the courthouse. Piper loved trees. I ran around them, looking up and around. She wasn't under or in any of them.

I tasted the bile creep up my throat.

Why hadn't I gotten Piper a phone? Tom had wanted that.

I turned toward Main Street, toward the town, scanning.

*Did that nasty man have her? I will kill him with my bare hands.*

I ran down the sidewalk. Midmorning, there were few people out and about, mostly folks on break from their office jobs, getting coffee or delivering something. No Piper behind that dumpster, or in that alley. She was just . . . *gone.*

*I should call the police.*

I pulled out my phone, and then my eyes settled on the familiar letters of a sign across the street. The orange letters, the awning. This one was brick, like it had to follow the town standards for New England design.

Dunkin'.

*Of course.*

*She had to be there.*

I took off at a sprint, scanning for Nick. I dodged a woman with a double stroller, yelling "Sorry!" as I flew past.

I pushed open the double doors, a bell ringing as they opened.

And it was there that I saw him, sitting with a cup of coffee. Hard eyes that watched my frantic entering. He was wearing his gray custodial suit and his brown curly salt-and-pepper hair looked wet. The coffee cup looked small in his hands. I ran at him.

"Where is she?!" I spat.

He shrugged, like he had all the time in the world.

He lowered his voice, almost a whisper. His mustache sat on his lip like a fat caterpillar.

"Stop asking questions. Or I really will take her next time. Would have been so easy."

I launched my body at him over the table. He pushed back in the booth, just missing my fingers.

"Ma'am?" one of the employees called. "Is everything okay?"

I righted myself and turned slowly around. The young woman, probably a teenager, looked wide-eyed, ready to call the police.

"A girl. A small girl. Did she come in here? Black hair, star leggings, sneakers?"

She looked around.

"No. I don't think so. But check the bathroom."

I ran to the two orange doors in the back corner, entered the women's bathroom.

Small spaces. Of course. Piper would have recognized this place, headed for the smallest, safest place she could find. I looked. Three orange stalls. No feet.

"Piper?" I called. "Piper!"

I heard a sniffle. "Mama?"

I hit the floor and looked under the door.

There, perched on a toilet, was Piper, arms and legs pulled into a tiny ball. Her eyes were red and puffy.

"Open up, sweetheart!"

The door clicked and I enveloped her in a hug and she threw her arms around my neck, sobbing into my coat. My whole body relaxed, my stomach settling.

"That man in the truck. He was scary. So I ran here."

"It's okay, it's okay."

*Jesus. He followed her.*

"Why didn't you get an adult to help you?"

"It happened so fast," she hiccuped. "I didn't know what to do."

I picked her up like she was a tiny baby. Piper's body wrapped around me. We stayed in the stall like that, quiet, breathing.

Maybe he was still here. Waiting for us.

I felt my phone in my pocket. I would call the police. Or I would walk up to the counter, and calmly tell the Dunkin' employee that the man was threatening me and my child, and that she should call the police.

I held on to Piper with one hand as I opened the door out of the bathroom with the other.

Took those few steps holding my breath.

But he was gone. The booth was empty.

His steaming coffee cup was still there.

"You found her! Oh, I'm so glad," the Dunkin' employee called from behind the counter.

I tried to smile at her as I scanned the rest of the store and the street outside.

Nothing.

My heart slowed its frantic pounding, but then I remembered his truck next to mine.

Would he be waiting there for us?

I set Piper down and stood, thinking. I heard the young employee whisper to another one, both in their baseball hats, watching me.

"Thank you," I said as I took Piper's hand, and we walked out the door. Like a deer looking out for predators, I scanned for him. The sun was peeking out in blinding bright spots, then retreated again behind darkening gray clouds. A few more people were walking on the sidewalk now as the clock ticked toward lunchtime.

*Good*, I thought. *More witnesses. He can't do anything to us in broad daylight, can he?*

I called Till.

"Listen," I said, "I want you to stay on the line. If anything bad happens, call the Manchester police immediately. That's where I am."

Till's answer and support was immediate. No questions. She must have heard the seriousness in my voice. The danger.

"Okay, I'm here."

I held Piper's hand and walked toward the crosswalk. Piper had used every bit of her energy to get to that Dunkin'. She moved so slow, like she wanted to lie down on the sidewalk and take a nap. But I pulled her along, my eyes scanning. Businesswoman, walking with focus. Dad with a baby on his chest. Older man walking a dog. All normal people, a normal scene.

We crossed the street, and I looked to the rows of cars where my truck was and beyond it. I squinted and saw another car in the place of the gray truck.

He was gone.

I felt relief wash over me, then a deep unease settling again in my stomach like a swarm of bees.

Who would believe me? What was my evidence that this man was stalking us?

*Stop asking questions.*

I let out a long breath.

"Liv. Is everything okay?" Till's voice was taut like a thick rope being pulled.

"Yeah, sorry, I'm okay. He's not here anymore."

"Good. Now, listen. I want you to get home safely. If it doesn't feel safe at home, I want you to stay here. Whatever's happening, we'll figure it out. You're not alone. I can protect you here."

What did I do to deserve Till? She was a New England superhero. "Thank you, Till," I said, my voice barely a whisper. "So much."

At the truck, I unlocked the door, let Piper get settled in. She instantly grabbed Clyde the hedgehog in a tight embrace, pulling him to her face, burying her head in his furry softness.

I walked around the truck, making sure everything was as it should be.

I was paranoid. Did he put a tracking device on my car? A bomb?

*Relax, Liv. This isn't a spy movie. Piper is back with you. Everything's okay.*

But it wasn't, clearly.

Nick had followed me to Manchester. And maybe he and Bob Stewart even knew the only reason I would be there.

Roger Shepard.

And if they were sending someone to follow me . . . ?

*What else have they done?*

I felt a deep sense of unease, of dread. I slid into the truck seat. Locked the door.

The sun blinded me intermittently as it peeked out from behind the clouds. I flipped the shade down. Fear lodged itself in my throat, but I swallowed it down.

There was no stopping now.

I just had to make sure Piper was safe. Nothing like that could ever happen again.

It felt like I was watching a movie about someone else's life.

I wished I had a gun. It was New Hampshire after all. Live free or die and all that. Didn't everyone here have one?

My energy drained from the spent adrenaline. I rested my head on the steering wheel.

Breathing. Thinking.

Just get home. Get back to Till and think through the next moves.

I looked up, set my jaw, then put the truck into reverse and pulled out.

I turned the truck north and got on the highway. Piper had fallen asleep quickly, her face still squished into the hedgehog, as if his coziness could erase all that had just happened. The clouds had lowered even farther and a mist of rain kept me turning on the windshield wipers. It was almost hypnotizing. Back and forth. Pause. Back and forth.

But the voice in my head was still in the background, keeping the events of the past hour fresh in my mind.

It had been a while since I'd felt that kind of panic, that level of sickening fear. At the firm, there were a few times when the fear had almost completely overwhelmed me. Like when I thought Mr. Alter, the charismatic sixty-something, well-groomed lawyer who acted like he was a gift to all women, would take it too far one day. But he was too smart for that. He knew exactly where the line was, and who had the burden of proof and who had the credibility. He mostly kept it verbal, commenting about what I was wearing and how it fit.

Comments about my husband, how lucky he was, and then about my pregnant body.

I never understood why people seemed to think that a woman's pregnant body was their own.

Their own for the touching. In the grocery store. By complete strangers. The commenting on its size. The personal questions.

"Are you sure there aren't twins in there?"

*Just shut up.*

Instead, I would smile and say pleasantly, "Yep! Pretty sure!"

Make my face say, *Aren't you all so charming?*

Except with Mr. Alter. It was as if my pregnancy was an affront to him—a visual reminder that I'd had sex, and not with him.

His chair was *right* next to mine. All the time.

His face, too close when we talked about cases. I always had to back up.

He didn't move when I needed to pass in the office, only made me press against him, scurrying to get by. His body was unyielding, even pushing forward against me at the last second.

I learned to keep doors open. To look for exits, sit near them. To never be alone in the office with him.

But I had never feared for my life. I had feared only for my dignity. For my body.

Which, as the rain came down and I continued along the highway with Piper snoring softly next to me, I guessed was one and the same.

Threats, in any form, were threats against being a free woman in the world.

And isn't that what so many want? Women to be less free. To not have control of a body.

To not have the agency to move around, be independent, take care of things.

And now Piper knew that same cold fear. The running. The hiding. I couldn't protect her from that. The knowledge of this settled on my shoulders like a boulder.

My decisions had done that.

I brought her with me. I put her in that situation.

It was my fault.

I needed help. I would get better locks on the doors. I would tell Till everything.

Maybe I would even call Tom.

But . . . no. He would just tell me how he was right. Always right. About everything.

How to load the dishwasher. What size pot to use when I cooked. How to wash his clothes.

About anything, really, and he had the very best way. And made sure to tell me all about it.

About how I couldn't possibly care for Piper on my own, keep her safe.

So how could I call now, tell him that his little girl had almost been kidnapped because I was pretending to be a lawyer on a case I wasn't getting paid for?

He would come get her. Or call me back into court about custody.

He would ride in on his white horse with a whole lot of feedback.

No. I wouldn't call Tom. Couldn't. But I would be way more careful. And make a backup plan.

Now it was like I was driving through a gray river. The windshield wipers were on high. All I could do was follow the highway, like pushing through a watery tunnel, as best I could.

# CHAPTER EIGHTEEN

It was the power of Halloween candy, in all its shiny wrapper goodness. Piles of it.

That's what motivated Piper to apologize for something she shouldn't have had to. To walk back into that place, face that salamander-killing boy, and a man who had tried to drag her by the elbow out of the woods.

Candy.

Kids were simple in a lot of ways. Many adults tried to hide their greed. Not kids. This was their night. Free candy. Simple, really. Piper had realized it was the week of Halloween, and all the decorating, card making, costume designing—and then, Friday night trick-or-treating?

She couldn't miss that.

So, I called Ms. Mitchell. Made an appointment to go in with Piper. To "reenter" school. To apologize. To check the boxes, do what we had to, so we could have a perfectly normal Halloween, a night to remember.

When I walked into that same dreaded lobby, I died a bit inside. My hand gripped Piper's.

I wanted to show her. *We can do hard things.*

Mrs. Patrick, the world's most unfriendly and inflexible administrative assistant, looked at us like we were a mess her dog had made on the carpet. She looked down her glasses at us, wearing a sickly beige sweater with an orange jack–o'–lantern button pinned to her chest. She simply waved us on, sighing and saying, "Go ahead," like we were a lost cause, barely worth the time it took for her to look away from the super important spreadsheet she was likely filling in. Or the enforcement of the time sheets of all the employees. Yes. I was certain she thrived on that kind of authoritative monitoring, the enforcing of set rules.

I felt my shoulders rising up to my ears. The place gave me the creeps. But I tried to breathe, to show Piper with my body that everything was okay.

But she was no fool. She tiptoed down the hallway, looking up at me, reading me like a book.

I tapped on Ms. Mitchell's partially open office door.

"Come on in," she called.

We took up most of the small office with our bodies. Ms. Mitchell was clearly used to this. "Here," she said, pulling up what had to be kindergarten chairs, bright orange, for us to sit in. She deftly slipped behind us and closed the door.

Ms. Mitchell sat in her office chair. I noticed duct tape holding the bottom cushion together. She was wearing a loose faded blue flannel dress, with what looked like pet hair stuck to it. Her legs were crossed. On the small table between us, there were coloring pages of mandalas. Small fidgets. A tube filled with liquid, with tiny bits of purple glitter and stars floating around. A jade plant, round leaves reaching across the windowsill. On the floor, a puffy, kid-sized blue chair.

This was clearly her domain.

"Thank you so much for coming in," she said, and her smile reached her eyes.

*Like we really had a choice.*

I nodded.

"Let's start by talking about what happened outside."

Minutes went by where we processed the event, and Ms. Mitchell, bless her soul, got Piper talking about how much she loved animals, especially salamanders, and how mad she was that anyone would harm one

Ms. Mitchell helped us make a plan. Piper was to start the day in her office, get settled in, and she would bring her down to class. If Piper ever needed a break, she was to come to the counseling office and sit in that puffy blue chair, which had several fidgets tucked into the side pockets.

Then Ms. Mitchell said she was going to go get Mr. Stewart.

Piper went to the chair, sank into it. It almost swallowed her. I held my breath. All of us, in this crowded office?

Before we knew it, Bob had stepped into the guidance office. He was visibly uncomfortable, stiff, looking like he was wearing a shirt made of thorns while in a place full of so many feelings.

Piper lifted her eyes to his, and I could tell that it took every bit of her energy to do it.

He waited, sighing.

Finally, after looking at him for a moment, her eyes turned down to that blue chair as she said she was sorry. That she would follow directions.

And maybe because he felt trapped there in that tiny place with posters about confidence and empathy, he just listened, then vanished.

Ms. Mitchell leaned over to Piper after the principal left and beamed at her.

"Good job, Piper."

Piper half smiled, twisting a curving plastic fidget in her hands.

And while I appreciated this, I still couldn't understand how she could work in this horrible place.

"Are you okay to walk to your class now?" Ms. Mitchell asked, tilting her head.

Piper sat there, in her purple sweatshirt and star leggings, considering. She looked at me, and I swear she was thinking, *See, I can play along too, Mommy, but I don't believe any of this.* Finally, she nodded, resigned to her fate. We were so tied to each other, I felt her resignation, her discomfort, in my chest.

I reached out and kissed the top of her head as she stood up. "I love you, Pipes. I'll see you later, okay?"

She disappeared, her braids swinging, out the door.

Piper was learning: The world is not fair.

The air changed after she left, like now we could get real. My thumb found the cold metal of my ring. I spun it once, twice, looking at Ms. Mitchell. She sat in this office—a safe place for emotions of all kinds.

"Let me ask you something," I said, my voice low. "How can you work here? I mean, for him?"

Ms. Mitchell pushed her fluffy, frizzy hair behind one ear, looked out the window of her office to a tree outside with a few yellow leaves lingering.

"That's the thing. I don't work for him. I work for the students. And their families."

I nodded. I understood that. Her mission was bigger than just one man.

It wasn't enough for me. I dug my fingernail into a dry cuticle crack.

"Is it safe here, for me and Piper? I mean, it certainly seems like Principal Stewart is out to get us. And I don't know if Piper will ever feel safe here."

"I know it seems that way. It's hard to start at a new school, especially in a town that hasn't really changed for decades. But my job is to make it feel safe. The change in administration has been . . ." She measured her words. "Difficult. But you have my word, I'll look out for Piper."

She looked back from the tree and right at me. I knew she meant it.

I had at least one ally in that school, other than Silas.

Finally, we left her office and were back in the sterile halls of the school.

I looked around. What would Halloween be like at Barnes Elementary? Would they even acknowledge it at school? I had no idea. But it was a good sign that Piper wanted to go back, even if they did nothing to celebrate Halloween. Then we could go trick-or-treating in the neighborhood like a normal family.

With no fear.

I needed candy. It was the first Halloween in our new house, and I couldn't be seen empty-handed in case we were back in time to receive some trick-or-treaters. That would be an embarrassment.

The hallways showed no sign of an upcoming holiday as I walked down the corridor. It radiated a sickly unease under fluorescent lights. My stomach clenched in a spiky ball. Leaving Piper here didn't feel right, but at least I knew Silas and Ms. Mitchell both had her back, and I had my new Halloween focus to distract me.

I pushed through the doors, knowing that Mrs. Patrick was watching me from her mission control location, thinking, *There she goes, that irresponsible parent.* I stepped out into flat gray light, and the wind hit my face, leaves skittering across the pavement in front of the school, like scrabbling fingers. Definitely a Halloween vibe.

One step at a time. We had done a hard thing this morning, and now we needed candy and to prep for trick-or-treating the next night. It was late morning by the time I pulled up to the grocery store at the other end of Main Street. Just one of those small-town grocery stores that tries to fit too many things into the small space it occupies, so it feels like it's crushing in on its customers, like the towers of food might bury someone at any given moment. The lanes were so tight, they could barely fit two carts passing at the same time.

I found the candy aisle right away, all that color and shiny wrapping, and stood there. My favorite was peanut M&M's but with all the allergy concerns, that was a nonstarter.

Around the corner came a man pushing a cart. He had on khakis and a nice flannel button-up, probably on his way to or from small-town work. His stomach pushed against the shirt where he had tucked it in.

He glanced at me. Then looked down.

I recognized him. But from where? His face—I knew I had seen it before. My feet were planted to the floor in front of the rows of candy as I stared.

Yes. His face. Definitely.

His eyes didn't meet mine as he walked by, even though we were the only two there. I kept watching him.

I grabbed handfuls of random candy bags, shoved them in my basket, and headed toward the front of the store.

"Chris! How ya doing?" the middle-aged grocery clerk called to the man, chewing her gum loudly.

I followed him to the checkout.

"Just fine," Chris said quietly. He looked back at me, then forward again to put his items on the counter.

"How are things up there at the district? You figuring out where all my taxes are going?"

*That was it.*

*He was the only face I hadn't recognized in the picture at the restaurant. He'd met with Bob and the school board president Brooke Bentworth. He had to know about Roger Shepard.*

Chris nodded. Forced a small laugh.

"And how about Jenna? How is that little sweetheart feeling?"

This woman clearly knew a lot about him.

"She's doing fine," he answered flatly, not looking back. He quickly bagged his groceries and headed for the door.

I cycled through what to do. Follow him?

"Hi," I said to the woman, short and stout and very into her gum.

She nodded, said nothing else as she moved the bags of candy across the checkout area.

I was confused for a second by her suddenly changed demeanor, but then remembered I was the newbie, the outsider.

How long would it be this way? Did it ever change, after five years, or ten? Or did you have to live generations in Whitebridge to feel known?

It didn't matter. They would see what happens when a town just protects itself at all costs.

I had work to do.

But first, I had Halloween to handle.

*Don't mess it up. This is Piper's night. Get it right.*

I said thank you and stepped out of the small grocery store with ten bags of candy. I resisted the urge to follow Chris and instead headed home.

The next night, I sat on the floor of the kitchen with pieces of felt all around me. At some point in cutting out large feather shapes in brown, beige, and tan, then hot gluing them to a sweatshirt of Piper's, I had moved to the floor. Small pieces of felt were in my hair and there was dried glue on my fingertips.

I was trying to be the type of mom who made Halloween costumes.

Because of course Piper wanted to be an owl. It was the perfect costume for her, really. Quietly beautiful. Skittish. Timid. But also wise, strong, somehow magical. Not missing anything, taking everything in.

That was Piper.

She had come home from school and said she wanted to be an animal that felt like her. After consulting with her hedgehog and her animal book, she said she wanted to be an owl. Far too many internet searches later, and digging into a messy and deep craft bin, I was splayed across the floor with felt and a sweatshirt, creating the body of a woodland owl out of felt and hot glue because I had never really learned to sew.

My own mom loved art and music but mostly paintings and ones that challenged the systems, said something, a critique of society. Not cookie or costume making. That would have been too domestic. My mom's head had always been in the clouds and influenced by counterculture. Creativity, ideas, abstract thought, not pragmatic life skills. It had been my aunt who had taught me things like not carrying debt, how to research something, how to change a flat, how to fix computer problems. As a kid, I had always made my own costumes, and some of them, like a boombox made out of a refrigerator box, were pretty great. Other years, they were barely passable.

I wanted to show love and respect for Piper by helping her do this, to be an animal that felt like her.

Next to me, Steinem batted around a piece of felt and

walked through the piles. I shooed her away. I only had a few more to go.

Piper came dancing into the kitchen wearing her gauzy brown wings. Luckily, Till had fashioned the wings out of one of her old dresses, clipping and gathering in ways that confounded me. The wings shimmered as Piper moved around the kitchen table. Steinem sprinted away from the movement.

"Is it almost ready?"

Piper looked happy, her little face upturned, her big brown eyes truly owl-like.

"Yes, almost. Why don't you try to eat something real before we go?"

I pointed the hot glue gun at the final beige flap of felt.

Piper got herself some bread, put it in the toaster.

I pushed the final piece down.

"Okay, we'll let that set, you can eat your toast, and then we can do your face."

I pushed a flyaway curl behind my ear. This felt like parenting Olympics. One phase down. Makeup next.

I climbed back to the dining room table, set out my tools. Brown and black eyeliners, eye shadows, and foundations of different colors.

Piper finished her toast and settled in on the chair before me. I pushed the jet-black hair off her face, light and feathery on my fingers.

Piper's long black eyelashes were stunning. They always made my heart skip a beat.

She blinked up at me.

"Ready?" I said, smiling.

"Ready!" Piper said, the happiest I had seen her in a very long time, possibly since we'd left Boston.

Minutes later, Piper looked up from behind successive

brown-and-white circles around each eye, and a solid triangle of yellow where her nose was.

I stepped back, checking out my work.

"How does it look?" Piper said, settling the headband over her hair, and now wearing the sweatshirt covered in felt feathers.

I clapped. "Fabulous. Owlish! Go look!"

Piper ran to the small bathroom and stared into the mirror.

I waited, holding my breath.

Piper ran back, her steps slapping the linoleum.

"I love it," she sighed softly.

I had won. No matter what else happened that night, I'd done something right.

It was a classic Halloween night.

There were high, thin clouds, with the almost full moon offering a glowing, gauzy light. The last of the sunlight was leaking away, leaving the sky an inky blue. There was a cold north wind, reminding me of what was coming, a solid six months of winter. But Piper, in her owl sweatshirt, wings, and headband, didn't seem to notice the chill. She skipped in circles in front of our house as the quiet street came alive with small people dressed up as ghosts, pirates, kings, and queens.

Laura pulled up and her girls piled out of the Subaru. Niki, almost too old for trick-or-treating, but clearly not ready to let it go, was wearing a cow onesie, and her sister wore a baby bunny costume with puffy, pink ears.

"Hey! Look at that. You made the owl costume."

I smiled. "Just barely."

"It looks great. Though I bet your house is covered in felt pieces."

"Totally."

"I'm telling you, a simple press of a button and I have a bunny and a cow."

I laughed. Things seemed almost normal.

Laura handed me a small silver flask.

"We're gonna need this to survive tonight. And to keep warm."

Laura was nothing like I thought she would be that first night at the board meeting. I unscrewed the top and took a sip. A burning sensation slid down my throat, settling in my stomach. I wiped my mouth, handed the flask back.

Laura's girls ran ahead, finding friends and moving at a breakneck pace for optimal candy gathering. Piper, instead, grabbed my hand.

"You ready?" I said.

She nodded and walked to the house next to ours. We had decided to make Till's house our last stop, on the other side of the street.

"Remember, you knock on the door, or ring the doorbell, say trick or treat, then say thank you after they give you candy."

Piper nodded again and with a few kids behind her, walked up to the house slowly, tentatively.

A middle-aged man opened the door and said, "An owl!"

He gave her a piece of candy, and she started walking back. We waved to him. But he just looked at us, then shut the door.

"Asshole," Laura murmured.

"Not very friendly."

Piper continued down the line. Some kids were cutting in front of her, laughing, some telling her to hurry up if she was moving too slowly. She wasn't skipping anymore.

Most of the adults didn't offer a friendly wave, but a curt nod, if anything at all.

"I don't think I'm liked very much here."

"They just don't know you yet." She handed me the flask again. "They don't know your awesomeness like I do. And you're from Boston. You know there's bad blood there."

"Yeah, what's that all about?"

The wind picked up. Piper had to be freezing. I zipped up my fleece jacket to my chin.

"You know, New Hampshire is kind of like the conservative older brother, the one that works in insurance, goes to church, hunts on the weekend, and Boston is the flighty younger sister, who's an artist, a vegan, and drinks twenty-dollar cocktails. I mean, who has more fun? Which one would you want to be?"

I burst out laughing.

Thank God for Laura.

There were now more and more people on the street. Teenagers started whooping and hollering, and the small kids were losing their energy and couldn't feel their toes. The night had the eerie feeling of being caught up in a crowd, but most of the people were wearing masks as everything got darker and louder—creepy, confusing. We curved between traveling groups and Piper waited in lines to walk up to houses.

She and several other kids walked up to one house that was close to the field that led down to Main Street. It was a white, two-story colonial, simple, straightforward. The lights were on, and a bowl of candy sat on a white rocking chair. A sign said *Take One!* even though I noticed that there was a car in the driveway and a small light on inside.

Before I could think to warn her, Piper walked up, taking small, unsure steps, as a kid pushed past her, grabbing a handful of candy. A screen door pulled open, and a clown, with orange hair, a brightly painted white face with black circles over the eyes and stripes down each cheek, and a large, blood-red smile, appeared, with a handsaw over his shoulder.

"Hey!" he yelled. "The sign says take *one*!"

Piper froze, a small deer trapped in headlights, then dropped her candy bag and ran for her life. She scanned the crowd and sprinted full tilt into me, her tiny force almost knocking me over.

The kid who'd taken the handful bent down to grab Piper's bag.

Laura came up to him and yelled, "What is *wrong* with you?!"

He looked up at her and dropped the bag. Some of the candy spilled out. Laura picked up the bag and walked back to us.

Piper was folded into my fleece jacket.

Her body shuddered in small cry hiccups.

"Hey, hey, it's okay. He was just pretending to be a monster. I know you were only going to take one. It's okay."

But Piper, the little joyful owl, was gone.

"I want to go home," she sniffed.

"Hey, let's not end on that. Why don't we do one more house."

Piper didn't answer. Filtered moonlight gave the street a gauzy glow. The few streetlights, widely spaced, revealed trick-or-treaters moving in and out of the deep shadows.

I turned to Laura. "I'm sorry. I'm going to take her home. We might stop at Till's before heading in if I can get her to."

Laura nodded. "I'm sorry people are assholes," she said. "Bye, Piper. I loved your costume."

"Mama, she said *asshole*," Piper sniffed. She looked up at me, her eyes puffy and red, the owl circles now smeared down her cheeks.

We walked back down the center of the road, staying clear of the mayhem.

We passed small groups of people, their volume increasing. Some little kids crying. Others running, using every minute of their Halloween freedom. I tried to see it through Piper's eyes.

Unpredictable. Dark. Sudden movements. Crowded. All things she didn't like. "How about we make our last stop at Till's so we can show her your costume."

Piper didn't respond but didn't resist as we made our way along the shadows.

Till had a simple jack-o'-lantern on her porch and pulled the door open when we knocked. She was wearing a black cloak and a witch's hat, and her face broke into a huge smile when she saw us.

"A beautiful little owl!" she exclaimed.

Piper sniffed and offered a small grin.

"Come on in," Till said. "Let's have some hot cider."

"But don't you have to answer the door for trick-or-treaters?"

"Not anymore! My most important one just came," she said with a wink, shutting her door and turning off the porch light.

After settling in with cider, I told her what had happened with the murderous clown.

"That Jerry, I don't know why he does that! Scaring kids. I mean, maybe his life in insurance is a little boring." Till laughed and it was like somebody had sprinkled fairy dust in the room. "Hey. I think you need to do two more doors of trick-or-treating."

"No," Piper said. "I'm not going back out there."

"I don't mean that. I mean right here. In a minute, you knock on that door and that door, and you'll get more candy."

Piper nodded, her eyes perking up.

Till grabbed me, handed me a crown and a red robe, and a small, stapled-shut bag, and pointed to the laundry room door. I ducked in, closing the door halfway behind me so I could still see what was happening.

Piper knocked on Till's bedroom door.

"Trick or treat!"

Till opened the door, using her most dramatic witch voice. "Who's there? A small child who can help me stir this cauldron?"

Till stirred a plastic cauldron with a wooden spoon.

"Let me see what's in here. Oh! Look! A treat for someone named Piper?"

"That's me!"

The witch reached into the cauldron, picked up a small bag, and handed it to Piper, who took it with wide eyes.

She then came to the laundry room door and knocked.

"Who is it? I am polishing my diamonds!" I shouted in as queenly a voice as I could muster.

"Trick or treat!" Piper yelled, smiling now.

"If you must!"

I opened the door with a flourish and said, "How dare you interrupt the kingdom! Take this and be gone with you!"

Piper took the bag I handed her.

It was safe, inside trick-or-treating. And it was perfect.

Later, Piper sat on the carpet, her new bags emptied, with her candy in organized piles, along with some Halloween socks and stickers.

Till and I sat drinking glasses of wine.

"Thank you so much, Till. You saved our night. Really. I just wanted her to have a normal Halloween."

"You made *my* night. It's the most fun I've had in so long. I just love you guys," she said, taking a sip, her cheeks flushed.

Later, we walked back across the street with some of the night recovered. At least Piper wasn't whimpering now. Once she was safely in bed, I settled into my own with my computer and another glass of wine. I'd done it. Created a somewhat normal Halloween for Piper.

Thank goodness.

But as I took a sip and then set the glass down on the bedside table, a name surfaced in my mind.

*Roger Shepard.*

*He didn't get to do Halloween with his family this year. He's been missing for four months now, almost five.*

As these thoughts swirled in my mind, I drifted off to sleep.

Then, a thudding sound jerked me awake. Then a high-pitched sound right outside my window.

I flew up and out of bed. Steinem was a furry streak. My brain was thick from sleep, and I stood listening.

Just as I started to relax, a noise came from downstairs. Someone was knocking—or battering their way in.

# CHAPTER NINETEEN

I ran downstairs, two steps at a time, toward the sound at the door. What weapon did I have? I had left my phone on the nightstand. No calling 911 now. I stopped in the kitchen and grabbed the first thing I could find—a giant chef's knife.

*I wish I had a gun.*

I flattened myself against the wall of the kitchen, slid toward the entrance to the mudroom and to the front door.

"Mama!" Piper called from upstairs. I didn't want to call back, to alert anyone at the door that I was nearby.

My breath came in shallow bursts, fingers wrapped tightly around the cold knife. I would do whatever necessary to protect my daughter.

Another thudding sound came from the windows, and then a louder one on the front door. I rounded the corner, my hand shaking as I held up the long silver knife and peered out the window on the door.

No one was there.

No masked face, no Nick, or even Bob Stewart.

Just a blob of fresh egg, the yoke sliding down the window, visible in the filtered moonlight.

*Eggs.*

*They were just eggs.*

*Not someone breaking down the front door.*

I sighed, my entire body relaxing. Maybe I was losing my mind. About this . . . about everything. Maybe I had created all of these mysteries because I didn't want to deal with my real life, with taking the bar exam, with building a life with Piper—and without my ex-husband.

"Mama! Where are you? What's happening?"

I set the knife down on the kitchen counter, mortified that I thought I could have saved us with it. I ran back up the stairs to my crying baby. I went to her bed, where she was curled up in a ball, comforter pulled up to her nose, big fat tears pouring from her wide eyes.

I leaned over, brushed her hair back.

"Shhh, sweetie, shhh. It's okay."

It was so totally not okay.

I stood up and walked to the window, pushed back the curtain just a little bit. I could see the two trees in our front yard, filled with toilet paper, draped like bizarrely placed Christmas lights.

And then I saw them: a couple of teenagers jumping into the back of a pickup truck. I heard them hoot and laugh.

"Go back to Boston!" one of them yelled.

Why would these teenagers be targeting me? What had I done to them? How did they even know who I was? It made no sense.

"Is it the mean clown? The man in the truck?"

I went back to Piper, climbed into the bed, pulled her to me. Her tears dampened my chest as she sobbed, her tiny body shaking. Seeing your kid suffer, the very worst kind of pain. It guts you, scoops out your center, leaves you desperate.

"I want to go back to Boston," she whispered. "I hate it here."

I nodded, my own eyes filling. Yes. I wanted to leave too.

Who was I kidding? I couldn't find a missing person. I would never figure out what was really happening here.

I hadn't even passed the bar exam. Had only told the truth about the harassment at the firm after the other woman had.

I was a fraud and a fake, and the only brave thing I had ever done was to leave my husband, which really, right now, I wasn't even so sure about. All of this would have been much easier if he was there.

Because if I was married to a man, who was living in that house with me, none of this would have happened.

The world was so messed up. Maybe it was just better not to fight it.

I sobbed with Piper, both of us shaking together like a little collective storm.

I cried for everyone who just gave up. Stayed with partners they didn't love or who didn't treat them well.

For those who gave up dreams for their kids.

For those unmet visions of themselves.

Me, a strong lawyer, fighting for human rights against big corporations run by rich, white men.

Except that I couldn't really fight them. They were winning. They *always* won.

I sank into Piper, until we combined into one sniffling heap. Steinem approached from the side, concerned. Rubbed against us.

*Maybe we should just move back to Boston, or home to Vermont. Sell this house and let someone else deal with this place.*

*It's the only way.*

"Jerks," Till said, crossing the street to where I stood on a ladder to wipe off the egg, now thick and crusty, stuck to my bedroom window. "And be careful up there!"

I pressed the paper towel with window cleaner across the glass, where it promptly began falling apart, adding bits of paper towel to the clumpy mess.

"Ugh!" I said. "Everything sucks!"

I climbed down the ladder, met Till as she approached.

Icy bits of rain came down out of the steely November sky. The air was a creeping cold, the kind that slowly freezes a person from the inside out. Stick season, the last of the leaves finally falling off, a landscape of gray and of bare, haunting trees.

"What you need is newspaper and a wet sponge. Can you go get that for me?"

I nodded and hustled inside, then reappeared with the goods. Till stepped up the ladder and got most of it off with the wet sponge, then sprayed the window and began wiping it with the newspaper. The eggy streaks began disappearing.

"Well, look at that!" I said.

"You can't make it through seventy years and not know a thing or two," she called from the top of the ladder, which wobbled slightly.

"Jesus, Till! Be careful up there!" I couldn't help but smile as she waved her hand dismissively and continued cleaning the windows. Till was the best thing about this place.

I turned to start pulling down toilet paper where I could reach it in the tree. It was falling apart—wet and gross. After a while, Till appeared next to me and started helping clean the tree. "Till. I was thinking. Maybe Piper and I should just leave this town." I grabbed a string of paper that broke as I pulled. "Shit."

She considered my words for a minute, and then nodded at the house. "Let's move the ladder over here."

"Okay," I agreed, wondering if she'd heard me.

We carried the ladder over to the tree, set it against the trunk. I took a few steps up while Till steadied it for me. I picked some more of the pieces away in silence. Finally, Till spoke, quietly.

"I understand why you feel that way. But this is your home. Your family lived here. You have every right to be here and to be treated well. I'm embarrassed of our town. You and your daughter are special, lovely people. If you leave, the bullies win. And it won't get better."

"But I don't know if we can take this. Or if it's safe for Piper."

"You can. Listen, you come from tough stuff. Your aunt was braver than most. And Piper? I can help with her."

*Tough stuff. Doesn't feel like it. Last night, I resolved to give up, to leave.*

"Thank you, Till," I said, stepping down with a handful of wet toilet paper. "Want to come inside? I have some coffee brewing."

Inside, we shook off our rain-covered jackets and sat at the kitchen table, steaming mugs of coffee next to us.

"Honestly?" I said. "Last night scared the hell out of me."

"Oh, I bet. That's terrifying. I'm sorry I didn't wake up this time. I would have grabbed Charlie's old rifle and given them quite a scare."

I almost spit out my coffee. "Till!"

"Those little shits. I think they were Nick's boys and their friends. Total jerks. Go around breaking stuff, leaving beer cans everywhere."

*Ah, related to Nick. Makes sense now.*

I imagined Till walking across her yard with a rifle, the boys squealing and running. I chuckled.

"Now that's more like it," Till said, smiling at me. "Listen, I won't try to convince you to stay. But just give it another week or two, okay? Then decide. I know you're doubting yourself, but you're doing important work here, and I'm with you. And I bet others are too."

I was quiet for a long moment.

"Let me ask you one thing," I finally said. It was the most important thing. I had to know.

"Ask me anything."

"Those last few days. With my aunt. Was anyone there? I mean, did Lydia visit?"

Till leaned over the table, took my hand.

"Yes. Lydia and I both were visiting every day with food and flowers, while the hospice folks were in and out as well."

Till's eyes clouded, but she kept looking at me. She knew about Lydia. Her gaze said it.

There was such warmth and kindness there.

"Lydia was with her that last day. I was out at the grocery store, and when I came back, I knew your aunt was gone." Till stared now out into the space beyond the table. "Then I saw Lydia pull out of the driveway, and I never saw her again."

We sat there together with this, Steinem rubbing the legs of the table.

"She just left?"

"After all that with the school? And the pain she was in? Yeah, she just left."

"Didn't come to the service?"

"No. All those people that had worked against them? And wanted her out? Coming to the funeral, pretending to honor her? No. She was back in Vermont with her family. And I don't blame her one bit." Till paused, picked up her coffee, held it in her slightly shaking hands. "I don't want to see you go like that—leaving suddenly, letting the town bullies win. I can't let that happen again."

It suddenly made sense to me. This was Till's fight too.

"They won't," I said, confidence rebuilding inside of me. "Not this time."

Later, I sat in Aunt Esther's office. I felt relief that she hadn't been alone at the end. And also a deep sadness about how everything had happened, and how I'd been too busy to notice.

I looked around the office. How many times had Esther herself sat here, pondering the cruelty of the world? I wondered how often she would sit and read the words of women who had come before her for inspiration.

I sat with the files and a web search open and a fresh cup of coffee.

The sleet had stopped outside, but the sky didn't seem to notice or care, a thick gray blanket muting any sun. I took a small amount of comfort from the fact that the door was bolted. Growing up in Vermont, we had never locked any doors. It was only when I moved to Boston after marrying Tom that I'd started to, and sometimes even then I would forget.

After clicking around on the computer for a while and not finding any new information, I went back and listened to some of my audio files. Especially the one I recorded in the truck after the candy run to the grocery store about that man who wouldn't look at me. Something about his eyes, his avoidance of me, the mention of his family, all of it felt off. It seemed like he was in over his head, and that maybe he had some humanity, some regret. He certainly had some knowledge.

Chris. That was his name.

I started looking for Chris on the district page.

And of course. There he was. The financial manager for the district. Chris Parker.

The money man.

He knew about these budgets, so he must have known about Roger Shepard too. And he was in those pictures, meeting with those men—and Brooke—at the restaurant.

I searched social media for him. Luckily, many of his settings were public.

He was quite a community man. A coach of soccer and basketball, and he had a little girl, Jenna, who looked about eight. Everyone commented that they "hoped she was feeling better" and that "they would get through this" and that "God has a plan." So it wasn't the regular sick, it was the big, bad sick.

I felt for him.

Well, if there was a sick child, that was bullshit. There aren't any divine plans or purpose when it comes sick kids. And anyone who says so needs a punch in the face.

*Call me sentimental, but someone who has a sick kid can't possibly be involved in a potentially violent school-level organized crime syndicate. At their own child's school?*

*Unless.*

*Unless he's piled under mountains of medical bills.*

*And he's complicit. Because he has to be.*

*Because there's no other choice for him.*

I was going to have to talk to Chris Parker.

The next morning, I woke, rubbed sleep out of my eyes, and my brain started spinning immediately, instantly on the treadmill of Roger, Chris, Bob. I had some idea of what was happening, between the budget, my notes, and observations. What I needed now was proof—and to stay safe.

I needed to think. And to think, I needed to run. So I

chugged some coffee and then asked Till to come over and watch Piper just for a bit. I searched for my windbreaker, which I hadn't needed since the move.

Once ready, I stepped outside and took a deep breath of cool air. That always seemed to set my mind a bit at ease, uncurling the vice grip of thoughts coursing through my brain. The air felt more like spring, smelled wet and earthy, water coursing just under the soil. My body was heavy from lack of sleep, but I pushed through it and started to run.

My feet fell into a familiar pattern, my arms pumping, as I headed down the street.

Sunday morning. Most of Whitebridge would be waking up and getting ready for church.

I knew I should stay away from Barnes after what had happened last time, and Bob's finger-wagging that I should stay off the school's property. But didn't I pay taxes? Have a kid at the school? I assumed there were security cameras. But it wasn't like I was going to break into the building—just run around the grounds and have a look. There were no laws against that.

I did, however, need to make sure Nick wasn't there first.

So I turned left out of the neighborhood and away from town, toward Barnes. The morning birds were chatty in the trees lining the road as I climbed the hill above Main Street and the town center.

What was I looking for, really? Maybe they were just a bunch of closed-minded assholes, nothing more.

But Roger Shepard. He was gone.

And Lydia, she was destroyed.

I came up to the school grounds, lost in these thoughts, stepped off the road to run behind the school in a wide circle, not getting too close, sticking near the tree line. I wobbled on the uneven dirt and long grass, feeling the wetness seep through my sneakers.

The huge garden, still a mystery, rose before me. It looked like they were starting to close it down for winter, cutting the dead plants out for compost, a large green plastic dome just outside the edge of the fencing. A few bags of mulch were lined up against the shed, ready to be set down before the snow fell in earnest, sealing the deal for the upcoming season.

I wondered again if the garden was a holdover from the last administration. I could imagine the kids of Barnes Elementary sticking their little fingers in the dirt to pull up baby carrots. Delighting in the planting and harvesting something themselves, of being allowed to get really dirty. I thought of my own parents, standing in their Vermont garden, which was usually planted with a strong spring fervor, then promptly ignored for months afterward in exchange for camping trips, swimming holes, and outdoor concerts. But the thing seemed to produce a wild bounty anyway, as if to reward my family for just living.

My mother would beam when she'd go out to pick out some fresh basil for dinner, and then come back in with a giant zucchini or two as well. I loved to go out there and see what was popping up, what was being eaten and destroyed by bugs, and what the deer or rabbits had taken.

It was like life—wild, unpredictable, full of drama.

I was so lost in thought about gardens that I missed the small black car tucked in under the awning at the back entrance to Nick's "man cave."

My body jolted as I spotted it, a zapping electric pulse, so I made a beeline for the back of the garden, where I could hide behind the composter, the largest hiding spot I could see. The ground was mushy under my feet, threatening to take my shoes or knock me off balance.

I crouched behind the green dome, then raised my head a little over the top, heart pounding. Scanned the area.

No movement.

I squinted to peer into the building. A small light was on, probably at that desk in the large storage room.

Someone was in there.

If I ran, it would be in the wide-open athletic fields and I risked being seen. And accused of trespassing. Again. And now I was stuck. Stuck behind a composter.

The wind picked up a bit, drying my sweat from the run. I shivered.

I ran through the options. I could make for the tree line, for the trail I could see at the back of the school property, beyond the baseball field. But that would be a long sprint on this mushy ground, out in the open.

And I wouldn't see who was in there. On a Sunday. In the "man cave."

I took out my phone, tried to snap a few photos of the car, but couldn't get a shot of anything beyond the garden without risking being seen.

So I took some photos of the garden.

Someone had started mulching the area in front of the composter. The new mulch looked dark and fresh, and its scent was strong, earthy. It looked like it hadn't been done with kid hands, but laid out on the ground in a deliberate, focused manner. The rest still needed a covering.

I sat waiting, glancing over periodically and watching the light inside the school for any movement.

Time slowed.

My legs cramped as the lactic acid settled. Despite Till's kind words, her support, the voice reasserted itself in my mind.

*What am I doing with my life? Is this what going crazy feels like?*

I heard a clicking sound and carefully glanced over again. The heavy school doors were open.

From my limited vantage point, the next thing I could make out was a thick hand—which held on to a large banking pouch with a zipper.

# CHAPTER TWENTY

I dared to lean slightly farther out, to scan up his body.

Thick neck, mustache, scowl. It was Nick, and he was making for the black car, quickly.

That pouch

He opened the door, then suddenly turned, as if he somehow felt my presence. He reached into his back pocket.

He must have seen me and was getting something. A phone—or a gun. I held my breath and prepared to bolt.

But he only pulled out a circular case of chew, and in one swift move, grabbed some, tucked it under his lip, dropped into the car, and drove away.

I watched him go, my body relaxing slightly.

Maybe he was headed to the district office. To get there, he had to head out and around town, and back up the hill on the other side of the river.

Not me. I'd noted that path behind the school, and was pretty sure it led to the district office, but I'd never run it before.

Well, it was time.

And if it didn't lead there, I would at least get a workout in.

Maybe it was because I'd seen Nick for the first time since the Dunkin' incident, or maybe something else, but I felt a deep unease, a sense that I wasn't quite alone in this garden. Somehow, the air felt instantly alive. Charged. Otherworldly. A cool breeze swept me, giving me instant goose bumps, my arm hair standing up.

Once the coast was clear, I readied myself to move. I would run as fast as I could just in case the cameras were trained over the garden, so hopefully I would be just a blur. I took a deep breath, let it out, my vision tunneling.

And then I cannonballed out of the hiding spot and sprinted across the baseball field, my feet squishing in the mud, my socks soaking instantly.

I was almost to the tree line when I dared myself to look back.

No one and nothing moving at Barnes Elementary School.

Into the trees. My feet pounding a wet trail.

*Concentrate. Can't afford a sprained ankle.*

The trees surrounded me, almost seeming to observe the frantic human passing through, so temporary, so fleeting. Yet I felt safer with them around me.

I'd always been able to run fast. When I drank too much in college and couldn't exactly remember the details of the night before, I always went running the next morning. To punish myself a little bit for being so stupid but mostly to regain control. To see the world, push through the guilt and heaviness, and be in my body again.

This felt a little like that, only the control I was seeking was of this town, this situation. Pounding my feet on the trail, catching myself from falling on roots, another voice called out from the back of my mind.

*I am alive.*

*I am in control.*

*I can do this.*

A sudden breeze whipped up, and the bare branches clacked together, the sound feeling like increased encouragement with every turn, up and around their trunks, and down short, rocky hills until I could see the forest ending. The field next to the district office had to be up ahead.

I slowed, contemplating where I could sneak to the edge of the woods and take a look—only about seven minutes had passed. I had crossed the trail in little time, my heart pounding, sweat prickling my armpits. I was exactly where I thought I would come out, on the backside of the district office land.

Looking around, I noticed a massive fallen tree, not unlike where Piper had hidden—a perfect hiding place. It was close enough to the building that I could see, but not be seen.

I ducked into the loose, muddy loam soil left by the fallen tree. As if the forest itself was there to help me. A small puddle splashed my feet where I landed, then I peered out, over the lip of the makeshift tree fort. I squatted down.

Damn, was I going to need to stretch after this. All my muscles ached from the sprinting and the positions I'd been holding.

Across the field, I could see the small black car was in the parking lot of the district office. On a Sunday. It just seemed sketchy.

Nick, who had no trouble threatening a little girl.

Had he done something to Roger Shepard?

And what the hell was in that bank envelope he'd been holding?

I checked my phone. No messages from Till. I let her know that I wouldn't be too much longer.

I could see that Nick had not gotten out of the car, but sat there, waiting. I had to stay hidden. Had he seen me running for the trees?

Before I could allow myself to worry about that too much, a large, silver SUV pulled in. After a moment, Brooke Bentworth stepped out, dressed in her Sunday best—a navy blue dress, with a matching jacket and white pearls, iron-straight hair sprayed up into a tight updo. She walked over to the black car like her bones were made of steel. She reached into her cavernous, leather purse, pulled out a thick envelope. Her eyes scanned the area, and I ducked lower, as she handed it to him. His sneer indicated he liked his power over her. He smiled but her eyes didn't meet his. She turned and briskly walked back to her car, got in, and was gone. Nick waited a few minutes, then left as well.

*Brooke.*

*Nick.*

*An envelope.*

They clearly didn't want anyone seeing them—otherwise they could just do it outside of church—but why not wait until the middle of the night?

Too suspicious. They could play this off as some sort of school business.

But why would the school board chair be handing off an envelope to the head custodian? I had to assume she wasn't having an affair with him. He was so "below" her. Stature, appearance, all of it. But then again, maybe she liked that.

And where was Bob Stewart in all of this?

I remembered the drunk man's words at the bar. The shiny tools, the questionable budget. My brain was gathering steam. It was all one big grift of the school system. Buying and selling equipment with school funds, giving construction deals to board members' families, and now, possible blackmail. But how to convince other people of what I suspected was happening?

I had to get my hands on that envelope. Or get into the "man cave" myself.

When the coast was finally clear, I ran out to the road and started the descent into town. Small-town Sunday morning, not much movement or activity. I stopped to look at the river as it rushed under the bridge, thinking.

All my life I'd had to prove myself. First, being the youngest in my family, with my genius older brother—everyone expected the same from me. I had to step into that expectation in every class I'd walked into.

*Oh! Alex's younger sister? Yes, welcome. You will be quiet, focused, hardworking, and follow directions. Even with those hippie parents.*

Except that my laugh was too loud. My emotions a little hot.

So I learned to tuck in my edges. To make myself smaller, and swallow emotions.

My parents, meanwhile, encouraged me to *lighten up! Put less pressure on yourself!* It was funny, really, like they had one genius, and that was enough.

The conflicting messages were confusing. So I set about to prove myself worthy—to my parents: yes, I am smart too. And to school: yes, I might be a little loud, a little passionate, but I also get good grades.

It was fucking exhausting.

And here I was having to prove myself yet again. To make this case believable, to uncover and tell the story of what I thought was really happening here, how it wasn't okay. It was, in fact, criminal. But how to do it? And in a way that would make my aunt proud.

Was my life just about proving my worth to people over and over again? When would that ever end?

I shook my head, watching the gray water twist along below me.

*After this, I would focus on passing the bar, settle into this place, and start practicing law for real. Not for anyone else, but for me.*

I ran through the rest of town, back up the street, and into our neighborhood. I looked forward to stripping off the wet shoes, socks, clothes, and jumping into the shower.

But first, on a whim, I stopped at Star Bakery. I always tucked my credit card into the thin pocket of my tights before heading out. You never know when you'll need a hot coffee and a pastry, and it seemed like a perfect way to thank Till. I had always wanted to stop here anyway.

I would just walk up the hill back to my house with the goods.

The bell sounded as I popped in. The Star Bakery was painted a bright white, with small metallic silver stars painted on the walls and stainless-steel silver counters. It was elegant, simple. This was mostly a take-and-go bakery—there were only two small tables to the right and left of the door. The case that held the baked goods popped out from this white-and-silver palette, with richly brown whoopie pies, bright pastel-colored macarons in stacks, croissants in so many varieties staring back at me.

Why had I never been here? It was immediately my new favorite place.

"Good morning!" The woman behind the counter smiled broadly. I felt better just being in her company.

But one of the fancy moms was in front of me. Why wasn't she in church like everyone else? She wore tight leggings that fit perfectly over her Pilates strong and thin body. Her hair was impeccably highlighted—her brows perfectly plucked. She looked at the case of gorgeous baked goods, each a perfect tiny package of sugar, butter, and goodness. She was on her cell phone, while the woman behind the counter waited, her smile twitching a little.

"I know, Mom, but they're doing Singapore math now, and

Phillip will be getting gifted and talented instruction from Johns Hopkins. Yes. They say he's already working on high school math in third grade! I know. Isn't he just amazing?"

Her eyes sparkled with pride.

I wanted to vomit.

The woman behind the counter started vigorously wiping down the back of the big stainless-steel case holding the creations while she waited for her customer's order.

The woman on the phone pointed to baked goods she wanted as she spoke.

The baker nodded and pulled the selections out one by one.

"Honestly, I'm so glad we got rid of the hippie principal and got someone who can get them ready for the ivies and help give them the challenges they need. And not make them feel guilty all the time for being who they are, you know?"

The woman behind the counter's smile turned down a few notches. After gathering the four baked goods and placing them in a bag, she hit a few buttons on the old-timey cash register and said, "That'll be fifteen dollars."

"Hold on, Mom. I'm at the bakery." She inserted her credit card and paused speaking. "No, it's not for me. I can't eat this stuff, not if I want to keep this body, no way!" she said with a laugh. "It's for the kids after church."

She tilted her head and mouthed *thank you* to the woman and was on her way with her white bag in hand, her phone still attached to her cheek as she walked out of the door.

I looked at the baker, who was still watching Pilates-mom leave.

"I'm sorry about her," I managed.

The woman nodded. "That's Whitebridge for you." She shrugged. Then, "How can I help you?" Her smile was back in place, full wattage. It must have been exhausting.

I walked the rest of the way home with the bag of freshly baked goods. I'd been so focused on my experience in this town, I had forgotten that other people here had it so much worse, dealing with the overwhelming privilege of the town as well as the inflexibility of the school.

The filtered sun was getting higher in the sky; it had to be almost 10 a.m. It gave off a gauzy light under thin, high clouds. I'd been gone awhile.

When I was just a few houses from my own, my phone buzzed as a text came in.

From Till.

*We have a problem. There's a police car in your driveway.*

# CHAPTER TWENTY-ONE

*Should we call a lawyer?* I texted back.

*It looks like Billy. He's not that smart. The scariest kind of cop.*

My brain went sideways, thoughts colliding. A cop. In my driveway. Certainly not to protect, I guessed. Another text.

*Stay calm, Liv. I'll keep Piper over here.*

I didn't feel my feet as I took the last straightaway to my house. I was soaked and shivering. Billy was standing outside his Whitebridge police car, leaning against it with his arms crossed as I got closer. He had closely cropped brown hair, neat, and his uniform tried to make him look older, but his round cheeks and smooth face betrayed his youth. Likely in his mid-twenties at most.

He was frowning, watching me approach.

I had dealt with men like this before, of all ages. Ones that needed to feel powerful. Lots of apologies and deference helped, even if it made me feel sick. I had avoided speeding tickets that way. Maybe it would work here. If I could stomach doing it.

He stood up from the car. Leaned forward.

"Good morning, Ms. Wilcox," he said, his voice also boy-like but serious. And none of the warmth of an actual greeting.

*Here we go. Showtime.* "Good morning, officer. How are you today? How can I help you?"

All sugar.

His eyebrow twitched, a thick brown brow, quivering. Probably something he'd tried to control, but failed.

Billy didn't take the bait.

"Where are you coming from this morning?"

"Oh, I was just out for a run," I said, smiling. The wind picked up, blowing my hair and chilling me even more. My baked goods hung from one hand.

"Did you fall?"

As if he cared. I looked down. My knees were muddy from where I'd crouched in the forest, watching the delivery of that envelope. My shoes, wet and muddy.

"Yes, I did stumble a bit. I was trail running."

"The trails over by the school?" He waited.

There was no way out of this.

"Yes, they're just so beautiful." *Time for a subject change.* "And then I headed to Star Bakery. What an amazing place. And the pastries look *so* good. Would you like one? I have a few extra."

*Baked goods. Common ground.*

I smiled. I wasn't going to make this easy for him.

But he didn't waver.

He took another step toward me, said, "My aunt did say you were nice, but that doesn't change the fact that you were warned by Principal Stewart not to go on school grounds, except when picking up your daughter."

*His aunt? Laura?*

*Who else could it be? How could she not tell me that her nephew was a cop—and one that was in cahoots with Bob Stewart?* I rolled back the tape in my mind. What had I told her?

*Every. Single. Thing.*

I tried to control my breathing, but I could feel the panic rushing across my body. He watched me, a tiny smile playing at his lips. It was clear he'd enjoyed surprising me with that information.

"And it sounds to me like you were just there, on school grounds. Did you—"

"Well, no," I injected. "I was just running in the area. You know, on public grounds? We runners take advantage of all the public places we can."

His face clouded. He didn't like the interruption or the fact that I had corrected him. "Yes, well, I can check the surveillance video of the grounds. I know you were escorted off the property once and then went back again and were trespassing on the site another time." Laura had known all of these details too. What exactly had she shared with him?

The walkie-talkie clipped along his collarbone crackled with some voices. He reached up and turned it down, lost his train of thought. Like a student in a class who raised his hand, then got called on, and forgot what he wanted to say. His mouth formed an O as he searched his mind for what to say next.

I almost felt bad for him.

Until he snapped to and said, "I'm going to need you to come downtown with me."

My pleasant veneer broke. "What? Why?"

"Because you're being charged with trespassing."

"I'm sorry," I said, now shivering, "but where's your proof?"

Billy stopped. He had been challenged again, and he wasn't amused.

"You're serious." His voice was no longer boy-like.

The curtain in Till's window moved, and I knew she was watching, trying to figure out how to help.

"Yes, I'm serious. Do you have any proof about any of this?"

"I'm looking at it," he said, and he came right at me, twisting my arms behind my back before I even knew what was happening. The bag of baked goods dropped to the ground, its contents spilling out across the driveway.

What the actual fuck was happening?

I squirmed but his grip was too strong.

"You're under arrest for trespassing on school grounds," he managed before a sharp voice rang out.

"Billy Sullivan, just what do you think you're doing?"

"Mrs. McHale, this doesn't concern you," he said as he began leading me to the squad car.

*What would happen to Piper? What would they do to me?*

"You bet it does. She's my neighbor and friend. What are the charges?"

"Criminal trespass," he said quickly, as if he was answering the teacher right away for extra credit.

"On school grounds? Nonsense. That's public property, and you know it. Don't embarrass yourself. She's a member of this community and the parent of a student at the school."

"But Mr. Stewart said—"

"I don't care what Mr. Stewart said!"

He paused for a moment, tried to think of what to say. "I'm sorry, Mrs. McHale, but I have to bring her in."

"She hasn't committed a crime."

"We'll have to see about that," he responded, a bit more confidence in his voice. And with that, in one move, he opened the door and shoved me into the back seat of the cruiser. I stared at the black cushions where other small-town criminals had sat—domestic abusers, thieves, and drunk drivers—in disbelief. My knees knocked into each other with chills from both temperature and fear.

Till was still arguing with Billy. She was gesticulating, her hands and strong voice making the case. She waved over at her house, pointed, and then pointed back. Billy nodded.

Opened the door suddenly, pulling me back out into the morning air.

"Okay. Here's what we are going to do. Thanks to your neighbor here, you're not coming in *right now*. But I *will* print out and deliver the no-trespass order against you. You are in no way to go onto school grounds for any reason, including running, unless you are dropping off or picking up your daughter. You got that?"

"Yes," I managed. It came out like a quiet chirp.

"You're lucky your ass isn't sitting in a jail cell at this very moment," he added, trying to get his power back, pointing at my chest. "But next time? I won't be so nice. You think you're so smart, just like your aunt. Smarter than the rest of us. She was always sticking her nose where it didn't belong too."

I nodded even though his words caused my knees to buckle with rage. I needed to keep standing.

"Thank you, Billy," Till said, dismissing him like a class of first graders.

He glanced at her, then climbed into his cruiser and drove away.

Till came immediately to me and led me toward the front steps of Esther's house. I looked over her shoulder, across the street, and saw Piper, in Till's living room window, watching with wide eyes. I waved at her, forcing a smile that said, *Look! I'm okay!*

Till watched this then said, "Don't worry. I'll explain to Piper that Billy made a mistake, and I'll bring her back over."

Her voice soothed me. I hoped Piper wasn't too upset. It was just all so much.

Once in my bathroom, I immediately stripped down and turned on the shower. My body was violently shaking as I waited for the water to heat up.

*This town will be the end of me.*

What did Till say to make it possible that I wasn't sitting in a jail cell right now? The woman was freaking magic.

I stepped into the steam, my numb toes aching as they met the hot water. My body temperature was finally rising, calming my shivers.

*How did I get here?*

*Almost arrested. Kicked out of a school. Racing through the woods, hiding.*

I stepped out of the shower, wrapped myself tightly in a towel, sat down on the toilet, not wanting to leave the steamy heat of the room.

Then, after a long moment, I grabbed my phone and texted Silas.

Hey. I almost got arrested for trespassing at the school.

Another moment, and then:

What? Jesus. Are you okay?

Yeah

Billy?

Again:

Yeah.

Ugh, that guy. Acts all tough. Not much going on upstairs. Hothead.

You should have seen Till. She talked him right out of it like schooling a little boy.

I really would have liked to see that

There's some shady shit happening at that school. I have to tell you what I saw. Maybe you can help.

I'd be glad to. Can you talk now?

Yes, but just for a bit. Till is waiting downstairs. We're going to figure out what to do next.

I paused, then:

Did you know that Billy is Laura's nephew?

Three dots appeared. Then none. Then three dots again.

Yes. I don't know why she didn't tell you right away. This town is real small, Liv. Everyone knows everyone.

It stung, this withheld information. I wondered why Silas

hadn't warned me. I'd trusted Laura since my first moments of meeting her, way back in that dark parking lot. Now, I wondered what she had told her nephew about me, and if she was really a friend at all.

I texted Silas, *Can I call?*

*Yes,* came the response, lightning-fast.

So I called, told him everything. But I didn't want him to get involved—he could get targeted, just like Lydia was. In fact, he might already be a target just for knowing me, and certainly would become one if he helped me in any way.

I drank in his kindness and attention, even though the subject was dark and the stakes were high. We brainstormed ideas for what to do next, then I said I needed to go. I knew what I really needed. And that was Till, and a plan. But first, Piper.

I put on my robe and headed downstairs to meet her.

"Pipes!"

She ran into me with force and buried her head in my robe. I wrapped my arms around her back.

"Mama, why did the policeman want you?" she asked, her voice muffled from the fabric.

I looked at Till, who nodded her encouragement.

"He was confused, honey, that's all. Thought I did something wrong, but I didn't."

She popped her head back up so I could see her face. I smoothed her hair.

Her eyes searched my face. "Why do people keep thinking we're doing things wrong?" *Great question, Piper.*

I kissed the top of her head. After some snuggles and hot chocolate, we settled Piper in front of a show.

"Till and I will be in the study, sweetheart."

I looked at her, curled around her hedgehog, hair fanned around her.

"I love you, Pipes. It'll all be okay."

Piper nodded, her eyelids heavy. I knew she wanted to believe me.

With our hot teas in hand, Till and I headed into Esther's study. Till sat at the small recliner where Esther journaled, and I sat at the small desk. Steinem came busting in the office, startling us both.

"Okay," she said. "Show me what you have."

So I made the case. I pulled up the budgets, where I had highlighted excessive maintenance and tool costs, the numbers increasing every year. New construction contracts with the board member's firm, his sick daughter, as a financial motive. I detailed the meeting between Nick and Brooke, an exchange of a bank pouch.

Till listened. Rubbed her face.

And Roger. I explained how he was the state rep on the case, how he came up to visit four months ago and never returned.

At this, Till's face contorted into a grimace. She was silent. The sun made shadows across the office, the dust hanging there, glittering as I waited.

*Maybe she thinks I'm crazy.*

Finally, she spoke.

"And then there's Nick. He followed you and Piper to Manchester. He threatened you in the Dunkin'." She said this in almost a whisper. Her eyes stared ahead into nothing, mind clearly working through all of these details.

"Yes. He also followed me to that restaurant."

"They're watching you, that's for sure." She went silent again, looked up at the ceiling, still thinking. "But we have no physical proof. No hard data."

"Well, not exactly. We have the budgets, a missing person, a motive . . ."

"It's not enough. We need something solid linking all of this together."

I sat back against the chair, deflated, feeling like I'd failed the test. I thought there was enough there, that we could do something with this information. Finally.

Till leaned forward, hands on her chin. "It's in the man cave," she said. "On that computer. It's so simple and obvious. They have to have files of all of the grift—who they're buying from, selling to, the amounts skimmed from construction contracts, files on Roger. It has to be there. They make that the center of the operation, because no one would ever look too closely at the custodian's computer. It's kind of brilliant. Where else would it be?"

Of course. The man cave is the center of the operation.

I sat up. I knew I had to get in there.

"Okay then. I'm going to go get what we need."

Till nodded. "Okay. Let's plan the shit out of it."

We launched in, reviewing all the files, the layout of the school, and how I could get in there, what I would do when I did.

Till's eyes were focused for hours as we pored over every detail. We googled how to handle security cameras, ran through various escape scenarios, thought about what I would need to bring.

I knew our plan was crazy. So did Till. But something about sitting there, taking control of the situation, felt right. Hours flew by as we worked, honing the timing and the route. The sun sank low in the sky, then started to set.

If it didn't go right? I would be arrested, and Piper would probably be sent back to live with her dad. I was gambling *everything*. But I was also doing it for her.

It *had* to go right.

This was the only chance I had to create a real home for ourselves.

And I wasn't going to walk away now.

When we couldn't keep our eyes open any longer, Till made her way across the street in the chilly November night. I watched her go. She waved from her front step and then I saw her go safely inside.

Once in bed, my brain refused to settle down.

*Everything needs to appear normal.*

*Piper will go to school.*

*I'll work on creating a solid case file that is indisputable to send to Manchester, to the state police. No local cops. No Billy, who's apparently in Bob Stewart's pocket.*

*In the meantime, I need to find Roger.*

I thumped my foot against the mattress. Spun Esther's ring, heavy on my finger.

*What would a good trial lawyer do?*

*Retrace steps. Go back to the beginning.*

*Lydia Brown.*

Where I first learned the scope of this madness. Learned how she and Esther had worked on the case together, had fallen in love.

After I dropped off Piper, that's where I would go. Now that I knew more, maybe Lydia would let me further in.

If she was in her right mind.

If her mom would let me see her. That hadn't gone so well the last time.

But I had to try. All the pieces were there. I just needed the evidence.

But Roger? Still missing. No clues.

And maybe Lydia knew more than she was letting on.

The next morning, I dressed to look the part. A lawyer or investigative journalist, in my white sweater, black pants with stylish boots, and long black jacket. I could play this game. As Piper pulled on her sneakers, I looked in the small wooden mirror with moons carved around it that I'd gotten in college from a friend and smoothed my hair, smiled at myself. A plastered-on, fake-it-until-you-make-it, everything-is-fine smile.

Piper stared at me.

"Why are you smiling like that, Mama?"

God, this child didn't miss a beat.

"Just getting ready, honey," I said.

I wondered what I was teaching her at that moment—to put on a smile for others? That looks matter more than anything? I grimaced, silently cursed the paradox of being a feminist mom in this world. A constant supply of feelings of hypocrisy and questioning.

But really, I wanted Piper to be proud of me—for wanting to fix something that wasn't right. For trying to make Whitebridge safer for her, for all the kids. For focusing on a problem and not letting up until it was solved.

As usual, Piper was quiet in the back seat of the car on the way to school. I looked at her in the rearview mirror, the wide brown eyes, staring at the trees outside the window. Winter was on the wind. Monochrome skies. Creeping cold with some tiny bits of sleet starting to spray the windshield. The kind of cold that crept under jackets, into socks—damp, clinging.

I pulled up to the school, hopped out, smiling, nodding, *everything is fine.* I opened the back door while Piper unclipped, not in a hurry. After a moment's hesitation, she stepped out, resigned to the school day.

I kept my eyes on my baby.

I didn't look for Bob Stewart or Ms. Mitchell. Didn't scan for them or look at the other moms.

Whatever.

"Have a good day, Pipes. I love you." I bent down to give her a kiss.

Piper shrugged on her swirly purple backpack, almost as big as she was, and gently placed her small warm hands on both of my cheeks.

"You too, Mama. Whatever you're doing. You look nice."

It was like Piper had a silver stream, a river, connecting her brain to mine. She knew that I was up to something, didn't know what, but supported me anyway.

My heart feeling full of her love, I got in, shut the door, and drove away like everything was normal.

That girl had a sixth sense.

Or maybe she just hadn't seen me wearing anything but a hoodie for a while.

I parked the truck and walked into the Sunshine Café. The ice pellets stung my face as they hit.

The whole northeast could have used a bit of this café's name. The sun was an infrequent guest in November, and it showed. People rushed from place to place with stretched grimaces, hunched under zipped-up jackets, pulled-down hoods. Maybe the Sunshine Café was a plea, a display of optimism, or a show of resistance while living here.

I focused on the heavy door.

While there was still cheery light and plants everywhere inside, the atmosphere was subdued. Almost empty at 9 a.m. on a Monday.

I didn't see anyone behind the counter.

There was no music playing, but I could hear someone in the kitchen.

I walked to the table I'd sat at before. There was only one other customer: A man in a thick flannel, scruffy goatee, reading a paper and drinking coffee. He looked like he might have been out all night, and didn't glance up at my arrival.

I waited. The bell on the door had rung when I'd entered. I knew they had heard me come in. After a few minutes, the woman who I remembered as Lydia's mom peeked quickly from behind the block of coffee machines. She looked surprised, then set down what she was doing and walked to my table.

I knew right away that something was wrong. Her eyes were swollen and sunken, like she'd been punched. Her hair was piled on her head in a messy bun but falling out everywhere.

Her mouth was pulled into a thin line, forehead wrinkled with apparent worry.

"Have you seen her?" she said as she practically ran to the table. Her eyes, like her daughter's the last time I'd been here, darted around.

She sat down and leaned forward, her face right in front of me, her hazel eyes, yellow flecks like broken glass, locking onto mine.

"Lydia? No, I—"

"Then why are you here?" she interrupted, her face turning angry.

"I'm sorry, I don't know what you're talking about."

"Lydia has been missing for eight days," she said, voice trembling.

*Her* baby. Gone.

# CHAPTER TWENTY-TWO

"What? I had no idea."

The woman shook her head like she was clearing a bad dream.

"You come in here," she continued, arms gesticulating wildly toward the door, almost hitting me, "you bring up the school she left three years ago. You start digging around Whitebridge. Then my beautiful daughter is gone. What the fuck do you think you're doing?"

She was inches from my face. I was stunned, words stuck in my throat.

"I'm so sorry. Did she leave with someone? Have you called the police?"

I slid back in my seat, away from her face, which continued to twist in despair.

"Oh, I don't think so. I don't think I'm going to share more information with you. I have no idea what's going on here, but I know Lydia loved your aunt. They worked together, tried to make a case against Whitebridge, but somehow they were stopped. Your aunt got sick, died, and my baby up and quit, though they might as well have fired her for all they did to her. She was getting back on her feet, getting counseling, managing that constant anxiety, until a couple weeks ago when you showed up."

I had focused so much on my own grief of losing Esther that I didn't even think about Lydia, this loss, amid all the drama at the school. It must have been truly awful. And I certainly hadn't helped. I didn't even show up to say goodbye before Esther died. Only made it to the service, briefly, because I had to get home to Piper.

"I'm sorry," I repeated, "I didn't mean to . . ."

"Yeah. Well. She started disappearing for hours at a time, missing shifts here, coming home late, until I barely saw her. And then one night, she didn't come home at all. No note, no texts, no nothing."

Her eyes glazed over. The world had not been kind to her. Again.

Is there anything worse than a missing child? And a person is always, in some way, a baby to their mother. And this woman looked hollow, gutted. I felt her ache, felt a weight in my chest. I had done this. I had caused Lydia to come unglued. But how?

"Who had she been with? Do you know what she'd been doing?"

Anger flared in her eyes again. "You don't get to waltz back in here and pretend you care. You didn't know her. You just came in, asked questions about that place, and then you were gone. You didn't see her unravel. She can never really leave that town behind. Not ever. The scars are always there. Your aunt was the best thing that ever happened to her, and she's gone."

I looked at her, trying for connection.

"I miss Esther too."

Her eyes softened a bit.

The sleet made tiny clicking noises against the windows. I felt my phone vibrate in my pocket.

"You know, Lydia wasn't even going to stay in Vermont or New Hampshire. She was going places. She wanted to take her teaching where she was needed. She had so much energy and was so creative, even when she was little. Endlessly curious. Younger kids would follow her around. She read to them, drew with them. And now it was all for nothing. I wish I had never shown her that job in Whitebridge. It was selfish. I wanted her near me, not off in a city, but that was so totally wrong. She would have been safer there, with more open-minded folks."

A parent, being wrong. What a painful, recurring feeling. I knew it well. A tight, blaming energy seemed to seep out of Lydia's mom, mostly onto herself. She stared across the café and out into some distant space of parental regret.

"I'm close to figuring it out, I'm sure of it." I reached my hand out to her. "If I find something that might help you find Lydia, can I reach out?"

"Yes, of course." She snapped back from her ten-mile stare, took a restaurant receipt from her apron pocket, wrote her number on the back. "But don't involve her in any more of this. She's already done too much. Given too much." She grabbed the crystal around her neck, her thumb rubbing the top of the shiny purple cone.

I nodded, seeing years of parenting behind her eyes—Lydia as a baby, a toddler, a ten-year-old. Years of caring for another, only to have them disappear.

And I might have been the cause.

The effort to stand was a burden, the weight in my chest still thick and heavy.

"I'm sorry," I repeated again, the words feeling hollow in my mouth. "I'll figure this out."

I headed toward the door.

I looked back, but Lydia's mom had already disappeared behind the counter.

Once back at the truck, I realized I was shaking. My hands rested on the steering wheel, which I gripped to try and steady myself.

First Roger.

Then Lydia.

At least with Roger I was removed, had never met him, only looked around the office he had inhabited and into his smiling eyes on the missing persons listing. But Lydia—she had sat across from me, in her slouchy, scattered aliveness. I had come seeking answers. But maybe I had just dragged things out of the closet that Lydia didn't want to think about or see again.

What was this whole thing anyway? Some sad attempt to make up for not speaking up at the firm? Or for not becoming a lawyer yet?

An obsessive, broken, scrambling for redemption?

I gripped the wheel, closed my eyes, heard that familiar voice.

*It's all your fault.*

*You, pretending to be a lawyer.*

*Even if you did dress up today.*

*When you are nothing.*

*You let all those women down. Just like you let down Lydia's mom.*

*Just like you will let Piper down.*

Over and over.

I couldn't hear anything else. The words pelted me. They were winning.

I felt my pocket buzz again, snapping me back.

The sleet was now more like icy rain, blurring the outside

of the truck. I pulled my phone from my pocket. It was Silas. A string of what felt like breathless texts.

> One of my students found something
>
> I think it's important
>
> It's really freaking me out
>
> I didn't think so before but now I do
>
> These people could kill someone.

# CHAPTER TWENTY-THREE

It was the sign I needed. The plan had to happen now. It would never be the perfect time, and if Lydia was still out there, if there were others in danger, I had to make my move now—before someone else got hurt.

I tapped out a message to Till.

It's go time tonight. We have almost everything we need.

She responded almost immediately.

Tonight? Are you sure? We still have some details to work out.

It'll be fine. It has to be tonight

The rain continued to pound the roof of my truck.

A long moment, and then: *Okay.*

I tossed the phone onto the seat, nodded my head.

*You have to see this through,* I told myself. *Esther started it, and you need to finish it.*

Just maybe not the exact legal path that she and Lydia had been on.

I put the car in reverse, headed back toward New Hampshire in the gray icy soup, barely a distinction between sky and road. I pushed the haranguing voice into the background—there was no time for that now.

Hours later, I pulled the small duffel bag over my shoulder. Clyde the Hedgehog stuck out of the side that wasn't zipped, having been hastily shoved into the bag. I held a rolled-up sleeping bag in the other hand.

"What about Steinem, Mama?"

"She'll be fine. It's only one night."

"Why am I having a sleepover on a school night?"

"I told you—I have to do some work."

"Instead of sleeping?"

"Yes, honey, instead of sleeping. But I'll stay with you and Till for dinner. She made her homemade mac and cheese. And maybe before school, you can have those maple rolls." Piper smiled at the thought, but then looked to the sky, thoughtfully. Knowing something big was happening but not sure what. The promise of delicious food only took things so far. I watched her tie her purple sneakers. This girl, unfolding, becoming smarter and more aware of everything each day. I couldn't afford to mess this up. They would take me away, my heart would never mend, and I would miss this curious, loving soul as she grew up without me.

I shook my head, trying to clear the thought and the sudden constriction of my throat.

*I won't let that happen.*

She stood up from the bench, we walked outside. I closed

our front door and locked it. The November tree branches reached toward us like icy fingers. The air was cool and still, mirroring how I felt inside.

Till opened the door and her house breathed life and color and warmth.

"Why, hello there! Welcome."

We pushed into the small entryway, Snowflake running up to see what all the commotion was about, white fluffy tail straight into the air. Piper, bent down, talking to the cat. Those two, since the moment they'd met, seemed to understand each other.

Till pulled me into a hug, whispered into my ear, "Silas will be over later to show us what he has. But Liv, this might be too dangerous. I know I said you had to go in, but we're talking about a possible murder. I don't want anything to happen to you."

I breathed Till in—a classic rose scent, but with soapy edges, clean, floral, comforting. This is what it was like to be mothered, to be fussed over. My own mom had been full of life, had been consumed by her creative work, had been encouraging but only vaguely present. Parenting seemed like a distraction from what she really wanted to be doing, something she wanted to escape from. Till was a whole new species for me.

I nodded. "It'll be okay."

Till turned to Piper and said, "Wait until you see the little nest I have for you up by my bed!"

"Really?" my little girl beamed.

"Yes! It's piled up with blankets and books and drawing materials—which Snowflake has already laid across, of course. Let's go put your stuff up there."

Later, after dinner and a game, we sat in the living room, with Piper tucked into the nest beside Till's bed upstairs. A quiet tap came from the door.

Till jumped up, in her white fleece sweat suit, hair pulled into a neat braid down her back.

She let Silas in.

He filled most of the mudroom in his blue puffy jacket and his brown Carhartts. His face was slightly ashen, pale blue eyes dim with worry. It was slightly surreal to see him inside Till's house. I'd only spent time with him at the bar or at school—though I'd imagined him in plenty of other places.

"Is Piper asleep?" he whispered.

"Yes, we think so," Till said. She took his jacket, hung it up.

"Come on in. We're just going over plans for Liv tonight." She said this like we were going shopping or having a luncheon.

He walked into the living room but didn't sit down.

"Liv. I don't think you should go. We need to call the police."

"Hold on, Silas," Till said. "Take a breath. Come in, sit down, let's talk about everything. You said you have something to show us. But first, we all need tea."

I was beginning to realize that this was just how Till did things. Get comfortable, and then dive in.

She retreated to the kitchen to get three mugs of tea ready. Silas sat down across from me, his shoulders up by his ears, his whole body tight.

"Hey," I said. "You okay?"

He looked up at me, his eyes landing on mine, the connection still taking my breath away, even in his diminished, worried state. Maybe even more so.

When he spoke, his voice was hushed, ragged with concern. "I don't want anything to happen to you. Or Piper." He looked around the room. "It's way more messed up than I ever imagined."

I was taken aback by the emotion in his words, the look in his eyes. I couldn't remember anything even vaguely like this from any man. Mostly, I was just the person to dictate plans to, to figure out schedules with, to make the food and give the rides. It had been forever since I had felt cared for by a man. Seen, noticed. Maybe never—Jesus, maybe this was the first time.

I smiled. Then felt the moment evaporate.

Because I knew. Knew it in my bones. The feeling landed like bricks.

"They killed him, didn't they." A statement, not a question.

"I think they did."

Till came back in with three steaming mugs. Set them down, looking between us.

"What did I miss?"

She sat down on the tattered yellow chair, a delicate white handkerchief covering the spot where Snowflake routinely sharpened her claws.

Silas reached into his pocket and pulled out a small, shiny object. Held it up to us. A tarnished, intricately carved class ring, like the one I wore, with dirt in each of the small carved lines. The ring itself was thick and solid, a man's ring, with a dark blue stone recessed into its base.

"Someone just lost their ring," Till said. "Happens all the time."

"That's what I thought too." Silas set the ring down gently on the coffee table, like a live bomb, and took out his phone.

I looked closer. On the side of the ring, barely legible because of the mud, was the number 90, and the letters MHS.

Manchester High School. 1990. Roger Shepard's graduating class, his hometown. I had built up his file, his story, knew this was his.

Silas held up his phone, showing a Facebook group from 1990, Manchester High School graduating class. There stood Roger Shepard in the second row.

"And here."

He clicked over to Roger's profile and pointed to where it said that he'd graduated from: Manchester High School, class of '90.

"Where did you find it?" Till asked, looking pale now too.

Silas looked down, recalling the scene. "I took my class out to the garden to hang our pine cone bird feeders on the fencing, on the far side, by the composter. I thought it would be the best place for the birds to access the food because it's on the opposite side of the school, so it might be safer for the birds there. Some of my kids went inside the fence through the gate with my aide and some were on the outside with me."

I imagined the little faces of pre-K students carrying pine cones covered in nut butter and sunflower seeds out to the garden.

"One little boy, Finn, was waiting for my help and then started digging with a stick in the mulch at the corner of the garden. I was helping them wrap the string around the wire, and also trying to make sure the kids didn't throw mud at each other. I guess Finn just kept digging."

I nodded, silently encouraging him to keep talking.

"I was chatting with another student, and then Finn held something up, shouted, 'Look!'"

"Oh God," Till said, her face now looking green.

"Do you think he's . . . ?" I started.

"Yeah. Under there," Silas said. "I don't know why else this would be there."

"But how?"

"The ring. Right. Well, I thought of that. Based on my social media stalking, it looks like Roger lost a lot of weight, and maybe it was loose and fell off when they buried him there, or maybe they destroyed the body but somehow missed the ring . . ."

We sat in grim silence. Silas finally continued, even paler than before.

"I took the class back inside, trying to stay calm. I asked Finn if I could have the ring, so I could find its owner. He didn't want to give it to me at first. You know, 'finders keepers' and all that, but he finally did."

"Did anyone see you? Did anyone else come out with your class?" I asked, imagining Nick there, watching.

"No, but the security cameras. They're bound to see it."

"If they're checking them. Monitoring them closely," Till said.

"Oh, I'm sure they are. If there *is* a body there . . ." He shook his head. "If Roger is there, that means he's . . ." Silas stopped talking again, rubbed his hands together, finding the words. "Somewhat fresh. He's only been missing for four months. And in that case, they're watching and waiting for the snow, so their secret is safe for the rest of the year."

I felt a sudden stab of pain in my chest. I'd hoped we could find Roger—that sweet smiling face, round cheeks, glasses on a nose—alive and well.

Silas continued. "The thing is, Finn's dad is in construction, at the local firm that has contracts at the school. If he tells his parents what he found, and somehow they know about this . . ."

We all heard the wood floor creak under a foot on the stairs.

And there stood Piper, Clyde hooked under one arm. Her eyes were round, full, glassy.

"Piper, sweetheart, what are you doing up?" My heart jumped into my throat. What had she heard?

She looked as if she was on another plane, in another reality, like she didn't hear me at all. Maybe she was sleepwalking.

Her voice was barely audible. "They spend a lot of time around the compost and that part of the garden. I watch them out the window. I thought they liked composting." Like she had been part of the conversation all along.

Piper was certainly a window dweller.

I called back softly. "Who does, sweetheart?"

"The mean man. The one who scared me and I ran to Dunkin'. He rakes it, he checks it, all the time, then he goes to the shed and does stuff."

I looked at Silas.

*Nick.*

"Sometimes I think he sees me looking out. So I duck down real quick. Mama. Is there a man under there?"

Tears suddenly overflowed from her eyes, brimming over the bottom lids, cascading down her small, puffy cheeks.

"Oh, sweetie," I ran over, grabbing her in a crouched hug. "We don't know for sure."

"I'm never going back there," she said.

I looked at Silas and Till. "I know, sweetheart, I know. Not like this."

Till came over, placed a hand on Piper's back.

"Piper, honey, I have some hot chocolate in the kitchen. We can use the whipped cream."

If there was ever a moment for whipped cream, this was it.

Piper looked to me to see if she could do it. Sometimes things are bad enough that an evening sugar infusion was not only okay but necessary.

I nodded.

When Till and Piper went to the kitchen, Silas started urgently whispering.

"Liv, you can't possibly go to that school tonight. You can't. They might be covering up a *murder*. You don't think you would be next? You *have* to go to the police."

"What, go to Billy? Sure. He already wanted to lock me up."

"You have evidence now."

"A gold ring in a garden? Come on. Billy's in the board's

pocket and you know it. The ring would be 'lost' as soon as we turned it over, and then we'd have nothing. We need evidence of the crimes, the whole system of selling and contracts and grifting the district. I know how to get it. I'm going in tonight."

"What about Piper? What if you get arrested? What if they take her away from you?"

"That won't happen." Despite my words, the idea took my breath away. Still, I felt like I had no choice.

"How can you risk that?" His whisper climbed up louder, strained.

"How can I *not*? If these people are murderers, how can I not do this? It's not like there's anyone else in this town who even knows about it."

Silas rocked back and forth. Shaking his head.

"Then I'm going with you."

"What? No, you can't. You could lose your job."

"*You* could lose your daughter."

He had a point. But I shook my head, regained my mental footing. "No, we need you to appear separate from this, removed, to talk about it objectively when we finally do turn them in."

Silas stepped closer to me, and I could feel the heat coming off his body, had to stop myself from wrapping my arms around him.

"I can't do this, Liv," he said, hardly more than a whisper. "I can't just let you go there and risk everything." Despite the emotion in his voice, his words ran over me like a cold shower. I pulled my hands away from him.

"I'm going anyway. You're not 'letting' me do anything. I'm in charge of myself, and I'll do what I have to."

"I know that. I wasn't saying . . ." He rubbed his forehead in exasperation.

"You know what? I don't need your opinion right now. I don't need to be rescued. I don't need to be saved."

His voice got louder now. "I wasn't saying that. I wasn't saying I could save you."

I didn't respond, just tried to control my wildly spinning emotions.

"Liv. You have to know I'm not like them. I'm a preschool teacher, for god's sake."

"You grew up with the same bullshit we all did."

"I just want to help you. Really. You don't need to do this alone."

"Actually, Silas, I do."

I looked past him, my mind going back to the firm, where I'd been utterly alone, even while married, while being a parent consumed every inch of me. Where I'd decided to be silent, to let more women suffer, because I needed that job, needed to feel like I had some control of my life.

But not this time.

I would be in charge. Make things happen. Do the right thing. And I would do it alone.

"I'm going, Silas."

He looked at me, eyes wide. And then he nodded. Let out a long sigh.

"Okay, Liv, okay. Jesus. Be careful. And take this. No need to use all those tools and lose time."

He held out his keys and key card to me. As I took them, he explained how it worked, where to go. He told me he had lost his earlier in the year, and this was one of the generic extras they had given him. I memorized the details, repeating them in my head.

"Liv," he said. "Till and I, we have your back. We'll be waiting for you."

"Thank you," I responded.

"Keep me posted," he said as we heard Piper and Till

finishing up in the kitchen. "And text me if you need me and I'll come get you, no matter where you are or what time it is. I'll keep my phone on and next to me."

Full of milky chocolate, Piper came out into the living room, eyes half-open. "Let's get you tucked in," Till said from behind her.

I kissed Piper on the cheek, gave her a huge hug, and mouthed "Thank you" to Till, and then they walked upstairs. Silas looked at me for a long moment and then left the house without saying another word. I supposed there was nothing more to say.

Standing in the empty room, I wondered for a moment if he was right. Maybe I should have let him come with me.

No. This was my fight now. And there was no turning back.

It was time to do the right thing.

# CHAPTER TWENTY-FOUR

I stepped out into the cold air just after midnight.

Unfortunately, the sky wasn't cooperating. The clouds had broken, the sky a wide scattering of stars and a half moon, lighting up the neighborhood. The illumination wouldn't help me. I needed darkness, needed not to be noticed. I supposed it could have been worse, could have been the same rain and sleet from a day earlier. Instant hypothermia.

I looked down at myself. All dressed in black, tools in my pocket, running shoes tied.

High school track, cross-country, running regularly since then—at least I was trained for this.

Maybe I had been working all my life for this.

Since that first board meeting, some part of me knew that I was going to take on Bob Stewart. Only then I didn't know the true horror of what he and his board were capable of—but really, couldn't I see that in the way he looked at me? The way his hand shot up so suddenly, violently? Don't people often show who they are right away?

I walked past my truck to Till's slate gray Subaru. The car

of New England. This would make it harder to identify me, a car similar to so many others in this town.

I looked up at Till's bedroom. All the lights were off, but I knew Till wasn't sleeping. I also knew that she would protect Piper with everything she had.

I opened the car door and looked up one last time, wishing I was curled up next to Piper in the nest that Till had made. I turned on the car, wishing it was one of those hybrids that was much quieter. Who heads out at midnight for anything good?

I sealed myself in, started to back up. My stomach turned over with nerves. The trick would be to stay calm. Methodical.

I drove through Main Street, quiet at this hour.

I wondered if Billy was working. Who might be up now? Donovan's wasn't open. Even the bars closed early. The stools were up at Star Bakery. I drove over the river, which now had ice forming at its edges, chunky pieces narrowing the flow. I turned up the hill toward the district offices, the cape house. I pulled off partway up the hill at a small spot where the town high schoolers probably partied sometimes, tucked the car into it, turned it around and backed in, facing toward home, and slipped it in under a few trees. It was ready for a quick getaway.

I opened the door, my eyes adjusting to the dark. Checked again to see I had everything I needed, took a deep breath, and then set off running down the trail just beyond my car. My stomach continued to churn. I'd tried to eat the mac and cheese but had only a few bites, settling instead for some strong coffee.

The night was still. Mostly it was my own heart I heard in my ears as I padded down the path. My feet connected with rotting leaves that had lost their crunch. My mind went hazy, filled with white noise, something that happened sometimes when I ran. My past rose up in flashes before me.

What crimes had I committed in my life?

Underage drinking. But I was smart. I could sense when things were just about to get out of control, before someone would get hurt or the cops would come. I'd always been able to read a crowd, sense the vibe like a turning sea. Once my friends started getting loud, breaking stuff, disappearing into bedrooms, I would look around for someone to get out of there with, catch a ride home to my family's cabin, come in late, my parents oblivious and fast asleep.

There was a bout of shoplifting in the eighth grade, which I lost sleep over for a week. I'd had this friend, Crystal, who couldn't keep her hands off anything in the stores. She was from a family where they pretended everything was perfect all the time. Amazing farmhouse, golden retriever, supportive parents, cute little sibling. Crystal was supposed to be perfect too—school, sports, boys. It exhausted her.

So we'd drive in her family's spotless Volvo to the big city of Burlington, Vermont, wandering on Church Street, in and out of stores. She was an impressive actress too. She'd say a bright hello to the managers and clerks, in her tidy outfit, high ponytail. They never suspected she was dropping earrings into that cup she was carrying around, layering dresses and shirts onto her tiny frame under her sweatshirt. Me, I would be physically ill, almost unable to move, the gnawing in my stomach so bad, the bile rising in my throat as we walked out. My parents may have been free-loving homesteading hippies, but stealing? That was a bad-karma-filled no-no.

For me, it was seeing that my future could evaporate in just a few seconds. Crystal, on the other hand, seemed not to care one little bit about that.

And then, as an adult, ignoring the sexual harassment in the office. I'd turned a blind eye and deaf ear to their comments, the dirty jokes, the too-close conversations. I pretended not to notice when they did it to the newly hired girls. For my own gain. Putting my own future first. *That's just how it is here. Better get used to it if you want to make it.*

Didn't that make me an accessory to a crime?

And now, here I was.

Breaking and entering.

Theft.

Trespassing. That same shoplifting bile crept into my throat. But this would be so much worse. I could lose all hope of ever becoming a lawyer. Worse, I could lose Piper.

The trees loomed overhead, black against the sky, as I skirted the field, making for the backside of the district office, to the path that connected to the Whitebridge Elementary School.

I concentrated on the feeling of my feet hitting the earth. Grounding me in reality.

*You can still turn back.*

*Move away from this town.*

*Never look back.*

The voices called from the corners of my mind, so I ran faster, trying to quiet them.

But really, where could I go? I couldn't move back in with my parents—they were barely functioning on their own, still in that tiny cabin, cluttered with half-done home improvement projects, art supplies, books, and weed plants; no room for us.

Back to Tom? Or even just to Boston, back in our old neighborhood?

No.

I could never heal that wound. Not after finally separating our lives, friends, and stuff. Going back would be admitting that I'd never had my shit together, could never really do it without him.

Even if we weren't together.

Not to mention, the settlement money wouldn't last much longer. At least we had a house. If I had to go on unemployment, I could. Then I could search for another paralegal job and try to finally pass the bar.

The truth was, ever since the moment I'd met Bob Stewart and the hand went up, I knew I had to bring him down. He stood for every male who had silenced me, starting in fifth grade, when that boy took credit for my project idea. It was irrational. Dangerous. But nothing could stop me, not even the nausea turning my stomach. I barely recognized myself, dressed for crime. The only thing centering me was the sound of my feet on frozen grass, the way my body moved forward, over the field, past the trees.

After another few minutes, I could see I was in the tunnel of forest leading to the elementary school.

A twig underfoot sounded like a gun crack. An owl hooted in the trees, far away, but it was as if the stereo was turned to ten, cranked up, the forest on full blast. My skin even seemed to be paying attention, noticing the air as it fell on my face, wrists, and ankles, the parts that were exposed. Like a prey animal, in a place full of predators, I moved.

I made it through the tunnel and could see the school across the baseball field. Painted white, it practically glowed in the partial moonlight. I slowed, felt around my waist for the fanny pack of tools. Still there. I searched the grounds for a sign of anyone else. No gray truck. No Nick. No sign of anyone. Just as I remembered and had studied, a spotlight shone out onto the back door and garden, and another light lit the side parking lot. Other than that, the building was draped in darkness.

I rehearsed in my mind what would happen next. I stood in the shadow of a large maple tree, leaned against the deeply grooved bark, poised and ready. I spun Esther's ring on my finger, summoning everything it symbolized for me—her boundless intellect, her daily perseverance providing truth and stories and resources to all who asked.

My body moved almost without my awareness now, doing what I had been preparing for all night. I skirted the edge of the field, staying in the safety of the edge of the forest, in case someone pulled in, appeared from nowhere. I could still get back, to the tunnel, to Till's car. My feet almost floated, making my way around, crossing over to the far side of the school, away from the parking lot light and the garden spotlight. Then it was time. Time to take that big step away from the trees to the back of the school.

I took a breath and pushed myself forward, out across the open expanse between the forest and the school. Closing the gap, my legs pushed as hard as they could. I knew I'd be under the light in a matter of moments and had to move fast. Heat surged through my body, my heartbeats were so fast they almost felt like a single steady thrum.

I reached the awning. A stack of milk crates from the cafeteria sat by the door as always. I spotted the video camera that was pointed across the space and at the door to the building. In one move, keeping my head and body away from the camera, I pulled a milk carton under me, stood on it, and withdrew a small LED light from my pocket, some duct tape from the other, and stuck the light on the camera lens.

Now the clock was ticking. Either they would think it was broken, or exactly what I had done would be clear. If someone was watching. If someone was awake.

But I had cover. It was time to go in.

I reached around my neck for the key card Silas had given me. Touched it to the lock, which clicked. I heaved it open and entered the school.

As the heavy metal door closed silently behind me, I scanned for the alarm system. It was right where Silas had told me, to the left of the door. I flipped it open, tapped in the code. It powered down.

I was in.

The man cave.

To my left was equipment, several snowblowers, rototillers, shiny chainsaws. So much more than a school needed. It looked like a full hardware shop. To the right was a long workbench, with rows of tools above it. Next to that was what I was looking for. The computer, tucked in next to a mustard-yellow living room chair.

I sat down and booted it up, then entered the password Silas had found for me to access this computer, and then shoved the blank memory stick into the port. I scanned, searching for files, my fingers flying until I located the spreadsheets.

Download.

I tapped my fingers on the desk. It would be a few minutes. How long did I have before they came for me? I would hear the sirens. Or would they keep them off, storm the school in silence?

I walked over to the workbench, started opening the drawers underneath.

One full of *Hustler*, *Playboy*, and *Penthouse* magazines. Fake tits, air-brushed bodies. That was certainly on brand.

One with a partial bottle of whiskey. The amber liquid sloshed back and forth with the opening of the drawer. Very on brand.

I hustled back to the computer to see if it was done copying. Nope. Not even halfway. I needed to be patient. An impossible task.

Back at the workbench, I pulled open the third drawer.

It held a fat stack of file folders with names printed across the top of each one.

The first one read *Brooke Bentworth.* I opened it and two photos fell out, taken from far away, but I could see the shapes of two lovers, naked, standing by a window, together, both facing forward. The woman had her hand up and behind herself, around the man's head, and the man looked down at her, hands wrapped possessively around her waist.

It was Brooke, for sure. But her expression was uncharacteristic—expressive. Her lips were parted, open in pleasure, a gasp. And the man? From the bald head, the close-set eyes, I knew.

It was Bob Stewart.

I stopped, forgetting what I was doing. These two. Wrapped up in each other—though the power dynamic looked off. Maybe I was just imagining it. But seeing them, usually so formal and rule-abiding, in shadows, intertwined, it unsettled me, my brain going sideways. Their unfiltered, unmanicured selves caught, suspended in time, so exposed. So wholly out of character, so vulnerable—while outwardly, to everyone else, it was rigid rules, hierarchy, all about appearances. It was as if the photo itself was on fire, electric, pure energy.

And under the image, a chart that held an array of numbers—dates of payments. To whom, I didn't know, but could imagine. I fumbled for my phone, hands shaking. This wasn't part of the plan.

I quickly took pictures of the file and the photo, my flash flickering in the dark, hoping they were good enough.

I continued to flip through files, not recognizing names, until I came to one simply labeled *The Garden.* I opened it but then saw a flash of light in my peripheral vision. Someone was here.

I dropped the files, ran back to the computer, which was almost done downloading. But *almost* wasn't good enough.

The original plan wasn't going to work.

But now I had new evidence.

I just had to get out of there alive. And with my phone.

I pulled out the memory stick, shoved it into my pocket, and ran for the door I had come in through.

But then I saw the door of the gray truck open, saw the shadow of the large man emerging, knew that my exit was blocked. I turned on my heel, ran for the other door, the one that led directly into the main part of the school, and hauled it open with a heave.

I would have to make it to the front door, then dash for the woods.

The hallway was dimly lit, the moonlight casting an eerie glow. The door hit the wall as I careened it open, making a violent, metal-against-cement clanging sound. I felt my feet accelerate under me, the rubber of my shoes squeaking, leaving muddy prints as I sprinted down the main hallway of the school, in survival mode, no time for conscious thought. I was almost there, to the lobby, my strides large, my arms pumping. But then behind me, I heard the same metallic sound and knew Nick was behind me, in that same hallway now.

I pushed through the nearest door off the hallway, the administrative suite, and ran for the only office I knew had a functioning window—Bob Stewart's. My eyes scanned the darkness, noticed the lights on the copier, the computers. I ran by the teachers' mailboxes, the employee bulletin board, a faux gold *Principal Robert Stewart* nameplate. I pushed open the door to his office.

There was no time to think. I found the window, a table underneath it with a printer, binders stacked with school policies, budgets, operations, neatly lined up end to end. I jumped up onto the table, scattering its contents. Heard a door open in the distance, twisted the locks, and used all of my force to push open the window, just enough to fit my body. I dove through the gap, my heel catching on the frame with a painful whack. I rolled onto the ground just as the office door behind me flung open. I turned and saw thick hands reaching through the window where seconds ago my body had been. Like I had pictured it in my mental map, I was now outside the school, the garden to my right, the fields and forests just beyond that.

I sprinted for the shed, feeling pain in my ankle, my entire body exhausted from the continued adrenaline coursing through my body. I heard the window snap shut behind me as I made it to the shed, and ducked behind the far side, chest heaving up and down. I scanned the area, trying to focus on the next sprint, across the field, into the forest, around the district office grounds, and back to the car. It suddenly seemed impossibly far. The stars twinkled above, the cool air moving around in small gusts, reminding me to move.

But as I stood there, I noticed the compost bin to my left, the corner of the garden with the most mulch. I noticed the pine cones covered in peanut butter hanging there from the fence, swinging in the wind, near where the little boy had found Roger's ring.

I wasn't alone. He was there. I could feel it in my bones. What exactly had they done to him? And what would they do to me?

It almost felt like he was urging me on.

*Avenge me.*

I ripped my eyes from the spot, heard the back door of the school open, heard Nick grumble, his voice rattling, "Look who's caught now. You can't win."

*Go.*

I took off at a tear, bold and furious, right down the middle of the baseball field. There was no way that big dude was going to catch me. I pumped my arms, sprinting toward the woods. It was coming up fast—I was going to make it.

But then I heard a rumble and the sound of tires on gravel. Was he going to the district office to block my exit, or was he coming to run me down?

I could tell from the sound that the truck was following, gaining, flying across the field behind me. I would be run down like a bowling pin. I had probably four hundred feet to go, to move to the safety of the trees, where the truck wouldn't fit. My legs burned, lungs heaving, trying to keep up.

I forced myself to go faster.

I wanted to see Piper again, feel her tight hug, smell her hair.

Only two hundred feet now, but the roar filled the night air around me with its churning mechanical sound. I ran for the biggest trees, the grand maples that stood near the entrance to the trail, hearing the crunch of leaves and twigs under the tires of the truck.

A hundred feet to go. I could see the tunnel now, the safety of the trees. My legs were fading, the sprint starting to slow. In that final stretch, I dipped into some sort of power that lay dormant most days. Maybe it was Esther, or my need to see my daughter again, or maybe it was just plain survival. But I ran faster and covered most of the ground before hearing the truck grind to a sudden stop—and just as I reached the first of the trees in the tunnel, ducking around trunks, I heard a click, and a muffled explosion, then a high-pitched sound by my ear, something slamming into a nearby tree.

There was the same sound again, whizzing by me as I ducked into the trees, zigzagging now, pushing up the tunnel of branches. I knew I didn't have much time before Nick would see what I was doing, retreat, turn his truck around, and try to block my exit from the district office grounds. Cut me off on that dirt road. Or maybe he'd already called the police, and Billy was on his way.

Jesus, I had made it this far, and it was time to finish what I'd started. I finally had everything I needed.

Out of the woods now and into the field around the district office. I covered the field but could feel the energy draining from my limbs. I couldn't keep this up. My body started shutting down, becoming sloppy. I was at the side of the field, could almost make out the little spot where I had tucked Till's car.

Looking ahead, I missed a small hole in the ground and stepped right in it, turning my ankle sideways, tripping forward, catching myself with my hands on the dirt. Despite the intense pain that radiated up my leg, I forced myself back up onto my feet and pushed forward. I could see the small Subaru waiting for me. Heard no sirens.

I dove forward, opened the door, piled in, turned it on, and slammed on the gas despite the increasing pain in my ankle, jumping with a burst out onto the dirt road. There was no sign of the gray truck as I pushed the car to sixty miles per hour, covering the hill in seconds. The clock read 1:38 a.m. as I eased off the gas pedal and turned left onto a quiet Main Street, my chest heaving up and down from all the running, my body starting to come down from the adrenaline rush.

*Don't speed now.*

*Don't draw any attention to yourself.*

*Just make it back.*

I turned onto my street, now out of sight of anyone on Main, and gunned it up the neighborhood road.

*Almost there.*

*You have the proof.*

I pulled into Till's driveway, right into the garage as planned, and the door instantly shut behind me. Till had been waiting, her finger on the button to close the garage, for who knew how long. I exhaled, could barely move. I needed to get inside to safety. But my body had decided that it'd had enough.

Finally, I pushed the car door open, and there she was.

Till stood framed in the doorway, with the dull light from the kitchen behind her, and a rifle in her hands, stretched across the expanse of her whole body. She looked perfectly at home and in command holding it there. She was clearly not messing around, took her job to protect Piper seriously. And she'd been ready to do whatever it required.

Till set down the rifle and ran out to me, helped me out of the car.

I suddenly realized I could barely put weight on my ankle. Till scooped me under the armpit and led me inside. We immediately went up the stairs and into Till's bedroom, where Piper was asleep, curled on her side, in the nest that had been made for her. Till led me to her bed, set me down, and I let her.

I laid back, all scratched and covered in mud. Till took off my sneakers, then my shirt, and helped me into some pajamas. I was a limp doll.

At last, Till whispered, "Did you get it?"

"Yes. In there," I gestured to the running jacket she had just taken off.

Till nodded, tucking me in.

"Okay, you rest now," she said quietly. My body had started shivering and shaking, finally catching up to everything that had just happened. "You did it, Liv, you did it. I'm so proud of you."

Instantly, tears prickled my eyes.

"But where will you sleep?" I whispered.

"Oh, I'll be fine," she said, and I realized she hadn't intended to sleep at all; a chair stood by the window. I heard her pad away as my eyes began to flutter.

After a few minutes fighting sleep, I opened them one last time to make sure everything was okay.

Till was sitting at the window, the curtain parted slightly, the giant hunting rifle laid across her lap, her long gray hair hanging down her back, her white pajamas almost glowing there in the night.

I felt myself drift off, finally safe and snug.

My brain loosened, and a final thought rose up, silencing all those voices once and for all:

Maybe I had finally made up for those years I was silent, when I did nothing to protect others.

# CHAPTER TWENTY-FIVE

I woke up and stretched, then immediately felt all the ways I had punished my body. My ankle throbbed, and my limbs felt like they were thousands of pounds each. But I opened my eyes and saw Piper peeking back at me, sitting up on her pillow, holding her hedgehog.

"You slept in Till's bed!" The concept was clearly outrageous. "Why did you do that?"

"We had a sleepover, remember?"

"But where did Till sleep?"

Piper was so chatty in the morning. My head pounded, my body ached. I needed coffee, but I was so happy to see my girl.

"I don't know, little bird. Why don't you go look for her?"

"Okay!"

Off Piper went, bounding down the stairs, on a mission to wake up Till, if she had slept at all.

I rolled over. Closed my eyes. Thoughts poured in.

*Did last night actually happen?*

*Why haven't the police come for me?*

*What did Nick do after he tried to run me down? Did he actually shoot at me?*

But the truth settled on me, even though I ached.

*You made it. You did it.*

The sun shone brightly through the white curtains in Till's room, the same curtains Till had kept watch from.

Maybe we would be okay. Maybe things would work out, and justice would be served.

For the kids in that school. For Lydia. For Roger.

Snowflake sat on the bed, looking a bit confused. I wasn't her normal companion. She watched me, suspicious. I closed my eyes, tried to drift off back to sleep, felt the warmth of Snowflake as she finally laid down next to me, apparently deciding that I was acceptable.

A few blissful moments passed before I heard footsteps in the room, Till appearing, her mouth pulled into a straight, worried line. Little lines around her mouth stood out and the skin around her eyes sagged.

She sat on the bed, a steaming cup of coffee in one hand, my phone in the other.

I sat up quickly on the pillows, instantly realizing that something was very wrong.

She wordlessly handed me the coffee. I grasped the handle, took a big sip, and felt the bitter goodness slide down my throat.

Then she handed me the phone. It was a little after 8 a.m.

"It looks like this came from an unknown caller," Till said, "But I think we both know who it's from."

> You don't have what you think you do. But look. I do.

There was a picture under the text. It was of me, caught in action, running down the hallway of Barnes Elementary School, with a date and time stamp from the security camera. Red-handed. Breaking and entering. It was blurry and in low light, but it was definitely me. There was more writing under the photo.

> Would you care to discuss options?

I felt the air and comfort leaving my body.

> If you want to keep Piper, meet me at 7 p.m. at Sullivan's with everything you have.

I hadn't made it. Not at all. I had proof, or so I thought. But now he had iron-clad proof of my breaking and entering at school. After I was warned by the police not to trespass.

"Maybe he's bluffing," Till said, though her eyes didn't look like she believed her own words.

I took one last, long sip of the coffee, felt it burn the back of my throat.

Snowflake jumped down as I stepped out of the bed.

"We need to go to Esther's computer and see what we have here."

Till nodded. We quickly changed and stepped out into the morning. My ankle burned as I put weight on it. It was frigid, had dropped about twenty degrees from the previous night. Our breath ballooned out in front of us as we walked across the street.

"Brrrr, I don't like this," Piper said, her teeth chattering.

"Me either," I responded, my mind turning.

*Please let the hard drive be enough. Maybe he was lying.*

But somehow, in some way, I knew I had been defeated. Men like Bob Stewart usually won. Everything was always on their side.

It was baked into the system. People constantly believed them. They were leaders. They were solid. Women were emotional. Fragile. Not to be believed.

I shook my head.

"Mama, what's wrong? You look tired."

"I am, baby bird. I am *so* tired."

"Yeah," Piper said, "Sleepovers are hard sometimes. Maybe you can take a nap."

I smiled at her as we walked into the house. Nothing looked disturbed. Steinem ran up to greet us, meowing her annoyance that we'd been gone for so long.

Piper ran off to her room, happy to be back with her bed and belongings.

Till and I made our way to Esther's office.

"I feel smarter just being in here," she said. "This is where all that big thinking happened. Your aunt was so brilliant."

I tried to reply but couldn't. My mind was a stressed, jumbled mess.

I clicked the computer on and grabbed my running jacket where I had shoved the memory stick. I pulled it out, pushed it into the slot in the computer, clicked the finder, and the new device.

Immediately, the file said: *Access denied.*

I tried clicking anywhere. But the gray box stayed there. Unmoving.

"Oh God," Till said. "No." So this is what he meant. "What about your phone?"

I pulled it out, looked at the pictures I had taken of those files. But all of them were blurry, barely usable. Nothing, really.

I had worked so hard, had used almost every inch of my body for this. And it wasn't enough. And now he had even more control of my life.

I pushed back from the computer. Sank to the floor. Stared at all those books about feminist power, science, and theory. About creativity and resistance.

I had lost. Just like Esther and Lydia and Roger had lost.

And now I had to go sit across from him. Beg to keep my child. My house. A silent cry started at my center and worked upward. My body shook in heaves, and I felt like I'd been cracked in two.

After a couple of minutes, a blanket was placed on my shoulders. Then Till bent over me, put a gentle finger under my chin, lifted it, and said, "Look at me. All is not lost. She's still here with us."

# CHAPTER TWENTY-SIX

I looked at myself in the rearview mirror. I had dried my thick brown hair which hung in waves around my face—wore silver hoop earrings, red lipstick, a fitted dark blue dress, with my black peacoat. The outfit played into my assets, into my foreseen submissive role. Concealer covered the dark circles under my eyes. Till and I had been working the previous two nights with very little sleep. I nodded to myself, glanced at Esther's tiny book that hung from the mirror, strung with iridescent beads.

Sullivan's was about thirty minutes away, outside of a town named Wayside, which lived up to its name, because most of the buildings were boarded up, empty. The only businesses I saw were a gas station and a dollar store, like many small towns in New England. I passed them and made my way down a rural highway.

It felt like I was driving right into a death trap. But there really wasn't any other choice. Not anymore.

The chill from the morning had remained, and gray clouds had come in behind the cold front. Tiny flecks of snow began to pepper my windshield, forcing me to turn on the wipers.

Everything about the day was oppressive, but I forced myself to focus.

*Go in there with dignity. Do not be scared. Use what you have. It'll be over soon.* An old rusty sign hung over the sidewalk, a deep orange-red like a used-up license plate, the white letters faded. *Sullivan's.* Neon bar signs for Bud Light, Corona, Sam Adams shined through dirty windows. The inside was dark, with several TV screens showing various sports. I sighed as I pulled into a parking spot. Most of the bars I'd gone to in Boston were full of college students, not townies, and felt urban, a little chic. Or they were classically Irish, with the black front, red doors, name in an Irish font.

Instead, this place looked like bad shit happened here. Shady. Perfect for an exchange of evidence and blackmail, where no one would notice anything, and the objectification of women was probably a regular occurrence.

I checked my phone. Everything was in place.

My hands shook as I opened the door. I had a role to play, and I needed to sell it. Needed to look meek and fragile, to convince him that he'd won, that he held all the power. And wasn't that what the first part of my life had been about? A performance? I remembered high school, trying to look cute but not too confident. Innocent but interested. Sexy but not slutty. Exhausting.

Then meeting Tom and feeling like I could let down my guard and finally be myself. But when I had Piper, I stopped being available to him in the way I was before. I focused on being a mom for a little while, and he just stopped paying attention, stopped showing me that he cared, but still expected me to stay with him no matter what.

And I'd done a special kind of pretending at the firm. One of the boys. A girl who would laugh at dirty jokes just to make the men comfortable. To get them to share the power. The truth was, I could see that kingdom of power and privilege, but it was never mine. Where did that get me in the end anyway? Certainly not supporting my fellow female employees.

Maybe this was my final chance for true redemption

Seven o'clock on a Sunday night. Mostly middle-aged white men at the bar, talking loudly, looking at the game. Or digging into nachos with bright orange cheese.

I scanned the back room, back toward the pool table, the dart board. I spun the thick silver ring around my finger. Finally, my eyes landed on him. Back corner table. Bald head, tiny eyes. Boring into me.

My stomach flopped around. I found him repulsive, and now I had to face him directly. The last time, which felt like years ago, was when he took me by the elbow outside, shook his finger at me, reprimanding me, warning that I could no longer be on school grounds.

Well, I had certainly done that.

I walked toward him through the bar. The floor was sticky, as if covered with several years' worth of grime and spilled beer. Which it probably was. About ten people were sitting along the bar, and I searched for any other woman but saw none.

I willed my feet forward anyway. Pushed them to go to his table, to sit down across from him, and to twist my face into a demure, small half smile.

"Hello, Principal Stewart," I said. His name felt gross in my mouth, attaching the *Principal* to it, like I had to defer to his power right away. I hated myself for it.

He nodded, a small shake of his head. "Olivia."

No one called me Olivia.

"I'm going to need to see your phone to make sure you aren't recording this," he said.

I tapped the back of my phone discreetly as I pulled it out, set it on the table between us, face up.

"There you go."

"So you're following directions. It's about time." His lips barely moved, but he was clearly enjoying this. He was going to take his time with my dismantling.

I pulled off my jacket, sliding each arm out, taking my time, before settling it on my lap. I used my body. Watched him watching me. I leaned forward toward him, even though I wanted to be anywhere but here, with this man.

"Yes. Yes, I am," I responded, delicately tucking my hair behind my ear.

*Look how harmless and feminine I am.*

"Well, that's good to hear. You've finally come to your senses."

I nodded, placing my hand on the table near his. "I don't know what I was thinking."

Maybe I was pushing this too far.

He didn't notice. He looked at me like he owned me, like I was his good little girl. His mouth pulled into a tight-lipped smile.

"Do you have what I need to make sure the photo of you in the school doesn't fall into the wrong hands? I have Billy on speed dial, you know."

I nodded, keeping my eyes open—doe-like, repentant.

"Yes, I have it. It was worthless anyway."

"Yes, encryption, a modern miracle."

"So smart."

Maybe this was too much—but no, he ate it up, by the fistful. His cheeks grew rosy, and he looked as if he might be getting turned on by all this power, his dominance over me. Is that how it had been with Brooke? He leaned forward greedily.

I could see the stubble on his cheeks, a tiny place where he had nicked himself shaving.

I kept looking at his eyes, trying to force my face into a look of admiration.

He broke free of my eyes and took a sip from his beer.

"But how did you do it?" I asked, wanting to let him fill in the gaps here, to leave this open.

"We have a perfect system, one where everybody wins."

Except for Roger Shepard. Or Lydia. Or the kids. Or the taxpayers. But I didn't say it.

Couldn't. I swallowed the words. Sealed my lips.

He stared at me, a glint of suspicion playing out on his face. It was clear that he wasn't going to spell this all out for me.

"It must be hard to run it all," I said, and he looked over my head at the TV screen behind me, some football game blaring there. I had gone too far.

"Do you have it?"

"Yes, it's right here."

I set the memory stick down on the table, and he quickly picked it up, put it in his pocket.

"You're lucky I don't press charges, you know," he said. Now he looked back into my eyes, hungry. He was showing off.

He could still get rid of me. Could get me arrested.

The first woman I'd seen since entering the building, a waitress, came over to the table.

Her platinum blond hair was pulled back, her makeup thick.

"Can I get you anything, hon?" she asked.

"No," Bob answered for me. "We're leaving soon,"

She looked between us. I nodded as if to say I was okay with him being my mouthpiece.

Letting him decide what I needed.

The woman shrugged her shoulders and walked away.

The men at the bar cheered at the TV.

I felt myself falling. I seemed to be sliding away from myself, all of my outward qualities, my sense of self, disappearing.

The feeling was familiar.

*Keep putting on a show. Keep your head down, don't say anything. Just play along.*

I was just so tired. Down to my bones, my cells.

My voice sounded like a mouse in my own ears, a child.

"How will I know you'll delete the photo?"

He didn't answer.

"You really gave Nick a good chase, I'll give you that." He licked his lips—they were a shiny, purple pink. "You must've really thought you were all that. Thought you won."

He couldn't hide his sideways grin now. Like a boy in class who'd gotten away with it.

I felt ill, trapped. I needed out of here, and fast. A mounted deer head stared at me from across the wood-paneled room. Fading male faces from sports newspaper clippings looked on from the walls.

Bob's voice was quiet now, but razor sharp. "You'll never know if I've gotten rid of the photo. You'll need to stay in line the whole time Piper is in school if you want to live in Whitebridge."

That was the last straw. I couldn't do it any longer. It was time to go. Just as I reached for my phone, a text came in from Silas.

*Are you okay?*

Bob looked at it, then slammed his hand over mine, grabbing my upper arm in a tight squeeze.

"That little prick. Did you tell Silas you were coming here?"

"No!"

I twisted my arm but he held on. I felt the tendons move under my skin as I squirmed.

"He's next, you know. I know he likes you, that he helped you."

I panicked, my eyes searching the room.

He squeezed harder.

"If you tell a soul about any of this, you'll lose more than just your kid." A little spit appeared in the corner of his mouth. Principal Stewart was losing control.

My forearm ached, burning.

My eyes found the waitress at the bar. Pleaded with her. Startled, she set down her tray of beers, wiped her hands on her white apron, and started walking over.

I felt Bob's thumb digging into the fleshy part of my arm, but his eyes finally looked away from me to the waitress approaching, and he loosened his grip.

I twisted away, grabbed my phone, stood up, and ran past the waitress, my shoulder grazing hers.

I ran, even though my legs were collapsing underneath me, all energy gone, ran by the crowded bar where not one of the men looked up from the game, and then I was out the door. I barreled down the dark sidewalk, my eyes trying to adjust, pulled open the door to the truck, got in, and heaved it closed.

Locked the doors.

Pulled out my phone. Tapped the back twice, turning off the voice recording app.

I called a number and said, "I got it. He's in there."

I tried catching my breath, but sobs rose in waves of their own. Sobs of fear, and of triumph.

*I'm safe. I made it out.*

I kept repeating these lines to myself like a chant. I rocked back and forth a bit, feeling the safety and comfort of the truck. Esther's truck. I rubbed the place where Bob's fingers had dug into my arm.

I wiped my tears with my hands, flicked them away. Sat up

a little taller. Breathed in deep, filling my lungs. The first deep breath in months. It felt like freedom.

I looked at myself in the rearview mirror. My eyes were puffy and tired but steady.

*There she is*, I thought. I'd done it. The state cops would be heading there any minute.

A second later, I heard something shift in the backseat. I turned to look.

Then there was an instant explosion of pain, white light, and then nothing but darkness.

I woke up later, no idea how much time had passed, my head pounding in the dark. It was like swimming to the surface of a pitch-black pool.

I tried to open my mouth to scream, but felt adhesive pressing my lips together. My body was curled up in a ball, my arms stuck behind my back, the plastic zip ties biting into my wrists. I couldn't see anything but felt the rumbling road beneath me.

A realization of cold hard truth settled on me. I hadn't won anything. They'd found me, and now they were going to take me somewhere and kill me, just like they did to Roger.

It'd been a setup. The whole thing. I was so stupid.

I kicked my legs into the trunk of the car, even though I knew it was useless. This made me breathe hard out of my nose, the air stuffy and unmoving, like breathing through a straw.

They had won. Bob Stewart shut me up that first day, and he would shut me up now.

Forever.

The back of my head pounded, and I let myself slip back into nothingness. It was easier.

I snapped awake at the change of the road, bumpier, a switch to dirt. I saw Piper's face, filling up the dark space like a movie screen, her freckles, eyelashes, all of it crystal clear.

My eyes filled. I would leave her. After all this. I'd leave her alone in the world.

The vehicle rattled and bounced over potholes, turning once, then twice left. No one would find me. I squeezed my eyes shut tighter and prayed.

*Please let Piper be okay. Take care of her. Get her out of this town and let her be safe.*

The vehicle slowed to a stop.

I swore to myself. No matter what, I would fight until the end.

The trunk creaked open, and I was blinded by a flashlight in my eyes. I squinted, turned my head. Two shadows lurked behind the light.

"Here we are, sweetheart," came a raspy voice that must have been Nick's. "I hope you had a nice ride."

His beefy arm reached in and pulled me out, my legs getting stuck on the lip of the trunk. I fell unceremoniously to the rough, frozen dirt below. I looked up but the forms were silhouetted, impossible to make out.

A female voice cut through the rattle of the car engine and my thudding head.

"There you are. Not so high and mighty now, huh?"

My brain cartwheeled, trying to figure out what was happening, what to do. Grasping, finding nothing but the icy cold ground.

"You must have thought you were pretty smart back there, figuring it all out. Thinking you were capturing the mastermind at the bar. You and your aunt always thinking you're smarter than everyone else."

I looked up from the ground, eyes squinting together, trying to focus. *Who the hell is talking about my aunt?*

I pushed up on my knees and could see the angle of a curtain of hair, and my brain suddenly clicked into gear.

Brooke Bentworth. Board chair. Here, in the cold dark, at some sort of gravel pit, at the end of a dirt road, ready to oversee my murder.

She wasn't just Bob's mistress, that much was clear now.

I had to stall. Tried to speak, but the duct tape held tight.

Brooke reached down with her manicured nails and ripped the tape off along with what felt like half of my lips. I doubled over in pain.

I spit out the words, "What do you even know about my aunt?"

"That she never belonged here. That she had all that information at her fingertips and fancied herself powerful. And she poked her head where it didn't belong."

Maybe using her name would help bring her back to the reality of what she was doing.

"Brooke, that was a long time ago. I can move away, and we can forget any of this ever happened."

Brooke chuckled, said in a forced whisper, "If there's anything I know about you and your aunt, it's that you won't forget. She and her little girlfriend had gotten close to us, but we took care of them."

*Took care of them?*

My heart jackhammered in my chest.

"Oh, sure, she was on her way out. We just might have helped the timeline a little. You know . . . we have friends everywhere."

I exploded to my feet and ran at her. My head barreled into her chest, knocking her back, the sudden compression of her lungs forcing a rush of air out of her mouth. Then I felt thick hands grab hold of my bicep, dragging me along the ground.

"You nasty little bitch," Brooke hissed. "I knew from the moment I saw you that you didn't belong here."

Nick dragged me forward, and Brooke walked beside us.

I quickly ran through my options.

*Twist away. Run for the woods. But then one of them would shoot me from behind.*

*Wait for the right angle, then knee him in the balls and sprint for the trees. He was probably the one who had the gun—that was too uncivilized for Brooke.*

But he was dragging me along, my feet barely touching the ground, grunting as he did so.

I felt the soft breeze before I saw what was causing it. The wind coming up from the bottom of the shale pit and on to my face. We stood at the large, dark hole's edge.

It was here he would shoot me, then dump my body.

Nick stopped moving, stood me up. This was my chance.

"Here we are, your final—"

I drove my knee as hard as I could up and into the space between his slightly spread legs with every bit of force I could muster.

He made a small, surprised sound, his face going completely white. Then he doubled over, dropping his grip on me, stumbling forward with a gasp, the rocks slipping under his feet. I picked up my leg and kicked him from behind, then turned and ran. I heard the sound of rocks shifting behind me, and then nothing at all.

I only made it a few steps before I heard the bullet sail above my head. I fell to the ground and looked up.

Brooke walked forward and placed her foot onto my hip, the heeled boot digging into my side. She pointed the barrel of the gun at my forehead.

"You didn't think it would be that easy, did you?"

I didn't say anything, didn't move. Tried to think of a way out.

Brooke shook her head. "You never learned the rules, did you? Just go along with the order of things, then take what's yours."

She smiled.

"You don't want to do this, Brooke. You don't want to go to prison."

"Oh, don't you worry. The cops around here? We're real tight."

I had no more options. It was over. I squeezed my eyes shut and thought of Piper, her dark eyes, her half smile, one last time.

"Goodbye, Liv."

A gun sounded, shattering my hearing. But no pain, no blood.

I looked up, and there she was.

Till stood with her husband's rifle trained on Brooke's chest. Her white hair flowed behind her, her jacket covering her pajamas.

"Drop it, Brooke."

But the pistol stayed pointed at me.

The night was quiet, waiting. I saw a flicker of light or movement behind Till.

"You don't want to do this. Now you've got witnesses."

"Not for long."

Brooke took a step toward me, gun inches from my face. I could smell metal. I coiled my body tight.

*They're going to win. They always did.*

I pointed my face downward and tucked my chin into my shoulder, trying to protect myself.

A sudden sound blared from behind me, a shattering of still night air. Brooke looked up for a moment, and then there was a rush of movement: Till, a blur. There was a sickening thud, and a body dropped beside me on the ground, the dirt and dust around her rising into the air.

Till stood with the barrel of the rifle in her hands. She quickly flipped it around and pointed the it at Brooke. But she was unconscious, her perfect hair cutting an angle across her face in the dirt.

Without looking up from Brooke, Till said, "Don't worry. The real cops will be here soon." She adjusted her stance and looked at me. "*She* saved us, you know."

I looked from Till in the direction the sound had come from, her car, and could just make out the silhouette of someone in the driver's seat, her hands pressed to the glass.

Piper. My baby.

My head rang, and I shook from fear, shock, and the cold, but could only think: *We got them, Esther. We're free. For real this time.*

# CHAPTER TWENTY-SEVEN

Piper, Till, and I slept for almost two days straight. The hit I took on the back of my head was a large, pounding egg. The doctor told me I was moderately concussed from the impact.

All I wanted to do was rest. We would gather for comfort meals in our pajamas and slippers, watch cartoons and comedies, then fall back asleep. I was in and out of dreams where I was running through the woods, trapped in a trunk, saw flashes of their faces, and where I didn't get away this time. Where I pushed Nick over into the pit but this time he pulled me in with him.

I'd wake up in a cold sweat, jolting Piper and Steinem off me.

And then there were the police interviews. The state police showed up and looked enormous as I shuffled around in my slippers, answering their questions. I knew enough to have my former colleague, one of the new female partners at my old firm, show up and sit in. She, in a suit with pearls, and two state police, a man and woman, all crammed into Esther's kitchen, asking me what happened.

Nick had died after his fall. I could still feel his hands on me, dragging me to the edge of the quarry. Of course I knew it wasn't my fault, he was actively trying to kill me, but I still felt a mix of horror and guilt that I'd done that. Heather made it very clear that we were dealing with self-defense here. She also told me that Principal Stewart and Brooke Bentworth were on immediate leave, both now under house arrest and part of an active criminal investigation. Relief flooded my body, yet part of me still worried for Chris Parker, the man who got mixed up in all of this, with his sick daughter. I couldn't shake his sad eyes in that grocery store. Because who wouldn't do anything for their kid? So much of life is a mix of both misery and joy, grief and hope, relief and regret.

During those groggy days, my phone constantly vibrated with messages. I ignored most but saw one come in that snapped me awake. Lydia.

*Thank you* was all it said, and a link. I clicked it and saw a staff listing with a picture of her, still hollow cheeked, but smiling. She was working at a small, progressive school in Ojai, California, as a new fourth-grade teacher. I looked at pictures of the school building, the walls covered with bright social justice–themed murals, and smiled into my pillow.

Lydia was okay. Lydia was doing what she was meant to do again.

A few hours later, I went down to Donovan's to meet Silas. Piper and Till had settled into a large tabletop puzzle, and they seemed okay for a bit. I just couldn't bring myself to tell him what had happened over text. I was sure the whole town was buzzing, but we had missed all of it.

I walked into the bar wearing jeans and a sweater and my leather jacket. It was the first time I'd left the house in days and one of the first times in recent history I had dressed just for myself. My head still hurt a bit, but I finally felt enough like myself to interact with a few people—well, one person to be exact. The bar was empty—maybe not even actually open yet.

Standing there, I reflected on the raw honesty of a bar in daylight. The greasy windows. The permanently stained floors. The vague smell of cigarette smoke still deeply embedded in the walls from decades earlier.

Hours later, a few drinks in, everything would look more glamorous, all the flaws falling away in the haze of alcohol and celebration.

There in the sunshine stood Silas, who looked up at me and smiled, that huge smile that filled up an entire room. He came around the bar and wrapped his arms around me.

"Oh my god, Liv," he said quietly. "Thank God you and Piper are okay."

He breathed a sigh of relief in my ear. Held on to me tightly.

"I've been thinking about you so much. Till and I have been texting. She filled me in on some of what happened." He paused, shook his head, and said, "I can't believe it."

"I know, it's all so awful, I'm still trying to process it. I don't know if I ever will."

"Come on, come sit down."

He pulled me to a small table by the window, then ran back to the bar and brought over a cider for me, a beer for himself.

"If you don't want to talk about it, I understand."

He wasn't going to force the story out of me. I could take my own time, and I appreciated that.

I looked down at my drink.

"There's going to be some changes at Whitebridge," I said, "that's for sure."

And to that we clinked glasses, took sips. A worried wrinkle settled between his eyes.

"I can't believe it was Brooke all this time, that she would do that to you."

"So much more than just me. Roger. Esther. Driving off Lydia."

"I thought we'd won. As soon as I had the recording of him, I thought that would be enough. But someone must have tipped off Brooke, and then she and Nick found me."

My breath began to shake and I stopped talking. The memories were still so raw.

"Hey, it's okay," he said. "It's over. You're safe now."

I nodded and thought maybe I was. For the first time since I'd left Tom, I realized that I might be okay. Not because this man wanted me, but because I finally felt like myself—calm, capable, and yes, still tired.

"No, I want to tell you the rest."

"Okay. All I know is that you were going to the school, going to find the evidence, and that something happened," Silas said. "And then I found out Stewart had something on you and that the whole thing might not work."

"Yeah. That's all true."

"And then you fought back. All three of you. Which is incredible. But that's all I know. Till didn't tell me what happened next."

"Well," I murmured, "I called the state police in Manchester. Skipped right over Billy. I didn't get off the phone until they came to my house and I showed them what I had. After several hours of reviewing everything, listening to me go over everything that had happened, showing them the ring, and contacting Roger's office, they said I needed to do one final thing. Go meet him, record it secretly, and they would follow me there, be ready to arrest him. And since I already had a plan to meet him, I knew I had to do it.

"And that's exactly what I did. I needed to convince him that he'd won. I needed him to say too much. I needed him to feel dominance over me in order to win."

"Oh, Liv. That must have been so hard."

"It was. I could barely bring myself to do it."

"But you did."

"I did. No, really, *we* did. I thought this whole time that I was the only one who could solve this. That it was me against him and the board. Me against the world. But really, I wasn't alone. Never was. I never could've done this if it weren't for Till, Esther, Piper, Lydia, and . . . you."

"What? I did nothing. I didn't even know your plan."

"You gave me comfort. You believed me. You saw the best in me."

Silas shook his head again, smiled, looked down at the table.

"But it wasn't enough. Someone from the state police must have tipped off Brooke because the police never came. And I think you know the rest."

Silas grimaced. "You don't have to talk about it."

"Thank God for Till."

"Thank God for Till," he echoed.

We were quiet.

"Nick is . . ."

"I know."

I felt a pit in my stomach. Silas reached out and touched my hand.

"You did what you needed to survive. For you. For Piper."

I took a long sip of my cider.

"You should see it at school. The teachers kept the school going this week, even with all the rumors that have been flying around. A lot of people have been brought in for questioning. It's been nonstop. Even Dolores at the front desk."

"Well, that must have been quite upsetting for her." I couldn't help picturing her smug face as she had looked me over from head to foot the day I was tossed out of the school.

"I can't believe you did it, Liv. People are talking about you. And they don't know the half of it."

"That's okay. They don't have to."

"I can't believe the full story hasn't leaked to the press. All they issued was a short announcement that they were investigating the school board and administration and that all of them are on leave. No mention of murder . . . but there will be. The rumor mill is wild and everyone's freaking out. I'm sure it's just a matter of time. All of this is more than this town—this whole *county*—has ever seen. We're gonna be flooded with reporters."

"Well, maybe it's time for me to hide out and start studying for the bar exam then."

Silas's face brightened into a smile. "It might be."

God, I loved that smile. I couldn't believe we'd made it to the other side of this, and he was still here—with me, believing in me.

He paused, looking down at our drinks, pink spreading to his cheeks.

It was time. Finally time.

I leaned over across the table, closing the gap between us.

His soft blue eyes lifted to meet mine, inches from his face. He took in a quick breath.

"Perhaps you could hide out with me," I said, and pulled his lips to mine.

### *PRINCIPAL, BOARD MEMBERS ARRESTED FOR SUSPECTED HOMICIDE AND EMBEZZLEMENT IN WHITEBRIDGE*

*Whitebridge, NH.*

*Brooke Bentworth, school board chair, was arrested on charges of embezzlement and attempted murder, and police say additional charges are pending. Bob Stewart, principal of Barnes Elementary School, and acting superintendent of the Whitebridge School District, was also arrested on charges of embezzlement and manslaughter. Nick Folley, custodian at Whitebridge, was found dead at the scene of the alleged crimes, at the Whitebridge Quarry. According to sources, the three had been embezzling funds from the school and awarding fraudulent construction contracts to board members. In September, New Hampshire state financial analyst Roger Shepard went missing, and the three are charged with his alleged murder. According to the Manchester police, Ms. Bentworth and Mr. Stewart have been in custody for questioning. "There may be other board members and school staff implicated," said Officer Hollingsworth in a press conference. More reporting to come as this story develops.*

I looked out across the long table in the school library.

"Come in, come in!" I said to the teachers and handful of parents who had gathered.

"Please feel free to sit with us at the table."

A few smiled, came closer, a little hesitant. Building trust, healing from what had happened, and the transition to this kind of school board would take time, I knew.

I looked down at the agenda for the meeting. A short one. I remembered how unwelcome and frustrated I'd felt at that first board meeting. Since then, the rest of the school board had resigned, as charges and media rained down on them. I volunteered to step in as temporary board chair and was appointed by the interim superintendent, who'd been designated by the New Hampshire Board of Education.

At this first new board meeting, I would be discussing the temporary administration of the school and some new positions the interim superintendent wanted to fill as a result of the scandal, to rebuild. At the table was Jada, the owner from the Star Bakery, and Star themself, from the gas station, both of whom I had recruited for the board. Just beyond the table sat Piper, her legs pulled under her, a journal in her lap. Close to Piper sat Till, her chin up, beaming at me. Behind both of them was Laura, her knitting in her lap. She looked up at me, head tilted, eyes soft with what seemed like a silent apology. I nodded at her, our first interaction since my almost arrest. I'd learned to be careful with small-town Lauras, but also hoped we could find our way back into a friendship over time.

I looked around at the other people gathered at the table and the reporters in the back and down at my welcome message, which I knew would be broadcast via Zoom to the whole town—another improvement over the previous board—and covered in the media.

I took a deep breath and thought of how wrong I had been. It had taken so long to see. I thought that I had to solve the mystery of what was happening at the school all by myself. That I was going it alone. But nothing could have been further from the truth. Esther still walked with me. She continued teaching me even after she was gone. And what a gift Till was, that wise elder and total badass. Then there was Silas, who truly saw me for who I was, who I could be, despite my flaws and the mistakes I had made before. This was my community, my home now.

And I had a job to do, a legacy to protect.

That night, I had come so close to losing it all.

I took a deep breath. "I want to welcome everyone here

tonight. I know the last few weeks have been very difficult for Whitebridge and our school community. I, too, am heartbroken about what happened here. And while I may be somewhat new to town, my family certainly isn't. My Aunt Esther lived here for over thirty years, providing a public service for the community, helping people gain the information and knowledge they needed. I hope to carry on that tradition in any way that I can. Tonight, we start the long process of rebuilding trust, welcoming teachers, students, and families into the school leadership process, and creating an inclusive, brave, and joyful learning environment for our students, where they take on challenging issues and work to create a better world. Thank you again for this opportunity, Interim Superintendent Latisha Jones."

Piper looked up at me, her head tilted, her chin lifted. I could see in her eyes what I had been waiting for my whole life: pride.

I gulped down the hitch in my throat and continued.

"The public comment period is now open, and everyone is welcome to speak. Let's listen to each other, respect each other's points of view, and work together to create a welcoming, compassionate, and supportive school and community for our kids."

I paused, and then panicked slightly when silence filled the room. Maybe I had been too optimistic, maybe this wasn't actually going to work. But after another moment, slowly, people began to raise their hands. It was a beautiful sight.

And then . . . the board got to work.

# ACKNOWLEDGMENTS

This book was many years in the making. First of all, a big thank you to Josette Blais and Kailea Silvers for connecting me with Brendan Deneen of Blackstone Publishing to launch this whole wild ride.

Next, a huge thanks to my big brother, Mike Farber, for brainstorming creative endings and plot twists with such gusto in the early stages of this book.

Endless gratitude to my family for constantly being there. To my husband, Kurt Budliger, for surviving in 2023 (no small task), for supplying me with endless cups of coffee, for the author photo, for cleaning up the kitchen again and again, and for being my hype man during the writing of this book (and always). To my brave, brilliant, and beautiful daughters, Elly and Addy, for listening to various plot ideas and helping me figure out what might work.

Special thanks to Addy for being the very last beta reader before this book was due, a Gen Z editor of the highest order. Thank you for taking the time to read the manuscript and for offering your brilliant feedback (and for creating the accompanying mix on Spotify—check it out!). A great big thank you to Elly for offering outfit support and near-constant humor!

Thank you to Chris Mihaly for your reading and editing of this manuscript and for your mentorship and support in coffee shops and on dirt roads in Calais. Thanks also to the Red Hen Writers for their inspiration, listening, and guidance even though my attendance and participation are less than stellar!

My heartfelt thanks to Jeanie Phillips for reading and offering feedback even during your most busy days. I'm forever grateful for your support, friendship, and astute reading and editing eyes.

Thank you to the incredible educators I have had the honor to teach alongside in public schools in Vermont for almost two decades. There are too many to name, and I love you all, but to my closest teammates for many years, Heather Bower, Julie Smart, and Sharon Spector: your tenacity, passion, courage, kindness, humor, and friendship have made my life infinitely better, especially during trying times (and we have had a few!).

Thank you to the Blackstone Publishing family. First, a great big multiyear thank-you to my brilliant editor Brendan Deneen, who inspired and then sharpened this story and helped it become better and better with each conversation and round of edits. Deirdre Curley-Waldern, thank you for your detailed editing and notes, and to Larissa Ezell for the gorgeous cover design that captures the essence of the story. Thank you to Katrina Tan, Grover Gardner, Nicole Sklitsis, and Bri Jones for their support in bringing this book to the world.

Warmest gratitude to Carol and Bob Budliger for asking me for updates, cheering me on, sharing your stories, and for your help with raising two incredible daughters.

Deepest thanks to all the brave women who have taught me and modeled an authentic way to live over the years. Starting with my grandmother, Catherine Mary Klees, and my mom,

Anne Farber, and the many friends, writers, musicians, scholars, and educators who informed this work, you are an army of bravery, brilliance, and vibrancy. I am eternally grateful for your work, lives, honesty, and guidance. You'll see their echoes all through this book.

Lastly, to all of the school board members and public servants who put the welfare, needs, dignity, and care of students, teachers, and families at the center of your tireless work, thank you.